Caught
Read-Handed

TERRIE FARLEY MORAN

BERKLEY PRIME CRIME, NEW YORK

BERKLEY
PRIME
CRIME

An imprint of Penguin Random House LLC
375 Hudson Street, New York, New York 10014

CAUGHT READ-HANDED

A Berkley Prime Crime Book / published by arrangement with the author

ISBN: 978-0-425-27029-5

PUBLISHING HISTORY
Berkley Prime Crime mass-market edition / July 2015

PRINTED IN THE UNITED STATES OF AMERICA

10 9 8 7 6 5 4 3 2 1

Cover illustration by S. Miroque.
Cover design by Rita Frangie.
Interior text design by Kristin del Rosario.

Penguin
Random
House

Berkley Prime Crime titles by Terrie Farley Moran

WELL READ, THEN DEAD
CAUGHT READ-HANDED

continued . . .

"I've long enjoyed the short fiction of Terrie Moran, and I'm thrilled to see her expand her talents to the novel with *Well Read, Then Dead*. Set in a paradise Florida island town, with lovable and quirky characters and a combination bookstore/café that I wish was in my own hometown, Terrie's well-plotted novel tells a tale of murder, old secrets and friends-for-life who will do what it takes to protect their loved ones and way of life. Very much recommended."

—Brendan DuBois, two-time Shamus Award–winning author of *Fatal Harbor*

"[A] fun change of pace for Florida cozy readers looking for a series that offers an alternative to the hustle and bustle of Miami or the laid-back calypso beat of Key West. The close-knit cast of characters in *Well Read, Then Dead* should appeal to fans of Elaine Viets's Dead-End Job series, while food-loving fans of Lucy Burdette's Key West Food Critic mysteries will find their mouths watering at the mention of *Old Man and the Sea* Chowder and buttermilk pie (for which a recipe is included). I look forward to the next pun-filled book in the series."   —*Florida Book Review*

"The mystery is a good one with plenty of suspects, motives and opportunities to have done the murder. The characters are likeable and full of quirks, making the Read 'Em and Eat a place readers wouldn't just like to see but a second home where they can hang out with friends. Pull up a chair during the Potluck Book Club, have a glass of sweet tea and relax. It's Florida, good books and good food."   —*Kings River Life Magazine*

Joan Moran Schlereth:
best daughter ever

Chapter One

Bridgy Mayfield's aunt Ophelia tapped her extra-long, shocking pink fingernails impatiently on the countertop beside the cash register.

"Really, how long can it take to pack a few scones and fill a thermos with tea?"

I held my tongue, reminding myself there was no point in answering Ophie. She never paid the least attention to what anyone had to say unless they were spouting lavish words of praise directed at Ophie herself. Everything else flew right past her.

Bridgy came out of the kitchen. She placed the tea-filled thermos and a box of scones in front of her aunt. "I tied your pastry box with a fancy lace ribbon. When you open the box, each scone is resting in its own little doily. Do you want cocktail-sized napkins rather than lunch napkins? More festive, I always think."

Ophie's mood swung from frozen latte to southern syrup.

"Here you go gussying up the tea I'm sharing with a new client to make it look like I fussed to the moon and back. Why, honey chile, it's no wonder you're my favorite relative." Ophie reached across the counter to pat Bridgy on the cheek and spotted a cardboard box half filled with assorted books. "What is that? A new shipment? Shouldn't you get those books on a shelf? How can folks buy them if they don't know you have them?"

She turned to me. "Sassy, you're the book maven. What are you waiting for?"

I tried explaining that we were donating some used books from home and a few unsold books from the café book-shelves for the library fund-raising book sale, but Ophie was having none of it.

"Isn't that like helping the enemy stock up on weapons? Honey chile, if everyone got their books at the library, who'd buy books from you?"

Remembering it wasn't so long ago that Ophie suggested we expand the café and get rid of the bookshelves altogether, I needed to change the subject, and fast. I pointedly looked at the wall clock and asked, "What time are you meeting your new client?"

"Oh Lordy, I've only got about two minutes." She picked up her thermos and package. "Y'all know the smartest thing I did when I opened the Treasure Trove was mix local art with eclectic consignments. The interior designer I'm meet-ing this morning has the exclusive to decorate the model homes and apartments for Lipscome Builders. And they are plenty big. Right now they're building an apartment complex here on the island, and a private home development in Bonita

Springs. I've got some great pieces, guaranteed to make the models look beachy yet elegant. Moving down here from Pinetta is the best thing I could have done. It'll be raining money over at the Treasure Trove."

As I watched her trot out the door on impossibly high, spiky yellow sandals, I thought back to when she'd barreled in the front door of the Read 'Em and Eat, eager to help as soon as she heard that Bridgy and I were in serious trouble because our chef, Miguel Guerra, broke his leg. Hard to run a café without a chef. By the time Miguel was back at work, Ophie had fallen in love with Fort Myers Beach, its friendly residents and peaceful vistas. She rented a vacant store in our plaza and was soon earning enough to allow her to buy a tiny cottage on Estero Bay.

Bridgy and I hustled for another hour serving breakfast, which included book-related items like Agatha Christie Soft-Boiled Eggs and *Green Eggs and Ham*. When we finally hit the brief lull between the breakfast and lunch crowd I grabbed the box of books and headed over to the library.

I carefully edged my ancient but beloved Heap-a-Jeep into a parking space tucked between a well-polished silver Lexus and a flamboyant blue Corvette sitting with its top down. An overflowing ashtray in the Corvette's dash was wide open and as each gust of wind blew through the dwarf palms lining the parking lot, cigarette ash swirled around the seats and console, scattering gray and white specks on the smooth navy leather. The tiny whirlwinds caught my eye.

For a second, I toyed with the idea of leaning over the passenger side door of the Corvette to close the ashtray, but decided that could spell trouble if the owner came out of the library and thought I was fiddling, or worse, with the car.

The expansive glass façade of the Beachside Community Library always made me smile. The library was every bit as warm and welcoming as the Read 'Em and Eat. The staff worked tirelessly to meet the reading needs of the full-time residents of Fort Myers Beach and the ever-changing snow-bird community—winter residents who came to the Gulf Coast of Florida from all parts north. A car door slammed, breaking my reverie. Involuntarily, I looked toward the noise. The man who'd shut the door of a faded black Mustang covered with rusted-out dents and dings looked surprisingly familiar.

"George. George Mersky?"

When he turned toward me, I realized that he was not my former boss at the final job I held before Bridgy and I left Brooklyn. For one thing, this man was more disheveled than the always-neat and tidy George. Still, the resemblance was startling. The man shook his head, muttered something to himself and stared at the ground as he limped his way into the library.

I pulled the box of books from the rear of the jeep and hoisted it until I had it balanced on my forearms. When I passed the ancient Mustang, I couldn't help but peek. The entire car was jumbled with the fragments of a topsy-turvy life. Stuffed in the front passenger seat, I saw the jagged edge of a large tree limb. It crossed over the console, and its branches, most bare but some with dead leaves still clinging, straddled an assortment of bags and boxes piled on the car floor and spread across the backseat.

I shook my head. George would never tolerate such unsightly clutter. A few steps closer to the library door, I began maneuvering the box of books until I had it poised on my hip, leaving one hand free to reach for the handle. The box began to slip but I juggled it back to steady, and managed to open the door a few inches. From inside I heard a woman yelling something that began, "You can't . . ." Her screech threw off my equilibrium and the box began to slide to the ground.

The voice got louder, the words less intelligible, and then stopped abruptly when something metal crashed, followed by dead silence. A wave of whispers by patrons and staff quickly crescendoed to a flap of confusion. My box landed on the ground with a thump, and several books spilled to the concrete. As I bent to pick up the books, the man who looked like George pushed through the door, knocking into my shoulder. He was muttering incoherently.

He tripped over one of my books, and I couldn't help but say, "Oh, careful."

The man stopped short and looked directly into my eyes. He nodded his thanks for the words of caution, then he picked up the book and handed it to me. I felt an instant connection arise and then disappear when he dropped his head and went back to whispering indistinctly.

I gathered my books and went inside the library. Sally Caldera was assuring patrons that all was well while trying to straighten a book cart that was lying on its side. An elderly man, dressed in a loud Hawaiian-print shirt, kept insisting that he could lift the cart if Sally would get out of the way. I set down my box and rushed to help her set the cart back on its wheels before the old gentleman pulled a muscle or had a heart attack.

"Looks like I've come at a bad time." I pointed to the box I'd set down on the floor near the doorway. "I brought books for the book sale. Where do you want them?"

Sally pushed a mass of curly russet-colored hair off her forehead.

"Let's put them behind the desk for now. Do you want a receipt? For taxes?"

Great idea, I thought. I followed Sally to the reception desk and couldn't help but mention the man who looked like George.

"Alan. His name is Alan. He comes in all the time to use the computers. He doesn't bother anyone and we pretend he has a library card. I never forced the issue because I doubt he has an address he could use for identification. Still, he is clearly living somewhere on the island because I see him around town every now and again."

"No address?"

Sally nodded. "I think he is one of the veterans who've migrated south. They live outdoors, often in isolation, sometimes in small camps of three or four. They don't bother anyone and we certainly owe them our support. So if a vet needs to use our computers to write to the Veterans Administration or email family or friends . . ."

"I had no idea."

"Most people don't. That's one problem. The other is the people who don't care. Like Tanya Trouble. She was filling in for Marcie in the computer section a few days ago and—"

"Tanya Trouble?"

Sally discreetly pointed to a buxom brunette dressed in mile-high wedge sandals and a too-tight red skirt. She was helping a student-type go through research material.

"New volunteer. Thinks she's in charge of the whole place. Anyway, last week Alan came in and asked for computer time, but when he couldn't produce a library card,

Tanya went ballistic. He told her he needed to do some veterans business and she started yammering about no special privileges. She went on and on."

Sally shook her head.

"Confrontational isn't in Alan's DNA. I was in the back while this was going on but one of the clerks told me Alan ran out the door before anyone could intervene."

"Same as he did today?"

"He's skittish around people and would rather avoid interaction. I did have a heart-to-heart with Tanya, and explained how we liked to extend courtesy to our military veterans. She yessed me, made all the appropriate noises, but it was obvious she thought I was making a big deal out of nothing."

"If she's not interested in helping people, why volunteer here?"

Sally shrugged.

"Husband's a high-powered guy who spends all his time making pots of money. He golfs with the head of the library board of trustees . . ."

"So she may be here more to please her husband than to help patrons."

"Exactly. Oh, there she goes. She spends more time on cigarette breaks than being useful."

Sally's eyes slid toward the doorway. I turned and saw Tanya Trouble moving through the doorway, tottering on her wedges with far less grace than Aunt Ophie on spike sandals. She had a cell already at her ear and was carrying a small, shiny object I couldn't identify.

"You rarely see people smoking anymore," I said to Sally, who laughed.

"I'm not sure how much actual smoking Tanya does.

Mostly she waves the hand holding her cigarette while she talks on her cell phone. We've requested that all smokers stand away from the entrance, and we reinforced that by putting the upright trash can with the ashtray top at the far corner of the building."

I shrugged off the smoking area as something I'd never noticed, and that pleased Sally to no end.

"Out of sight, out of mind, even for the smokers. They come and go, never notice the ashtray so they don't smoke outside the building. Who wants cigarette smoke overtaking the fresh scent of a breeze off the Gulf of Mexico?"

I laughed. "Tanya Trouble, for one."

"I think she likes to show off that fancy lighter of hers. Claims her husband paid nearly a hundred thousand dollars for it as a gift for their first anniversary. She tells anyone who will listen that all those sparkly bits are hundreds of tiny diamonds and set in eighteen-karat white gold with platinum inlays. Carries it everywhere, even in nonsmoking spaces. Odd."

All this talk of cigarettes reminded me.

"By any chance does she drive a blue Corvette?"

"She left the top down again, right? Last week ashes were swirling around and flew right into a woman's eye when she stepped out of her car. I'm going to have to speak to her about the car, and about Alan. Here she comes. See you soon."

I headed toward the door, and as I passed Tanya, I got a good look at the lighter in her hand. It seemed too flashy to be real gold and diamonds. I would have thought it came from the dollar store. No accounting for taste.

In the parking lot, once I brushed away some ash that

had twirled from Tanya's ashtray to my windshield, I dismissed her completely. I hurried back to the Read 'Em and Eat determined that as soon as the lunch rush was over, I'd call George Mersky to ask if he had a relative named Alan living in Florida.

Chapter Two ‖‖‖‖‖‖

Within five minutes of walking through the door of the Read 'Em and Eat and tying on my apron, I forgot all about Alan, the library and Tanya Trouble. We were that busy.

Miguel had his *Old Man and the Sea* Chowder on the menu and from the way folks were ordering, I hoped he made enough.

Maggie Latimer, owner of our local yoga studio, Zencentric, came in with a woman who was as tall and lithe as Maggie but with dark auburn hair cut in an adorable pixie in contrast to Maggie's blond ponytail. They sat at the Robert Frost table. Maggie was pointing out the various Frost memorabilia laminated to the tabletop, copies of poems, pictures of the author, an article or two, when I brought over their menus.

"See the fruit poems, the one about apple picking and the one about blueberries?" Maggie pointed to the menus

still in my hand. "You'll find Robert Frost Apple and Blueberry Tartlets on the menu and they are yummy."

As I set the menus on the table Maggie introduced me to
her sister, Karen.

"Karen is here for a month recovering from a too-long
bout of pneumonia."

I welcomed Karen and she responded with an earnest smile.

"Maggie tells me that besides scrumptious food, you also
serve fascinating conversation at book club meetings. I look
forward to attending one or two while I'm here." She glanced
at the bookshelves that lined two walls of the café. "I'll
probably want to browse a little after lunch."

The sisters decided on *Old Man and the Sea* Chowder
with *Catcher in the Rye* Toast and sweet tea. I set the order
request on the pass-through shelf, and while I was pouring
the sweet tea, I decided to get a copy of this month's book
club calendar for Karen. I was reaching for the flier when
the door flung open and Jocelyn Kendall, her strawlike hair
even more askew that usual, stepped in. She looked around,
confusion mounting in her eyes.

"I didn't think I was that late. Did I miss it completely?"

I made the mistake of taking a step toward her. I was
close enough that she grabbed my shoulders and shook me.

"Why didn't you send out an email? Why didn't you call
me? I have so much to say."

When don't you? I kept that thought to myself and asked,
"Jocelyn, what are you talking about?"

"The Tea and Mystery Afternoons. *The Circular Staircase*? Mary Roberts Rinehart? For goodness' sake, Sassy,
you're in charge of the book clubs; I shouldn't have to tell
you what I'm talking about. You should know."

Then like an errant preschooler, she stamped her foot and fixed a bold, defiant stare at the book corner where the book clubs hold their meetings.

How convenient that I was holding a book club calendar in my hand. I thrust it at her and picked up the two tall glasses of sweet tea and walked to Maggie's table.

Behind me I heard Jocelyn groan.

"Tomorrow. The meeting is tomorrow! I rearranged my entire day for nothing."

I knew if I looked at her, I'd be subjected to a harangue of epic proportions. The fact that the error was hers was of no consequence.

As I set the tea on the table, Maggie whispered, "Don't turn around. Uh-oh, she's heading this way."

Feeling trapped, doomed even, I grasped for the handiest lifesaver.

"Jocelyn, have you met Maggie's sister, Karen?"

Jocelyn morphed instantly from offended book club member to helpful pastor's wife and greeted Karen as if she was a brand-new parishioner being welcomed to the flock.

"Maggie, you must bring your charming sister to late service on Sunday." She patted Karen's hand. "It's not that late, of course, ten fifteen. But the eight o'clock service seems so early. Still, some of the parishioners like it. Attend worship and get on with your day. I do envy the up-and-at-'em types. I'm a bit of a slug in the morning."

She drew a breath, smiling ruefully, and I took the opportunity to switch the topic entirely.

"I was at the library earlier and I noticed a poster for a palm frond weaving class."

"What do they weave? Grass skirts?" Maggie's laugh had the vibrancy of jingle bells.

"The pictures on the poster were of flower shapes. We should think about going. Karen, how long are you staying on the island?"

"Oh, I'm here for a month or until Maggie tires of my company, whichever comes first."

Both sisters laughed and it was a double jingle for sure.

Jocelyn sniffed. "I'll have to check the date. Busy, busy you know, pastor's wife. Lots to do." She waggled a finger at Karen. "Remember late service—coffee after."

She curved toward me and her "I'll see *you* tomorrow" sounded like a not-so-veiled threat.

The three of us silently watched her flounce out the door and on to terrorizing her next victim, who was more often than not her long-suffering husband, Pastor John.

As soon as the door closed behind Jocelyn, Karen opened her mouth but Maggie cut her off with a nod.

"Yep. She's always like that, a special combination of brusqueness and self-absorption, as irritating as sand in your sneaker."

"What's this about *The Circular Staircase*? It's one of my all-time faves."

Maggie pointed to me.

"Sassy is the book-meister for the book clubs that meet at the Read 'Em and Eat. Lots of different topics. At the Potluck Book Club we read foodie books; the Tea and Mystery Afternoons—Golden Age women mystery authors; Books Before Breakfast, well, I'm teaching a meditation class at that hour but that's more of a mix of all types of books, wouldn't you say, Sassy?"

"Yes, but all the clubs are open to suggestion. Sometimes I recommend a book, sometimes the members choose among themselves. It's all very casual."

"Sounds like fun."

"Oh, it is," Maggie assured her sister. "Come with me tomorrow afternoon. You already know the book. You can refresh with my copy."

When Maggie paid the check, I gave a book club calendar to Karen, who thanked me and then commented on how unusual but fitting she found my name to be.

"Mary Sassafras Cabot, that's my whole moniker, but my mother is a flower-power, earth-child type and called me Sassy from day one. It stuck."

The sisters left, promising to come back tomorrow afternoon.

Two sunburned surfer types lingered over a second round of orange juice at the Ernest Hemingway table while a young mother at Dr. Seuss was watching her preschooler dawdle as he played with his grilled chicken strips and apple sauce. I asked Bridgy to keep an eye on them all while I went outside to make a phone call.

I sat on a bench in front of the café and whipped out my cell phone. This was one of those times I was super glad that I'd always been neurotic about keeping any and all phone numbers in my phone. If I met someone three years ago, and we exchanged phone numbers so that the first one to hear about the next major sale on Celebrity Pink clothes in Belk's Department Store could call the other, believe me, that number is still in my phone.

So it was no surprise that even though I hadn't spoken to

George Mersky in a couple of years, his number was right there, waiting for me to push a button and connect.

He answered on the second ring and sounded harried as always.

"Mersky."

"Hi, George, this is Sassy Cabot."

"Sassy! What a pleasant surprise. How is life along the Gulf of Mexico?"

I could almost see his eyes move to the clock while his brain calculated how many minutes he could spare for social nice-nice before he cut me loose and went back to the stacks of papers filled with numbers that were his accountant heart's true love.

"Everything here is fine. I was wondering . . . it's none of my business . . . but do you happen to know someone named Alan? Someone who looks like you."

The silence was palpable for more than a minute.

"You've seen my brother Alan? Oh my God. Is he okay? Is he hurt?"

I hesitated. How could I explain the agitation I'd witnessed?

"He seems fine physically, but . . ."

Again I was at a loss for words.

"Sassy, Alan served three tours in Iraq. He suffers from post-traumatic stress disorder. Is he living on the streets? Does he need help?"

I was sure George was tugging on his ear as he always did when something upset him.

"No. No, he's fine. Nothing like that. I saw him at the library—"

15

"Then he's back to his old self, reading those adventure books he always loved?"

The hope in George's voice was distressing. How could I explain? Clearly, Alan still had problems. I gave it my best shot and George understood instantly. I ended by saying that when I called Alan "George" and he turned around, I felt compelled to get in touch with George on the off chance they were related.

"I'm so glad you did. And you say the librarian knows him? Wonderful. Perhaps she could ask him to call me. When we don't hear from Alan for long stretches of time, we try to find him but aren't always successful. And, even if they know where he is, the Veterans Administration can't give out that information—even to family."

I could hear such frustration in his voice that I offered to look for Alan. I heard myself telling George that Fort Myers Beach is a small town and once I started looking, I was sure to find out where Alan was staying and what he was doing.

By the time we said good-bye I was already certain I'd bitten off more than I could chew.

I went inside and gave the surfer dudes their check. I smiled at the toddler who'd fallen asleep in his chair and poured the mom another cup of green tea to enjoy along with the quiet. I bussed some dishes into the kitchen. Bridgy was loading the dishwasher and listening to Miguel go on and on about the wonders of Bow, his gorgeous black Maine Coon.

"She is the most extraordinary cat. Yesterday I was sitting on the patio when I heard a splash. Bow was roaming around, wandering back and forth between the house and the edge of Estero Bay but I thought no. She wouldn't jump in the water. Cats and water, ay, never. And a few minutes later, there she is on the patio, shaking her dripping-wet coat, with a fish in her mouth. She enjoyed it for her dinner."

"You let her eat raw fish?" Never a sushi girl, I shuddered at the thought.

"Of course not, *chica*. I skinned and boned the fish and sautéed it in olive oil. First, though, I dried and combed my beautiful girl's coat."

Behind Miguel's back Bridgy gave me an "okay" sign. We had been instrumental in getting Miguel and Bow to be roomies. The sleek, gorgeous but extremely uppity Bow once belonged to a frequent book club member, and when the woman died unexpectedly, Miguel adopted the cat. It turned out to be a true love match.

I thought I heard the toddler stirring so I stuck my head out the kitchen door. But he was still asleep and his mother was browsing the bookshelves. She gave me a wave and went right back to leafing through the fiction section.

"Don't run away just yet," Miguel commanded. "I have an idea for tomorrow's book club."

I turned my attention back to the kitchen.

Done with the dishwasher, Bridgy was pouring herself a glass of water. She held the pitcher, filled with lemon and lime slices, high in the air, as if asking if I wanted some, and I nodded.

Miguel motioned me over to the pastry work counter.

"Tomorrow the mystery ladies meet and I have a special treat for them."

He eyed a plate covered with a yellow gingham dish towel.

I made sure to "oh" and "ah," lavishly applauding his thoughtfulness. Finally, he waved two fingers, signaling permission to remove the towel.

Having gotten in trouble before, I knew to lift the towel carefully with both hands so as not to disturb the goodies underneath. And there they were—question mark cookies.

I clapped my hands.

"Goodness. Perfectly shaped question marks! And the icing!"

Miguel nodded. "I thought color would make the shape pop."

Every cookie was iced in white, but each one was edged with orange, red or yellow gel, clearly defining the shape. The display was guaranteed to wow the book club members, or as I called them, the clubbies.

I was still praising Miguel when I heard a wail from the dining room. The toddler had woken up. I rushed in. His mother was bundling him and his toys back into his umbrella stroller.

She handed him a plastic action figure, one I didn't recognize. He cooed and began to bang the toy on his knee.

"I was wondering. My mother lent me *Winds of War* by Herman Wouk and I loved it. I'm dying to know what happens to Pug and Rhoda and oh, just everybody. Could you order me a copy of *War and Remembrance*? I've got to know."

I took her phone number and tucked it on the bulletin board so I could call her when the book came in. As I wrote *War and Remembrance* next to her name, I thought of the soldier I'd promised to find.

Chapter Three

The Tea and Mystery Afternoons Book Club discussed *The Circular Staircase* peacefully with Jocelyn on her best behavior, perhaps because she considered Maggie's sister, Karen, to be a guest. But at the Books Before Breakfast meeting a few days later, she started a raging debate about the relevance of the novels written by D. E. Stevenson in general and her wildly popular *Miss Buncle's Book*, in particular.

"Compared to Stevenson's Mrs. Tim books, Miss Buncle lacks an element of adventure." Jocelyn smacked her hand on the book in her lap to emphasize her point.

"Writing under the nom de plume 'John Smith,' Miss Buncle published a thinly disguised book about her neighbors. That doesn't strike you as a daring exploit for a middle-aged spinster?" Ever since Blondie Quinlin had begun accompanying her neighbor Augusta Maddox to the early-morning book club, she'd delighted in tweaking Jocelyn's nose at every possible opportunity.

"Well, I wouldn't have the nerve." Lisette Ortiz shook her curly dark hair.

Irene Lester, the newest member, leaned over and patted Lisette on the arm. "You're far from middle-aged, honey, and I doubt you'll ever be a spinster."

Irene slid her reading glasses down from her forehead and opened her book. "You've only to look at the description of Silverstream in the first couple of pages. That bakery woman—ah, here she is—Mrs. Goldsmith, knows the morning breakfast habits of the entire village. Do you really think anything goes on in the village that everyone doesn't know? And while living in that atmosphere Miss Buncle chose to write a book with characters based on the local residents. I call that brave. And the book was funny. I love humor now and again. Anyway, I have a hair appointment. Can we choose next month's book?"

I sat back and let the clubbies wrestle among themselves until they narrowed down to two books. Most heads nodded when Lisette mentioned a fairly new Nora Roberts book, *The Collector*. Irene suggested that the eternally classic *O Pioneers!*, written by Willa Cather more than a century ago, still had a lot to offer.

Jocelyn snapped, "Willa Cather belongs at the Classic Book Club, not here."

I jumped in for the rescue. "Over the past few months the Classic Club has become more of a Teen Club with Maggie Latimer's daughter Holly and some of her friends. And Books Before Breakfast is the one club that has no theme. We read whatever strikes our fancy."

I beamed what I hoped was a gigawatt smile.

I was saved from having Jocelyn jump on me by Bridgy, who called me over to the counter.

She was talking to an attractive mid-twentyish woman dressed in what could have passed for a uniform of some sort. Her white man-tailored shirt, complete with button-down collar, was tucked neatly into a black pencil skirt. And, rather than the open-toed sandals that were de rigueur all over the island, she wore black low-heeled pumps. I wondered what she was trying to sell, and I guessed Bridgy wanted my opinion on whether or not we should consider buying.

I was still a few feet away when Bridgy started introductions.

"Elaine Tibor, this is Sassy Cabot, co-owner of the Read 'Em and Eat. Sassy, Elaine is a graduate student at FSU and waits tables during the dinner shift at the country club. Schedule permitting, she's looking for an occasional breakfast or lunch shift to supplement. You know how grad school goes."

I remembered well.

Elaine took a quick step to cover the distance between us and reached out to give my hand a strong and confident shake. She had a self-assured, personable way about her, which made me think she'd relate well to the customers. When I said so, I loved her response.

"I heard along the beach that you serve the best breakfast on the island. Everyone talks about the Read 'Em and Eat as being relaxed and fun. I thought it would be a nice relief from the stuffiness of my dinner job." Her smile was framed by two charming dimples.

Well, if she wanted a flavor the direct opposite of country club, she'd applied at the right place. Breakfast and lunch with a casual literary twist—our tables were named for authors with samples of the author's work, photographs and articles laminated on the tabletops. Lots of menu items with authors' names or book titles worked into the offerings. Two walls were covered with bookshelves filled with books of every description from chick lit to deep-sea fishing guides. The books and the book corner encouraged participation in the book clubs, which meet here regularly.

Impulsively, I decided we should give Elaine a trial. I exchanged a look with Bridgy, which she read instantly and correctly.

The voices coming from the book corner were getting louder and more insistent. I thanked Elaine for coming in and excused myself, leaving Bridgy to work out the details.

I stood behind my chair and listened to Augusta Maddox, never one for compromise, lay down the law. Tiny as she was, her booming baritone filled the room.

"We voted. Everyone wants to read *O Pioneers!* 'cept you." She gave Jocelyn a stern face. "Don't be such a horse's patootie. Lisette's willing to wait a month for the Nora Roberts book. Why can't you?"

Jocelyn opened her mouth and shut it. She gave her watch a swift glance and began to gather her things.

Crisis averted.

Everyone wanted me to order enough copies of the Cather book for the club members, except Jocelyn, who mumbled something about the library as she headed to the door.

Lissette asked me to order a copy of *The Collector*.

"My sister in Kansas City read it and was so gushy in her recommendation. I really don't want to wait. It doesn't matter when the club decides to read *The Collector* as long as I get it soon." And she waved good-bye.

Augusta and Blondie stopped at the counter, waiting for Bridgy's attention, so rather than straighten out the book corner, I popped behind the counter.

"Not staying for breakfast this morning, ladies?" I asked with a cheery smile. I had a special affection for Augusta and was growing fonder every day of Blondie, who had stepped up and filled in gracefully when Augusta's cousin and best friend died suddenly. It was nice to see two seventy-somethings hanging out and having fun. I hoped that would be Bridgy and me in fifty years.

"Ecology meeting got pushed up. Usually later in the day but our space at the community center is being painted. Carrie Trotter arranged for us to have a meeting room at that big hotel down toward Lovers Key. Free, o' course." Augusta hitched her jeans. "Can't expect us to volunteer our time to save the Earth and pay for the privilege."

Blondie nodded in agreement.

"We'd like to bring a dozen of those Robert Frost Apple and Blueberry Tartlets to the meeting. Could you cut them in half? One or two diabetics in the crowd. Some of the others are always on diets. We don't want to tempt them with too much sweet stuff."

"How about I add two or three Miss Marple Scones. Less sugar."

That seemed to please the ladies. When I came out of the kitchen with their box of pastries, Elaine Tibor was gone and Bridgy was taking an order from two women she'd seated at Barbara Cartland. A couple of fisherman came in, the salty

23

smell of the Gulf of Mexico still clinging to their clothes. I sat them at Robert Louis Stevenson. The man with the beard and a half dozen colorful fishing flies stuck on the patch pockets of his well-worn gray vest looked at the tabletop and began reading the poem we had laminated there among other Stevenson quotes and pictures.

"You expect me to believe that the same guy who wrote *Treasure Island* and *Dr. Jekyll and Mr. Hyde* wrote this little kiddie poem?"

I laughed and quoted, *"When I was down beside the sea* . . . it's called 'At the Sea-Side.' What better poem for a café at the beach?"

He shook his head. "Doesn't sound like the same guy who made up Mr. Hyde."

"That's the beauty of fiction," his tablemate interjected. "It's all made up."

He turned to me.

"How about some coffee while we check out the menu?"

I brought their coffee, then passed their orders to the kitchen.

Judge Harcroft, retired from traffic court not so very long ago, came in, picked up the *Fort Myers Beach News* from the counter and went directly to his usual table, Dashiell Hammett. He opened the broadsheet and ignored the world around him. I placed a cup of coffee on the table and turned away, knowing he'd signal imperiously when, having read the menu two or three times from top to bottom, he was ready to order his usual, Hammett Ham 'n Eggs.

So I was surprised when he stopped me.

"Er, Sassy, I was wondering . . ."

I stood, waiting for the rest of the sentence. After a while, it came.

". . . about Augusta Maddox. How is she doing since, er, you know."

A while back, during a really stressful time, the judge and Miss Augusta had a falling out. He'd been studiously avoiding her ever since.

I dropped into the seat opposite him and said softly. "Of course Miss Augusta won't ever forget the tragedy, but the rest of what went on, well, wasn't that all a big misunderstanding?"

He nodded. "I didn't mean to cause difficulty. I was the nephews' lawyer. I thought they were in the right. I was representing their interest."

"You haven't been to any book club meetings in a long time. Why not come back to one or two? We could use your level head."

Knowing the judge could take only so much intimacy, I stood up and held my order pad and pencil at the ready.

I put the judge's order on the pass-through and picked up the fishermen's breakfast, when the door flipped open with the force of Category Three hurricane winds. I nearly dropped a plate of toast. I hurried to Robert Louis Stevenson and was pleased that I set the orders down correctly. Double order of bacon and eggs for the poetry skeptic and *Green Eggs and Ham* for his fishing buddy.

When I turned toward the door, I was grateful that I'd served the food before I looked. Aunt Ophie was leaning against the jamb with her hand, palm outward, resting against her forehead like a 1940s femme fatale. Still as a statue, she was waiting for attention. She'd block any and all doorway traffic until someone, or more to her liking, everyone, started to worry over her. I was debating whether to give in or ignore her, when Bridgy came out of the kitchen with a plate of oatmeal. She took one look at Ophie, thrust the plate at me with such force that I nearly didn't catch it and whispered, "Cartland, the woman facing front."

Then she turned, and in a voice that could surely be heard from the beach to the bay, she said, "Aunt Ophie, my darlin', what on earth is wrong? Come over here and sit down. You look like death."

Ophie began to preen like a beloved kitten, delighted that she now had everyone's attention, until she heard Bridgy utter that final word. In that exact second, she started to wail.

Bridgy took her arm gently and led her to Emily Dickinson.

"Sit down, poor thing. What on earth has distressed you so?"

Every customer in the café was murmuring, voices filled with concern, but I'd seen Ophie carry on worse than this when she broke a fingernail, so I walked on back to the Barbara Cartland table to serve the oatmeal. Thank goodness I had set the plate on the table, or the oatmeal might have landed in the customer's lap when Ophie began wailing again. This time there were words.

"It was murder, y'all. She's dead. And it was murder pure and simple."

Chapter Four

Nothing like shouts of "Murder!" to stir up a crowd. One of the ladies at Barbara Cartland let out a scream so bloodcurdling that you would think she was sitting in the first row of a 3-D movie and the ax murderer had jumped out from behind the bureau.

The two fishermen stood up, looked around, realized we were not under immediate attack and sat down again. Judge Harcroft continued to turn the pages of the *Fort Myers Beach News*. I guess he was almost as used to Aunt Ophie as I was.

Bridgy took a deep breath and by the time I reached her, she was whispering to Ophie. "Who is dead? Who was murdered?"

Ophie swung her eyes back and forth between Bridgy and me. It wasn't like her to be the least bit hesitant, and yet, she was. Unless she was heightening the drama.

"I don't know who. I only know that right here in Fort Myers Beach a woman was murdered. In. Cold. Blood."

I was always less tolerant of Ophie than Bridgy was. I wanted to end the spectacle sooner rather than later. I asked Bridgy to fetch a pitcher of sweet tea. She headed for the counter and I sat down.

"Ophie, how do you know this?

I kept one ear on our customers but I kept my eyes firmly on Ophie.

Again, a slight hesitancy. Finally her shoulders sagged and she let out a sigh. "Never occurred to me that she'd tell a lie that bold in order to get out of a meeting."

Bridgy set a glass of tea in front of Ophie and sat down. "Who, Ophie? Who told you there was a murder?"

"Remember that upscale designer? Y'all fixed us that nice box of Miss Marple Scones. Anyway, her assistant called early on to say something came up and did I have time to reschedule later in the day. Well, of course I agreed. Pays to accommodate a client of her stature."

Ophie leaned to her right and peered over my shoulder, checking to be sure that all the diners were following her story. I heard the rustle of Judge Harcroft's newspaper and Ophie gave a slight frown, followed by a shrug. She'd have to be satisfied with having the attention of nearly everyone in the room.

"I took the opportunity to tidy up some and rearrange a thing or two. Next thing I know the time of our second appointment has come and gone. So I called Frederica, that's her name, the designer. Pretty isn't it? She didn't answer right away and when she did, she was crying loud enough to call the farmhands in for supper. That's when she told me about the murder."

The ladies at Barbara Cartland both gasped as if their purses had been snatched and one of the fisherman gave a loud, "Whoa." That's when I realized we should have had this conversation in the kitchen. Too late now.

Ophie sat back and relaxed, having told her tale and received a grand reaction in return. But we still had no idea who, if anyone, had been murdered.

I threw out a prompt. "What exactly did Frederica say?"

"Between sobs she told me that a woman she knew had been murdered right here on the island. Frederica said she hoped she'd be able to pull herself together and perhaps we could meet tomorrow."

Bridgy's turn to try. "Did she tell you the woman's name?

"She might have mentioned a name, but with all that crying . . ."

The door opened and Lee County Sheriff's Deputy Ryan Mantoni strode into the room. He took one look at the three of us huddled around the Emily Dickenson table and recognized a problem when he saw it. "Miss Ophelia, what's worrying you?"

"There's been a murder." And Ophie dramatically flung her arm across her forehead once again.

"So you already heard 'bout that. Not surprising. News travels around this island at warp speed. We're never on beach time when it comes to gossip."

I was relieved. Gossip. The murder was only a rumor.

"So there wasn't any murder?"

"There was a murder all right. Over on Moon Shell Drive. At the end of the road, past the curve. It's a little isolated there. A lady was sitting in her hot tub when someone snuck up behind her and cracked her skull. No one noticed for a long while. She was hard-boiled by the time her husband came home and called us. Emergency medical services couldn't do a thing. She's at the medical examiner now."

Totally unaware of the impact of what he said had on everyone in the room, Ryan switched topics.

"Could I get a sandwich to go? Bacon and egg on whole wheat toast. And a container of coffee. Maybe a muffin?"

He looked back and forth between Bridgy and me, and it slowly dawned on him that neither of us was writing down his order. "What?"

I stood, took his arm, pulled him over to the counter and whispered, "You announced that a woman was bludgeoned to death a mile or so down Estero Boulevard and then moved right on to 'Can I have a sandwich?' That's one way to stir up the crowd."

Trying to distract the remaining customers, Bridgy made the rounds offering more coffee or water. The ladies at Barbara Cartland were completely unnerved. One grabbed Bridgy's arm and told her they wanted to ask Ryan if they'd be safe in their rental bungalow until the end of season. Like anyone was willing to tell them they wouldn't be.

I looked at Ryan. "See what I mean?"

He nodded. As he ambled over to the Barbara Cartland table, I called after him. "I'll get Miguel started on that sandwich."

The fishermen were suddenly anxious to pay their bill, but not before telling me that we really should consider wiring the doors and windows with an alarm system. I guessed they were heading out to spread the word of the unfortunate victim's demise. If they mentioned hearing the news in the Read 'Em and Eat, it was sure to bring in an afternoon rush of customers wanting to find out what else we knew about the tragedy. I made a mental note to make sure we had plenty of sweet tea and pastries.

I noticed Ophie's shoulders slump. She usually didn't lose her audience so quickly. Ryan escorted the two Barbara Cartland ladies to their car, telling me he'd be right back for his sandwich.

As soon as the door closed behind him, Ophie brightened. "Ryan knows more than he's saying. I bet we can get him to tell us all the gory details."

I already envisioned a bloated body with a smashed skull. Honestly, how much more gore did we need? I held off answering Ophie because Judge Harcroft came up to the counter, bill and cash in hand. As I rang up his total, he shook his head.

"I remember a time when no one in Fort Myers Beach ever locked their doors. My father never worried about losing his car keys. He left them in the car, right in the ignition. And now, well, I'm glad I don't have a hot tub." He separated two one-dollar bills from the change I'd given him and slid them, his standard tip, across the counter to me. "Sad state of affairs." More head shaking and then he spoke his customary exit line, his homage to Hammett. "If you'll forgive me . . . I must *Dash*."

Ryan opened the door and held it as the judge walked out. Then as he stepped back inside, he took a look at the empty tables and raised his hands in front of his face in mock horror. "Was it something I said?"

"Honey chile," Ophie commanded Ryan, "you sit yourself down right here and tell me all about this horrible murder. I need to decide if I should order new locks. And the gentlemen who left a few minutes ago suggested alarm systems for everyone."

"Sorry, Miss Ophelia, duty calls. I've got to get back to the Lipscome house—still lots to be done."

Ophie and I both jumped on him as soon as he said the name Lipscome.

"Is Tanya Lipscome dead? The woman who volunteers in the library?"

"Lordy me." Ophie clutched her chest. "Is this dead woman related to the folks at Lipscome Builders?" Then she dropped her hands and gave me a look steeped in pique. "How do you know any of the Lipscomes?"

At that moment Bridgy came out of the kitchen carrying Ryan's meal all neatly bundled in a brown paper sack. I heard her murmur, "Uh-oh," under her breath. If she thought she could get away with it, I'm sure she would have run back into the kitchen. Instead she tried a diversionary tactic.

"Ryan, you didn't say what kind of muffin you wanted so I packed a double-chocolate chip." And she picked up a pot of coffee and started to fill a takeaway cup.

Ophie and I were glaring at Bridgy but she continued to put the finishing touches on Ryan's coffee as though she hadn't walked in the room and interrupted a conversation that was important to both Ophie and me.

Ryan was waiting at the cash register but when Bridgy started to hand him his meal, Ophie stood up and shouted.

"Don't you dare give him that food. He'll waltz out of here. We want answers."

Ryan laughed while pretending to duck as if Ophie had thrown something at his head. "Miss Ophelia, the victim is the wife of Barry Lipscome, who owns Lipscome Builders. What else what would you like to know?"

Ophie sat back down and, elbows on the table, she dropped her head in her hands and began rocking back and forth. "There goes my money."

Bridgy rushed over and put an arm around Ophie's shoulders. "Don't worry, sweetie, I'm sure it will take some time for him to recover from this loss, but sooner or later Mr. Lipscome will have to pay attention to his business or he'll starve. Before you know it Frederica will be designing gorgeous rooms with your treasures as focal points."

Listening to Bridgy soothing Ophie, I was getting antsier by the minute. Ryan hadn't answered my question. He had his hand on the door handle when I asked again, "And her first name? What was Mrs. Lipscome's first name?"

"Tanya. Her name was Tanya Lipscome. I have to get back to work. See you later."

"Tanya Trouble." The name burst from my lips. Everyone looked at me. Ryan let the door close and turned toward me. "You know her?"

This was awkward. How much did I want to tell? I made an instant decision to leave Alan out of it for now. "Sally calls her that." I hoped I didn't sound defensive.

Ryan looked directly at me. He'd gone from friend to deputy in two seconds flat. "Sally?"

"Sally Caldera. Tanya Lipscome is a library volunteer. And she smokes." I could still see Ryan waiting for the tie-in to the nickname. "Cigarettes. She smokes cigarettes and once got ashes in a library patron's eye. See, trouble," I finished lamely.

"Okay, thanks." Ryan was anxious to get out the door.

"If you think of anything else I should know, call my cell."
And he was gone.

Of course Bridgy was all over me the second the door
closed behind Ryan. "You know something. I can see it all
over your face. Good thing Ryan doesn't know you as well
as I do or you'd be on your way to an interrogation room."

I waved her off. "What could I know? Until two minutes
ago we didn't even know who the victim was."

I turned toward the kitchen but Bridgy wasn't having it.
"Mary Sassafras Cabot, you stop right there. What did you
not tell Ryan?"

I knew she'd haunt me until I fessed up. I sighed and gave
in. "I saw Tanya at the library the other day. She was having
a monumental fight with a patron. That's all."

Bridgy placed her hands on her hips, and glowered. Once
she pursed her lips and tilted her head to the side, I knew I
was done for. I raised my hands in surrender. "Okay, I didn't
tell Ryan because it didn't mean anything. Alan wouldn't
hurt a fly."

Ophie pushed back her chair and stood facing me with
the exact same body language as her niece. Easy to see they
were related. "Who is this Alan?"

From the doorway, Cady Stanton answered. "Alan Mersky. Here, I have a picture."

He took out his iPhone.

Chapter Five

He was dressed in his usual Florida work clothes, khakis and a golf shirt; this one was light green and I thought it made his brown eyes appear more hazel. He ran one hand over his sandy hair, a habit he'd had for as long as I'd known him, and then held out his iPhone for all to see.

Bridgy and Ophie crowded around Cady, both eager for a close look at the picture. I held back. If Cady, a reporter for the *Fort Myers Beach News*, was carrying a picture of Alan Mersky on his phone, then I knew Alan was in serious trouble. I pulled my own cell out of my pocket intending to call George, but then realized I had nothing concrete to tell him. I dropped the phone back in my pocket and patted it for good measure. I'd make the call as soon as I'd gotten as much information as I could out of Cady.

After taking a long look at the picture, Ophie took a step back and exonerated Alan of any and all wrongdoing. "He doesn't look one bit dangerous to me. Maybe a tad lost, is all."

Hoping to keep the conversation focused on the picture and away from any more criticism of me for withholding information from Ryan, I agreed, perhaps a little too loudly. "That's what I thought. Why waste everyone's time pointing at a person who couldn't possibly be a killer?"

Cady gave me a sharp look. "What are you talking about? I'm not pointing at Alan Mersky. A little less than an hour ago the sheriff declared him a person of interest. How do you think I got the picture? The techs took it from the library security tape, and deputies are asking everyone to be on the lookout. If Mersky is on the island, I'm sure the deputies will have him secured at the station within a few hours."

Ophie shuddered and then shook her head. "Well, I hope they treat him well when they find him. I swear I can't see a smidgeon of danger in those eyes." She pushed the phone back toward Cady and planted her hands firmly on her hips, ready to defend Alan from any and all comers.

Since Ophie was usually more of a conspiracy theorist, Bridgy was confused by her defense of Alan. She shook her finger in Ophie's face. "Don't be so sure that the look in a person's eye is telling you the whole story. You never even met the man. And that reminds me." She turned to me. "What's your story? You know this Alan?"

I was grappling for an answer when the kitchen door swung open and Miguel leaned through the doorway. His white chef's hat was tilted at a rakish angle and covered most of his dark curly hair. "Cady, I thought I heard your voice. I have an apple pie straight from the oven. It's a new recipe. You want to try a piece, *sí*?"

We all knew Miguel wouldn't have to ask twice. Cady immediately sat down at Robert Frost. He nodded when I asked if he wanted a cup of coffee. When I put the cup and saucer in front of him, Cady latched on to my wrist, pressing gently, signaling me to sit. He spoke in a "whispering in church" voice that was destined to attract the big ears of both Bridgy and her aunt.

"Okay, Sassy, tell me. What do you know about Alan Mersky?"

Before I could make up an answer that would appease him, Bridgy was standing in the space between us with Ophie right behind her.

"Maybe she'll tell *you* what's going on. She's been keeping secrets from us, from Ryan, from everybody." Bridgy shook her head and raised her eyes heavenward as if my behavior would be incomprehensible even to the Lord Himself.

"That's so not true. I didn't get a chance to tell you, that's all. I didn't think it was that important." I sat back in my chair, crossed my arms and attempted, with not much luck, to stare the three of them down.

Once again, Miguel saved me. He burst through the kitchen door carrying a dessert plate rendered nearly invisible by a supersized wedge of apple pie that filled the entire café with the aroma of an orchard in early autumn with a tinge of cinnamon. In his other hand he held a glass bowl brimming with freshly whipped cream. He swung around both Ophie and Bridgy until he could easily set the pie in front of Cady. Then Miguel extended the glass bowl and raised a questioning eyebrow. At Cady's grin, Miguel waved his spoon with a grand flourish, scooped up a healthy dollop of whipped cream and splashed it on top of the pie. Cady instantly forgot about me, Alan Mersky and everything else in the universe. He picked up his fork, broke off a chunk of pie and opened his mouth wide.

Bridgy demanded, "Is that what you're going to do, sit there and eat, while Sassy is in trouble up to her ears?"

Cady's fork wavered for a few seconds in midair. Then, as if moving on its own accord, the fork disappeared into Cady's mouth.

"Mmm, mm." Cady gave Miguel a thumbs-up. "Best ever, hombre."

Miguel broke into a wide, satisfied grin. Nothing pleased him more than high praise for one of his new kitchen creations.

Out of the corner of my eye, I saw Ophie give a tiny push to Bridgy's arm, as if directing her to reclaim the spotlight so they could keep the focus on my flaws.

Bridgy tried to charm Miguel with assurances that Cady was only the first of many customers who would adore his new apple pie recipe. She piled the compliments higher than Miguel had piled the whipped cream. It was evident that she wanted him to bask in glory for a moment or two and then retreat to the kitchen. I could see Miguel wasn't having it. There was something else on his mind, and he wasn't heading back to the kitchen until he said his piece, whatever it may be. Bridgy's voice trailed off. Miguel never budged.

Oblivious to us all, Cady savored his apple pie. Eventually the tense silence punctured his bliss. He looked at us warily and decided Miguel was the safest choice. "Miguel, I don't know how you can keep developing recipes, each one better than the last."

Ophie made a *humph* noise deep in her throat, and I made

a mental note to remind Cady the next time he came in to order Ophie's buttermilk pie, which was a staple on our menu. Miguel surprised us all by doing something he rarely does. He pulled out a chair and sat down. "It is hard to create new recipes when I am so worried about the snake."

We all blinked simultaneously. Snake?

Cady had just taken a sip of coffee and he managed to get it down without choking.

Ophie leaned over Bridgy's shoulder, directing her questions to Miguel. "Y'all know how to cook a snake? Are y'all making snake soup? I've heard it has potent medicinal uses."

Miguel looked at Ophie as if she'd gone insane. "Not the kind of snake that people eat. The big snake that eats other animals. I'm worried about a green anaconda eating my beautiful little Bow. She's a feisty cat, *sí*, but she's no match for one of the biggest snakes in the world."

We all exchanged puzzled looks. Even Ophie was rendered speechless— a rare achievement for Miguel, or anyone else for that matter.

Cady's reporter instincts took over. "Miguel, why would Bow go up against a green anaconda? And where in Sam Hill would she find one?

"Ha! Don't you read your own newspaper?" Miguel stood, reached under his apron and pulled a folded scrap of newssheet from his pocket. He spread it on the table. "A giant green anaconda has been spotted swimming, happy as you please, in Estero Bay between Mound Island and San Carlos Island. He's huge. He swims very fast. And my yard borders Estero Bay. Every day my pretty Bow scampers along the edge of the bay exploring the mangrove roots, sea grapes and swamp grass. She swats at tree crabs, chases those tiny green lizards.

39

Once she found a sea turtle, she tapped and tapped on the shell. She thought she was inviting the turtle out to play, but the more she tapped, the more the turtle refused." Miguel smiled broadly at the memory, and then he swiftly returned to the present day and the topic at hand. "That area beside my house is her playground. As long as the snake is in the bay, who knows where he will turn up next? My Bow is in great danger. Every pet on the island is in danger."

He pushed the clipping toward Cady and flopped back in his seat so hard the chair's legs thumped.

Bridgy had the temerity to ask, "When you say 'giant,' how big are we talking about?"

Miguel pointed to the article. "The newspaper says that green anacondas grow anywhere from twelve to fifteen, twenty feet. And when fully grown, they weigh more than two hundred pounds.

Ophie gasped. "And here I'm thinking of something along the lines of a big garden snake, two, maybe three feet long."

Cady scanned the article. "I remember this now. There were a couple of sightings two or three weeks ago. Last week there were a few more and my editor asked Joe Slaney, who covers fishing and tides and such, to write up a notice." He slid the paper back to Miguel. "As I recall, he wanted to be sure the boaters and fishermen were aware so they wouldn't be startled if they spotted her swimming around. As the article says, Joe contacted the Florida Fish and Wildlife Conservation Commission. They told him if the green anaconda becomes a nuisance here, they'd come and round it up. The person Joe spoke to says it's most likely the anaconda came north from the Everglades and will eventually swim back south."

"Swim?" In my mind snakes were slitherers, not swimmers.

"Oh, yeah, big-time swimmers. According to Joe, green anacondas are aggressive swimmers, not landlubbers like pythons, who can swim but don't love the water like the anacondas. 'Landlubber' is Joe's favorite word. Believe me, he uses it freely. He calls me a landlubber and I own a boat and take it out whenever I have a chance." Cady stopped, sniffed and then shook off the insult. "Because I'm not out on the bay or the gulf every nonworking minute of the day, Joe doesn't consider me a true boater."

Miguel was sitting with his hands patiently folded, set at the angle where copies of Frost's two fruit poems, "Blueberries" and "After Apple Picking," sat side by side sealed to the tabletop by heavy lamination. I guess he was losing tolerance for Cady's rambling on and on about Joe Slaney, landlubbers and snakes, because he started tapping his fingers in three-quarter time.

I give Cady credit; he caught on fairly quickly. "I can see why you are concerned but I'm sure Bow will be fine. The anaconda seems to like the far side of the bay. At least that's where the sightings have been."

"Those Fish and Wildlife people do not seem to have any concern for the safety of our domestic animals. Did your reporter friend even ask about that?" Miguel pointed to the article. "There is no mention of it here."

Cady shrugged helplessly. "I don't know much about this, Miguel. I only know what I heard around the office while Joe was doing his research and writing his article. I promise. I'll check in with him first thing."

The door opened. I stood and took out my order pad, glad
to have customers come in and get me out of this ongoing
conversation about a problem with no apparent solution.
Then I saw the two people coming through the door and
realized I was going from one problem to another. Deputy
Ryan Mantoni was back. Lieutenant Frank Anthony was
with him. And they were wearing their serious faces.

Chapter Six

Still, I tried. With as bright a smile as I could muster, I asked if they wanted a table or needed a takeout order. Ryan took a step back and let the lieutenant answer.

Frank Anthony glanced over at the Robert Frost table, where conversation had ceased. Every pair of eyes was fixed on him. He swung his eyes back to me. "I expect you know why we're here. You were witness to an incident the other day and I need to go over your recollection. Is there a place we can speak privately?"

He head-butted toward the kitchen door, which made Miguel half rise from his chair, think the better of it and sit down again. But from the look on his face, if I allowed the deputies into Miguel's kitchen, I'd have to answer for it.

I shook my head. "No, the kitchen's very busy."

Frank raised both eyebrows. He looked once more at Bridgy and Miguel. "Doesn't seem busy to me."

That was enough for Miguel to pop out of his seat. He told Cady they would have to speak again soon and then he marched purposefully into the kitchen. From the look on Bridgy's face, I could see she was torn between following Miguel to reinforce the café kitchen as a "busy" place or staying where she was in the hopes she could overhear some juicy gossip. Even better, she might get the chance to hear Frank Anthony ream me out for not being forthcoming with Ryan earlier in the day.

The lieutenant made her choice easier when he said, "Okay, Sassy, let's go." And he turned and headed for the door.

Cady jumped up, his chair scraping across the floor. "Where are you taking her?"

Frank gave a tight smile. "Don't worry. We're not taking her far." He pointed through the wide glass window. "We'll be at the seating area right outside the door."

I hadn't taken so much as a step, so Frank signaled me to hurry along. I hesitated, but knew I really had no choice. I followed behind Frank and Ryan, with Chopin's Funeral March playing in my head. *Dum dum da dum . . .*

I sat in the middle of one bench so that neither of the deputies could sit beside me. I knew I'd be less on edge facing them head-on.

Ryan gave me a slight smile of encouragement. In past encounters I'd noticed it was always uncomfortable for him when he had to interrogate—the deputies call it interview—a friend. And we'd been friends since almost the first day Bridgy and I opened the Read 'Em and Eat more than three years ago.

Frank Anthony remained standing. Since we'd done this before, I wasn't surprised when he didn't say anything for a couple of minutes. As he was about to speak, an older couple approached. They were regular customers so they recognized me. I guess they assumed that the three of us were outside for fresh air and a social chat, because the husband decided to tease.

"You finally got her, huh, deputies? Pretty gals are always trouble. Like my missus here." He laughed and opened the door for his wife, who told us to "pay him no mind" before she walked into the café. Still laughing, her husband followed behind.

Frank gave the old gentleman a slight nod and then he turned to me. "I appreciate a man who knows trouble when he sees it." As he watched me bristle, Frank held back a smile but he couldn't keep his blue eyes from crinkling. Then he took out his black leather notebook and moved into deputy mode.

"I know you're aware that there was a murder last night. The victim is Mrs. Tanya Lipscome, age thirty-eight. She was killed by an intruder on her property."

He waited for me to nod in acknowledgement of the facts and then he continued. "I understand you were at the library when our victim had an argument with a man who we now consider a person of interest in this case, name of Alan Mersky."

I crossed my arms defensively but said nothing. Frank took my silence for acquiescence.

"Okay. Now, when did you first see Alan Mersky? Was it in the library?"

I shook my head and told him about my seeing Alan in the parking lot. I tried to move on to hearing Tanya Trouble screaming like a banshee inside the library, but Frank slowed me down with another question.

"Who entered the library first, you or Alan Mersky?"

And so it went. Questions. Answers. Repeat the questions.

Repeat the answers. A conversation, or as he calls it, an interview, that should have taken ten minutes lasted for more than half an hour until the lieutenant was satisfied that he'd wrung every shred of information out of me. The fact that I didn't know a single thing related to the murder was of no consequence. The man likes to waste time and annoy me.

By the time he closed his notebook, said we were done and asked me to get in touch if I remembered anything else, I was seething. Both deputies were in a half turn heading to their car across the parking lot when I found my courage, or insanity, not sure which. I stood up.

"Wait one minute. You may be done, but I'm not."

Frank's head swiveled toward me. "Really? You said you told us everything."

"I have one more thing to say."

Ryan's "Uh-oh" told me he had a sense of what was coming. Frank was still opening that darn notebook when I let him have it.

"How dare you, even jokingly, refer to me as 'trouble'?"

That stopped him. He shut his notebook and froze stock-still for a full thirty seconds or more. He stared at me but I refused to squirm. Then he looked up at the sky, moving his eyes from cloud to cloud.

"You know what's interesting, Sassy Cabot? I'll tell you. During the time I've been assigned to this division, this is only the second murder in Fort Myers Beach. Need I remind you that you were far more involved in the first murder than you should have been? And now, lo and behold, here you are on the witness list for the second murder. So pardon me for thinking of you and trouble in the same sentence."

He strode toward the patrol car without waiting for a response.

Ryan stepped closer to me. "Sassy, it was a joke and it wasn't even his joke. The old guy started it. And too bad you didn't hear the word 'pretty' as interchangeable with 'trouble' in what the old man said. Might change your tune."

I heaved a sigh as I watched them drive out of the parking lot. Lieutenant Frank Anthony was a true annoyance, but Ryan was a friend. I was sorry he'd seen me lose my temper. Still, I knew Ryan would get over it in a day or so. Bridgy and I had both lost our tempers countless times, often with each other, and we're still besties.

The thought of Bridgy reminded me that I'd have to face an inquisition and a lecture from her as soon as I walked in the door. I prayed for a few more customers to show up and delay the inevitable, but when I looked around, there was no one in sight. Time to face the music.

The older couple who'd entered when my interrogation had begun were finished with their meal, and Bridgy was refreshing their sweet tea and asking if they wanted dessert. The gentleman asked if "that scrumptious buttermilk pie" was still on the menu, which made Ophie, still sitting with Cady, throw her shoulders back and sit a little straighter. I thought she might saunter over and introduce herself as the baker who developed the recipe. Unfortunately, when she looked up at me, her face filled with expectation, I realized that any gossip I could provide would trump pie accolades.

Cady seemed honestly concerned. He stood up and pulled out a chair for me.

When I sat, he patted my hand. "I hope the interview

wasn't too awful." And he turned the tables on me by asking if I'd like a drink or something to eat.

Bridgy, anticipating my answer, set a glass of ice water with lemon slices in front of me. I would have thanked her but she bent down and whispered, "Don't tell them anything until I come back."

Really?

Like aunt, like niece. They both wanted to hear the gossip and hear it before anyone else did.

Well, I thought, at least Cady waited for me to come back out of friendship, not nosiness. Then he leaned in toward me. "So did you learn anything?"

I was about to tell them all off when the door opened and a large family group—infants to grandparents—walked in. I got up, counted noses and realized I'd have to push two tables together. By the time I got the family seated and served them glasses of water, I noticed Cady standing by the door patiently waiting for my attention. He waved and left. Ophie could sit there as long as she liked. I was busy and glad of it.

And then the door opened again and again. All the tables were filled and there was a line at the door. A pair of roller skates would have really helped me hustle around the dining room.

Bridgy and I silently crossed paths at the counter or the pass-through, even once at the kitchen doorway. Since Bridgy always had a quip or two, her silence was making me nervous. I broke out in a relieved smile when halfway through the afternoon she was able to bring herself to tell me she hoped my interrogation wasn't too terrible. Later, as I was passing her a pitcher of green tea, I whispered, "I'll tell you all about it after the rush dies down."

Soon after my arches started to feel as if they were about to drop, the flow of customers curbed down to a dribble and within half an hour only three tables were occupied. I made the rounds with a pitcher of water and a pitcher of iced tea. One lady asked for a refill on her Diet Mountain Dew and then all was quiet. I signaled Bridgy that I was going to take a quick break and headed for the door.

As I stepped outside, a salty fresh breeze drifted inland from the Gulf of Mexico. I took a deep breath and felt my stress level drop a thousand percent. I sat on the same bench where I had endured my interrogation and pulled my cell phone out of my pocket. I scrolled to George Mersky's number, hesitated and then punched the "Send" button.

He answered on the second ring.

We'd worked together long enough that George instantly recognized my "we're in trouble" voice when he heard it in my hello.

"Sassy, what is it? Is it Alan?"

I plunged into the whole story. I reminded George of our earlier conversation about Alan's problem with Tanya. When I told him she was murdered last night, he stopped me.

"Say no more. I'll be there as soon as I can get a flight. And Sassy, thank you for calling. If it wasn't for you, Alan would be going through this all alone. Now I'll be there to help. I'll call you when my plans are set."

The Diet Mountain Dew lady and her friend came out of the café. Each had a book club flier in her hand. They had a few questions and were delighted to learn that all the book clubs were small and informal. I invited them to stop by for any meeting that appealed to them, and they assured me they would.

I took another deep breath and went back into the café.

Bridgy gave me a questioning look and I signaled her over to the counter. In a hushed voice so as not to disturb the remaining customers, I asked, "Do you remember George, my old boss when we lived in New York?"

"George from Howard Accounting? Sure. Nice man, kind of dour. I seem to recall from your office holiday party that his wife was a very funny lady. The old 'opposites attract' thing. Are they coming down?" Always the social one, Bridgy brightened at the thought of company.

"Um-hm. But it's not a social visit. The man the deputies are looking for. He's George's brother."

And I watched Bridgy's face morph from happy to bewildered as she took in the news.

Chapter Seven

We were momentarily distracted by the man sitting at Agatha Christie who gave the universal hand signal for "check, please." Instead of making the check mark sign with his index finger, he lifted his arm and waved his entire hand, looking for all the world as though he was leading an orchestra. He only needed to be wearing tails and a bow tie. Bridgy gave him his check, then walked over to ask the two couples sitting at Hemingway if they needed anything else. Since they were all wearing Fort Myers Beach tee shirts, Bridgy made an educated guess and asked if they were having a good vacation. The ladies giggled when one of the men said, "This is the most invigorating vacation I've had in years. I feel like I'm forty again, and these two"—he pointed to the women—"are acting like teenagers. Isn't that right, Herb?"

While the women protested, Herb replied, "Oh yeah. You

had to see them at Times Square trying to make the mime talk. They were ruthless, but he didn't break."

Laughter all around.

Then Herb continued, "We all think it's a hoot that you plant a clock in a plaza and call it Times Square. I guess New York doesn't have a monopoly on the name."

In between chuckles, they asked for more scones and sweet tea. Bridgy and I assumed they'd be with us for a while so rather than having a hurried, whispered conversation, we commenced with our afternoon cleaning.

I loved the peace of our ritual. We each had assigned tasks. Bridgy helped Miguel tidy up the kitchen, which was usually a brief exercise as he managed to keep his entire work area nearly immaculate, even during our busiest hours. After his broken leg had healed and he returned to work, I was constantly grinning from ear to ear every time I walked into the kitchen. Ophie had been a Godsend when she filled in as "head chef" while Miguel was on sick leave. She was excellent with the cooking and baking part but never acknowledged that mops and brooms or even dishwashers existed. Bridgy and I did double cleanup duty during those months but the food was scrumptious and the customers were happy, which was all that mattered. Still, life became easier for us once Miguel was back to work and restored order to the café kitchen.

Miguel came out of the kitchen. He was a man of such strict habits that I knew his stark white tee shirt, apron and chef's hat had been tucked into the laundry bin and a pristine set of chef's wear now hung on a hook ready for tomorrow. His bold floral tank top, all greens and yellows, and his baggy tan shorts gave him the surfer look he cultivated. When he saw we still had customers, he tiptoed over to me and said in a low tone, "I am not finished talking about this snake. Something must be done. *Mañana, sí?*"

I nodded. What was I going to say? The green anaconda swimming around Estero Bay was the least of my problems. I waved good-bye and continued scrubbing the chairs around the Dashiell Hammett table. The door had barely closed behind Miguel when my cell phone vibrated in my pocket. During our busier hours I turned off the ringer to avoid the distraction. Often, like now, I forgot to turn it back on. I answered with a quiet "hello" and rushed into the kitchen, where Bridgy was mopping the floor. I pointed to the phone and mouthed the word "George." She set the mop aside, wiped her hands and went out to the dining room in case the vacationing foursome needed anything.

It was disappointing to tell George that I had no further news, but he subscribed to the "no news is good news" school of thought.

"Sassy, with any luck I can get down there before the cops pick him up. Once I explain how agreeable and kind Alan really is, I'm sure they'll realize he couldn't possibly have hurt, much less killed, anyone. My wife and my sister are both coming with me."

"Give me your plane information. I'll pick you up. And you are welcome to stay with Bridgy and me while you are here."

"Thanks but I think three guests would be a squeeze for anyone, and we're hoping to find Alan and have him stay with us for a few days, at least until we can evaluate what he needs. Could you find us a nice rental or perhaps a bed-and-breakfast that would take us knowing that we are unsure of how long we'd need the accommodations? We need at least two bedrooms."

"Sure, I'll take care of it." I immediately thought of the woman who had helped Ophie track down someone who'd been renting on the island a while ago. Charmaine was a young, cheerful woman starting out in real estate. I'd give her a call as soon as we closed the café.

George gave me his travel information. I wished him a safe flight and told him I would be waiting at Southwest Florida International Airport when his plane landed. I tapped the "Off" button on my phone and went to find Bridgy, who was bussing the dishes from the Hemingway table, the vacation-ers apparently gone off to their next fun-filled activity.

As soon as she saw me, Bridgy put down the dishes she'd picked up seconds ago and waved me to sit at Emily Dickinson.

"Water?" she asked.

I shook my head. Bridgy sat opposite me and prodded.

"Okay, now tell me the entire story. Start to finish. I promise I won't interrupt." She gave me a wink. We both knew it was extremely unlikely that I'd be able to talk for more than two or three minutes without Bridgy having a question or a suggestion.

I told her I'd first seen Alan outside the library and then what I'd witnessed with Tanya. I repeated everything Sally told me and then I finished with my two conversations with George Mersky. In fairness, Bridgy only interrupted me twice. Once to ask me to elaborate on my description of the lighter that Tanya purported to be mega-expensive and once to give her opinion of anyone who wouldn't go the extra yard to be kind to one of our veterans.

I ended by saying, "I'll take that glass of water now. And do we have any Miss Marple Scones left?"

Bridgy brought water and scones to the table and, lost in thought, we both nibbled and sipped.

"I think we should try to find him." Bridgy put her half-eaten scone back on its plate and, using both hands, she pushed the plate toward the middle of the table.

I hated to admit that the thought had crossed my mind. The last time we went looking for someone, we spent an extraordinary hour of tranquility while kayaking in Estero Bay. Of course we didn't find the person we were looking for but since he was a master boater, the bay was the right place to look.

"Bridgy, this isn't someone whose habits and haunts are familiar to us. Where would we even start?"

"Well, would you recognize his car?"

"Absolutely. The car is unforgettable. You should see it. An ancient, beat-up black Mustang filled with boxes and junk. There's even part of a tree stretched from the front seat to the back. A four- or five-foot-long limb with branches still attached and dead leaves all withered and curled. Inside the car."

Bridgy leaned her head forward, eyes open wide when I described the huge limb straddling the console and covering the backseat. She banged one hand on the table. "Well now, a car like that shouldn't be that hard to find."

I shook my head. "Bridgy, the sheriff's deputies have been looking for him all day and they haven't found him. What makes you think we can take a quick drive and come right across him?"

"Well the deputies have a picture and a description of the man. You, on the other hand, know what his car looks like."

I tried to squirm out of the hunt.

"I have more important things to do. I need to find George and his family a place to stay. On such short notice . . ."

"Oh stop. We can turn that job over to Aunt Ophie and she'll have them lodged in the Palace of Versailles in the snap of a finger."

I laughed. Ophie did have a way with miracles of that sort and she was friendlier with Charmaine than I was.

Bridgy gave me her "puppy pleading for a treat" look. I took a deep breath.

"Okay, if Ophie will take care of the housing issue, we can go for a brief ride around town in the car. No kayaks. No boats of any sort." I had to lay down some sort of rules so she wouldn't be confident that she could talk me into any crazy thing she wanted to do, which of course she could.

We finished cleaning the café, and then reviewed our closing checklist. Stove off. No water dripping in any of the three sinks. Freezer door shut tight. Ditto with the refrigerators—one for food already prepared, one for ingredients. At long last we turned off the lights, locked the door and stood for a moment enjoying the glorious Florida sunshine before walking across the parking lot to Ophie's Treasure Trove.

A consignment shop had occupied the site for many years. When it closed, Bridgy's aunt decided to take over the space and turned it into what she liked to describe as an "old and new shop with élan." Ophie was very selective about the items she agreed to sell on consignment. She opted for upscale and unusual, although she had a small corner set aside for the strictly kitschy items that lots of tourists loved to buy and bring home to show off and possibly win the neighborhood tacky souvenir award of any given year.

She frequently traveled up and down the Gulf looking for unique items and when she fell in love with something, she didn't hesitate to buy outright if she couldn't talk the owner into consigning.

"I hope Aunt Ophie is feeling better," Bridgy whispered to me a second before she opened the door to the Treasure Trove.

She needn't have worried. Ophie was breezing around the shop waving a feather duster. Occasionally the duster actually touched an item or a countertop, but mostly Ophie was waving it in the air, chasing motes that could only be seen when they danced through rays of sunshine.

Ophie gave us a big smile and then immediately frowned. I was afraid we were in for another harangue about serial killers invading Fort Myers Beach, but she was off on a different tangent.

"Have either of y'all seen Tom Smallwood lately? His shell and fishbone jewelry is selling quick as a hot knife cutting through butter, and I'd dearly love to restock."

Tom Smallwood was a jack-of-all-trades who rowed a weatherworn boat up and down the Gulf of Mexico, stopping here and there on the mainland and barrier islands. Most folks called him Skully because he'd once found a fifty-year-old skull up on Mound Key and carried it around for half a year before Ryan Mantoni and two other deputies could finally talk him into giving it up. He kept to himself, worked excellent craftsmanship on anything made of wood and was a man I much admired. Over the brief time I'd known him, he'd shown both character and grit.

Bridgy shook her head. "He hasn't been in to fill his thermos in a while. Last time he told me he was off to rebuild a staircase on Sanibel. That was weeks ago. He's probably traveled farther afield since. Auntie, dear, we need a favor."

Bridgy explained that the Mersky family was making an

unexpected trip to the island and would need a place to stay with an open-ended leave date. Did she think her friend Charmaine could help out? She finished by saying, "The thing is, they're coming in tomorrow."

Ophie was in the middle of a string of "of course, no problem" comments when she suddenly thought to ask why the Merskys were making such an impulsive trip. She was pleased with the answer.

"I told y'all when Cady showed us the picture there isn't a lick of danger in that poor man's eyes. A bit of family will do him good. Now y'all go do what you're doing and I'll see to the lodging."

Back in the parking lot Bridgy and I got into my trusty Heap-a-Jeep. Based on what I'd seen so briefly, we decided that it was Alan's nature to avoid the beach, public parks and tourist attractions like Times Square or Lovers Key. Our best bet was to search the side streets off Estero Boulevard and those that edged Estero Bay. We ambled around and about, dead-ended in a cul-de-sac, followed a few loop-de-loops and always wound up back on the boulevard.

It didn't take long for even the ever-optimistic Bridgy to realize we were on a fool's errand.

"At least we got a reminder of how beautiful the bay side of the island is," Bridgy said with a sigh.

I nodded and headed for home, hoping that tomorrow would bring better luck. We could help George find Alan and this whole mess would be straightened out.

Of course, poor Tanya Trouble would still be dead.

Chapter Eight ||||||||||||

At four thirty the next morning, a large flock of birds began chirping their version of "Here Comes the Sun." They probably assembled for reveille in Bowditch Point Park but they sounded as if they were inside my bedroom. I pulled a pillow over my head but it couldn't block the noise. Eventually the birds stopped, confident I'm sure that they had woken every sleeping soul from Bonita Springs to North Captiva Island. I tried to get back to sleep. For a few minutes I dozed fitfully. Then my eyes popped open of their own accord. I continued tossing and turning for the next hour and finally gave up the effort.

I padded into the kitchen and found Bridgy at the table, sipping freshly brewed coffee. She was never a cheerful riser and I could only imagine getting up this early would intensify her sense of cranky.

I was hesitant but decided to risk inquiring. "The birds?"

She nodded and pointed to the empty cup waiting for me

next to the coffeepot. I poured my coffee, added a drop of milk and sat down. After a few healing swallows, I ventured, "I guess it will do us good to get an early start. Busy day with George coming in. Oh, I wrote down the rental address that Ophie left on the answering machine. I forget where I put the paper."

"It's in your purse and don't worry, we didn't erase the message. Sounds like a nice place, an efficiency right on the boulevard and close to Publix. That will come in handy if they need anything, especially since they're leaving home in such a rush." Bridgy stretched her arms high over her head. "I guess we better get a move on and face the day. It's sure to be a doozy."

Bridgy had that right.

We decided it best that we each take our own car to work on a day when I would be making an airport run and trying to help George and his family settle in comfortably. I swung into the café parking lot and slid my Heap-a-Jeep right next to Bridgy's shiny red Escort ZX2.

Walking across the parking lot, Bridgy looked at the café, all lit up, bright and welcoming. "How does Miguel manage to get up so early every day and not be grumpy by noon? If it was me, Lord knows . . ."

I smiled. "We are so lucky to have him. If we learned nothing else when he broke his leg, we learned that."

"Ah! Hurricane Ophie wreaked so much havoc on the kitchen I thought we'd never recover. She's my aunt and I love her dearly but good as the food was—"

"It was delicious," I interjected.

"It was exhausting to contend with the messy kitchen, the lack of organization, not to mention Ophie's drama, drama, drama. We get along so much better when she spends her days forty yards away at the Treasure Trove. And I think she's happier there, too."

I was nodding in agreement while I bent over to pick up the pile of the *Fort Myers Beach News* that a delivery van dropped off each morning. I glanced at the front page, gave an involuntary squeak and dropped the papers.

Bridgy grabbed my arm. "What is it? Did you hurt your back?

In response, I picked up the newspapers and showed her.

The page-one headline screamed, "CAUGHT," and right below was the picture of Alan Mersky we'd seen yesterday on Cady's phone.

"Ugh." Bridgy said what I felt. "What are you going to do, Sas? Should you call George now?"

I shook my head. "If George and his family aren't at the airport already, they are heading that way. Maybe in a cab or even a limo. Either way, there's no privacy wherever they are. I'd rather wait and tell them at the airport. Then when I take them to the rental agency and George picks up a car, they will have private time to talk while they follow me back here."

We slouched into the café and I dropped the newspapers on the counter. We went into the kitchen to stash our purses and find our aprons.

"Good morning, *chicas*." Miguel was in the kitchen, chopping vegetables for omelets so he'd have plenty when the breakfast rush started. I glanced at the round clock over the stove. Hungry folks would start arriving in a few minutes.

I stopped in my tracks and sniffed. "Something smells delicious."

"Ay, banana bread baking." Miguel waved his hand, along with the very sharp knife it held, toward the oven. "When

I got here this morning, *your* bananas were looking, eh, kind of old. Certainly we couldn't serve them in the dining room, so I made banana bread. Don't forget to put it on the specials board. I would not want it to go uneaten."

Bridgy and I often laughed about Miguel's take on ingredients. If we had a gorgeous bunch of salad greens, he would talk about *his* arugula, *his* lettuce. But let the ingredient not meet his extremely high standards and it became ours. He had nothing to do with it.

I was tying my apron around my waist and Miguel was in mid-turn, his attention moving back to the vegetables, when he got a good look at my face.

He put the knife down, wiped his hands on a towel and moved directly in front of me. "What is it? Bad news from home? Oh, I'm so sorry. How can I help?"

Impulsively I gave him a hug. "Miguel, you are such a sweetheart. No, my family is okay, but do you remember the murder that Ophie was carrying on about yesterday?"

He laughed. "I am not laughing at the murder, oh no, but believe me, it will spin Ophie's drama-mill for a long, long time. Until she finds something else to get crazy about."

I couldn't deny that Miguel had Ophie's number. I assured him my trouble had nothing to do with Ophie and gave him the quick version of my friend George and his brother Alan.

Miguel looked directly in my eyes. "You do not have an easy job today. Again, let me know if I can help."

Bridgy moved to the kitchen door and opened it a crack. "I thought I heard noise in the dining room. Customers. We're on, team."

As soon as I went into the dining room I wrote "home-made banana bread" on the specials board and threw a price next to it. I didn't even think about costing it out. If I had underestimated, our customers would get a special treat at a special price. The thought of that small gift to the people who enabled us to pay our bills was enough to cheer me. Within minutes the tables filled up and I had no time to think of anything but keeping the customers happy.

Eventually the breakfast crowd slowed to a trickle. I was refilling the sweet tea pitcher and Bridgy was right next to me, packing up a box of muffins. She offered to hold down the fort if I wanted to leave for the airport. It was a little early but it would be best to make sure that I was waiting next to the showy 1908 Cadillac displayed in the main terminal when George and his family got off the plane. The Caddy was one of the many perks of having Thomas Edison and Henry Ford spend their winter months hereabouts a hundred or so years ago.

I was totally at ease until the arrivals board indicated that George's plane landed. Then the butterflies in my stomach started to flutter at warp speed. I began pacing back and forth, unable to put my thoughts in any semblance of order. How do you tell a friend that his brother has been arrested for murder? I couldn't seem to figure out a kind way to say it.

I was still rehearsing and rejecting potential speeches when I saw George walking directly toward me. I waved and a woman dressed in a periwinkle blue tank dress pushed passed George. Her hugely teased black hair was the exact color of her thick eyeliner and heavily drawn brows. She had a long, neon orange scarf wrapped carelessly around her neck, and it fluttered this way and that as it trailed behind her.

As if it were opening night on Broadway and she'd managed to see the show destined to be the season's smash hit, she started clapping her hands. Moving closer to me, she began shouting "Honey, I love you." I stepped to one side, not wanting to get in between the *Queen Mary* and her dock.

"Honey, I love you." She repeated and stopped in front of me. "Don't be shy. Give me a hug. You know how hard it is to get this guy to take a vacation. You worked with him; you know. Thank you. Thank you for getting me a trip to the beach."

I yelped when she threw her arms around me, gave me a gigunda bear hug and planted any number of kisses on both of my cheeks. I could imagine them covered with smears of her orangey lipstick that didn't quite match the scarf.

How could I have forgotten George's flamboyant wife, O'Mally? The great, never-resolved mystery that stymied everyone who knew them was how placid George and high-flying O'Mally had ever gone on a first date, much less got married and lived happily ever after for the past twenty-something years.

I wriggled out of her grip.

George gave me a shy smile. With a hand on the small of her back, he gently guided the woman who walked a few steps behind him toward me. "This is my sister, Regina."

I immediately thought of her as colorless. Not the kindest description perhaps. And maybe it was seeing her in contrast to her bright and shiny sister-in-law. Regina's dark hair had wide streaks of gray, matching her gray pantsuit. Her tightly laced walking shoes were black and matched her large over-the-shoulder purse.

Regina extended a shy hand. "Thanks for letting us know where to find Alan. We've been so worried."

Before I could respond, George was giving me a restrained hug and thanking me profusely.

I tripped over my words at first but got quick control. "The thing is, we have to talk."

I ushered the Merskys to a quiet corner of the terminal and told them as unemotionally as I could that Alan had been arrested. Regina stifled a sob.

O'Mally immediately became comforter-in-chief. She put her arm around George and softly murmured, "It will be fine, you'll see. We're here now to straighten this out."

George turned toward her. I watched as their eyes met, and the confidence in hers swam into the worry in his. At last I understood how these two oddly different people were entwined. It was such a warm, fuzzy moment that I almost forgot the horrible news I'd delivered.

George asked me when they could see Alan. I had no idea but said I'd find out.

O'Mally, displaying her practical side, suggested that we collect the luggage and set off to get the rental car. Within a few minutes we were transferring suitcases from the Heap-a-Jeep to a spiffy Buick LaCrosse with less than three thousand miles on the odometer. George was nervous about using a strange GPS so I gave him general directions, which O'Mally jotted on a small pad she pulled out of her sparkly silver purse.

I ended by telling him that I'd keep him in my rearview mirror but if he lost sight of me, he should call my cell. Happily, there wasn't much traffic along Daniels Parkway or Summerlin Road. San Carlos Boulevard was a little crowded but we got over the bridge fairly easily, and turned onto Estero Boulevard.

When I turned into the parking lot of Breezy Beach Apartments, I realized at once that Charmaine of Mid-Beach Realty had outdone herself. The lot was roomy and the entrance to each of the four apartments was alcoved for privacy. When we got inside, the two-bedroom rental apartment was clean, bright and sunny. Several windows had a view of the beach. While the Merskys were settling in, I excused myself, went out to the parking lot and stood by the Heap-a-Jeep.

I punched speed dial and within two rings, he answered in clipped official tones.

"Lieutenant Anthony."

"Frank, it's Sassy Cabot. I'm with Alan Mersky's family. They just arrived from up north. Could you tell me how to arrange for the family to visit Alan?"

As Frank talked, I was comforted because the procedure didn't seem at all complicated, but then he shook me out of my comfort zone when he ended by saying, "Tell them to get a lawyer. Things aren't looking good for Alan Mersky."

I punched the "End" button and walked slowly back to the building. I hoped O'Mally had a deep reserve of the confidence she'd imbued in George a little while ago. He was going to need a lot more of it.

Chapter Nine ||||||||||||

I stopped dead in my tracks in the middle of the parking lot. How could I go inside and tell George he needed to hire a lawyer? He'd been on the island less than an hour. Where was he supposed to find one? The yellow pages?

I still had my phone in my hand and I hit the speed dial for Cady Stanton. As a newsman, he'd know the who's who of the legal system.

"Hi, Sassy, how'd it go? Are your friends settling in all right?"

I had no time for small talk. "Cady, I need a lawyer. Pronto. Who should I call?"

His response was louder than my request warranted. "What on earth did you do now?"

"*I* didn't do anything. *I* need to make a recommendation to Alan Mersky's family and I want to recommend the best. Who do you think that would be?" I hoped I responded sharply enough that he would think twice the next time before assuming I was stirring up trouble, when all I was trying to do was help a friend.

"Oh, of course. Let me think a minute . . ."

I was tapping my toe in an ever-increasing cadence. I didn't have the patience to wait for Cady to mull over a list of possibilities. I wanted the best and I wanted it now.

"I got it." Cady sounded jubilant. "Goddard Swerling. I did a feature on him once. He's a top-rated defense attorney. He centers his practice in Fort Myers, but works trials all around the state. He guest lectures at Florida A&M College of Law in Orlando and a couple of other top schools. Given his line of work, he keeps his home address under wraps but I know he has a beach house near the south end of the island. He's your guy. Hold on. I'll get you his phone number."

I found a dog-eared receipt from Walgreens in my purse and fished out a pen so when Cady came back on the line I was ready to scribble the phone number across the back.

He was slower than I liked in getting me the information but I finally had what I needed, so I was gracious with my thanks.

When I rang the doorbell of the Merskys' temporary home, Regina opened the door instantly. "Sassy, you've been such a help. And this apartment is so nicely kept. It is a charming place to stay while we get Alan's troubles . . . sorted out."

I gave her shoulder an encouraging squeeze and went looking for George.

O'Mally was sitting at the kitchen table, writing a grocery list. "George, do you want me to look for some fish, maybe a nice piece of snapper, while I'm at the market? And I suppose you'll want your cocoa for nighttime?"

George was staring absently out the window but he managed to nod at each of her suggestions.

O'Mally looked up as I walked into the room. "Sassy, darlin', I was thinking Regina and I could run to that supermarket you said was around here someplace while you and George have a little tête-à-tête about, er, whatever you're going to do about Alan."

Shouldn't it be O'Mally talking to George? I didn't want to get any further absorbed into their family problem than I already was. I'd be more than willing to do chores such as shopping, but O'Mally had already stuffed the shopping list in her sparkly silver purse and called Regina to be ready to go. She stopped in the kitchen doorway. "Sassy, where exactly am I going?"

I gave her directions to Publix, about a quarter of a mile down the boulevard, and she flew out of the kitchen, her orange scarf swerving back and forth like a rudder.

When the door closed behind his wife and sister, George gave a deep sigh. He walked over to the table and sat with his elbows on it and his head buried in his hands. Finally he looked up at me.

"Sassy, what am I going to do? Regina and O'Mally are counting on me to make this right. I don't even know how to start. I guess I should find out how to visit Alan, see if he needs anything . . ."

I waited half a beat and then told George the procedure Frank Anthony had outlined over the phone. I ended with, "The lieutenant said they don't like hordes of visitors. You and Regina may be able to visit Alan together or may have to go in separately. It's likely they won't let O'Mally in to see Alan at all."

George waved my comment away as if the visiting regulations were inconsequential. He'd already moved on to the next item on his list. "I can't figure out what I should bring him. Oranges. He always liked oranges. I should have asked the girls to buy some. And I guess he needs a razor. Oh, will they let him have a razor? Maybe an electric? Better yet, battery operated."

He leaned back in the chair and placed his hands on top of his head and began staring at the ceiling. When we worked together at Howard Accounting, I'd watched him stretch into that position a thousand times while he puzzled out a client's finances when the numbers didn't add up. Apparently that was how he tried to work out all his life issues large or small, personal or professional.

I admit it was nostalgic for me to sit watching him ponder. In the old days, the signal that he had unraveled a knotty problem was a slam of his fist on the desk, and a suggestion that we break for a cup of tea. Sure enough in a few minutes he punched the table and said, "I hope O'Mally remembers to get tea and fresh lemons."

"Okay, now I have a plan. I wonder if there is any paper around here." He got up and opened the kitchen drawers one after the other and came up with a lined pad with more than half the pages missing. "This'll do."

He sat down at the table and in that half-print, half-script penmanship that was so hard for me to read when we first started working together, he began to write.

In no time at all, he put his pen back in his pocket and held up the paper. As I well remembered, George was always most confident when he had a list. Nothing made him more satisfied than crossing off his accomplishments one by one.

"Okay, I have to visit Alan, contact the Veterans Administration on his behalf and most importantly, find him a lawyer who can get him out of jail. Alan won't do well if he is confined for very long." George leaned back in his chair but in seconds his confidence began to slip. "How am I going to find a lawyer? A good one? Alan needs a savvy lawyer who knows the ropes around here."

"I may be able to help with that." I pulled the wrinkled receipt from my pocket, and pushed it toward George.

"Still saving your receipts like a good little accountant, I see." George smiled at his own joke and then looked at what I had written. "How do you know this Goddard Swerling?"

Of course I didn't know him. I told George how Cady had highly recommended Swerling, and George seems satisfied. He pulled out his cell phone and dialed.

George had to spend time negotiating with intermediaries but he was persistent and eventually Goddard Swerling got on the phone.

The lawyer's voice was so loud I could hear him from where I was sitting opposite George. I stood, planning to go in the living room to give George privacy, but he waved me back into my seat. Swerling played the mildly interested card while George pressured him to take interest in his brother's case. Apparently a high fee would solve all problems. After they agreed on a number, George asked, "When can I see my brother?"

Swerling told him that they could meet at the sheriff's office in about an hour. "You and I will conclude our business and then I'll make sure they let you visit your brother."

George hung up and gave me a tight smile. He seemed satisfied that he was making progress. He leaned across the table. "Sassy, I can't thank you enough for all you've done, for all you are doing. Look at this place. Plenty of room for Alan to join us once he is out of jail."

I smiled and wished I were as confident as George that Alan would ever see the light of day.

O'Mally and Regina came back with enough groceries to feed a hungry football team. O'Mally had her priorities in order. She put on a pot of water and set about making George a cup of tea while he filled them in on the current plan.

Regina asked about the lawyer's fee and even I blanched when George said the number out loud. "And he made it clear that is just for starters."

I decided to interrupt rather than listen to a family conversation about money. "I'd be happy to drive you to the sheriff's office to see Alan. It's on the mainland and might be tricky for you to find."

George nodded at the wisdom of my suggestion. "Thank you. We can leave as soon as I finish my tea."

I took the opportunity to call Bridgy and let her know I'd be gone longer than planned. She didn't pick up, so I left a voice mail and a few minutes later we were all in the Heap-a-Jeep heading back toward the San Carlos Bridge.

I was still throwing the gearshift into park when George opened his door and jumped out. He headed right for the front door of the sheriff's office and then stopped and turned, realizing he had to wait for the rest of us.

When we got to the door, gentleman that George is, he opened it and stepped aside so Regina, O'Mally and I could go in first. As soon as the door was opened the tiniest crack, we could hear lots of voices. One overshadowed the rest. He was screaming something about his wife. Regina and O'Mally shrank back but I took a couple of steps inside, curious to see what the ruckus was about.

A gray-haired man in a blue pinstriped suit was banging on a desk. The deputy behind the desk was standing and trying to soothe the man while gently refusing his request. Two younger men, dressed more casually, were also trying to pacify him. One took his arm and said, "Come on, Dad, this isn't the best place for you to be."

The man banged his hand again and screamed, "I want to see the man who murdered my wife."

Regina gasped and George quickly put one arm around his sister and the other around his wife. We all knew the man was Tanya Lipscome's husband and he was demanding to see Alan.

I suggested we go back to the parking lot and wait for the deputies to get everything calmed down. George nodded. The second young man decided to try. "Dad, please. This isn't doing anybody any good, least of all you. Think of your health."

Lipscome nodded his head as he took a step back from the desk. I noticed he had an odd look on his face, almost like an actor who was pleased the audience had bought his performance. He rested his hand on his son's shoulder. "You're right. Nothing I can do now will help Tanya. Let's go home."

He muttered a half-apologetic thank-you to the deputy he'd been harassing and turned to leave. That's when he saw George standing next to the doorway.

Lipscome tightened his lips, then opened them wide and let out a scream. "You. Why aren't you in jail? I saw your picture in the newspaper. I'm Barry Lipscome. You killed my wife."

Hands outstretched, he pushed forward and pounced on George, who was too stunned to react. O'Mally intervened, grabbing Lipscome by the nose and twisting.

It took four deputies to break up the brouhaha.

Lieutenant Frank Anthony was right behind the group of deputies who came running from the back of the building. He sized up the situation and immediately took charge, ordering two deputies to bring Mr. Lipscome into his personal office. Lipscome's sons followed along behind.

The lieutenant noticed me standing next to Regina and flashed those crinkly blue eyes of his. "I should have known. If there's chaos . . ."

Before I could offer a smart retort, a man carrying an elegant alligator briefcase stepped through the doorway and demanded, "What is going on here?"

He was so imperious that for a second I thought he was the actual sheriff, the one we elect every few years, but then he asked a second question. "And where is my client?"

Chapter Ten

Frank Anthony stepped forward. "Can I help you, Counselor?"

"I'm meeting . . ." The lawyer looked past the lieutenant, his eyes scanning the room. "Er, thank you, Lieutenant. I believe I'm here to meet that gentleman." He pointed to George and asked, "Mr. Mersky?"

George half nodded, still dazed by the incident with the victim's husband.

Frank stepped out of the way and the attorney moved closer to us. I noticed he was wearing a shiny gray sharkskin suit that looked expensive, yet seemed dated. But then, what did I really know about men's clothes? Still, he wore it with flair and confidence. Ophie, the empress of "strut your stuff" would be proud.

He thrust a business card at George and stuck out his

right hand for a hearty shake. "I'm Goddard Swerling. I believe you and I had an arrangement to meet here."

George thanked him for coming and for agreeing to represent Alan.

Swerling took a step back. "Not quite, Mr. Mersky. Not quite. I merely agreed to talk to your brother. He may not want me to represent him."

He gave us all a condescending smile and shook his head slightly as if no one in his right mind would decline to be represented by Goddard Swerling.

"But I thought . . ." George was flustered; clearly he thought the issue of representation was resolved.

"Please, please, Mr. Mersky. You, George, are the one who guarantees payment, but your brother, Alan, will be the actual client. He is the only one empowered to make decisions."

Then he shrugged, lifting his padded shoulders well past his chin as if to say, "That's the deal, take it or leave it." And he put out his hand for still another handshake.

His attitude was so grating that I wanted to smack his arrogant face, and I noticed O'Mally take a slight step forward probably with the same thought in mind. George grabbed her hand, and I guessed it was to stop the explosion he could feel building up inside her. Then he firmly took the lead. "Mr. Swerling, for now, I'd be grateful if you'd talk to Alan, let him know you are on his side and let him know that his family is here. We can work out the details later."

The two men shook hands for what seemed like the third or fourth time, but it was the first time the gesture helped George visibly relax, as though he finally believed they'd reached a gentleman's agreement. Swerling, on the other hand, grinned like a Cheshire cat. George was going to pay the bills and

Swerling had figured out how to keep him happy—access to his brother. George must have forgotten that Frank Anthony had assured me there was a procedure for family visits, or perhaps he thought of Swerling as added insurance.

"I'll do so much better than telling him you're here. I'll get you in to see him—as soon as Alan and I have a private word—I'll demand your right to visit. First I need you to sign this agreement." He handed George a few sheets of paper and a pen. "Right there at the bottom of page three. Once your brother signs, we'll be fine."

As George scribbled his signature, Swerling said, almost as an aside, "And the amount is flexible you realize. It may increase. Depends on how much work is required to, ah, straighten out this little misunderstanding."

The lawyer looked at the signature and brightened with approval. "Okay, now you wait here and I'll go speak to your brother, and then I'll get you in."

George was antsy, as he had every right to be. "Will it take long? We've come a long way and we're anxious to see Alan."

The lawyer looked at the flashy gold watch on his wrist. He mugged an "I don't know" face and snapped. "It will take as long as it takes."

Now that he had George's signature, he had no reason to be agreeable. Turning his back on us, he presented himself at the desk and asked for a deputy to escort him inside to meet Alan.

At that precise moment the Lipscomes, father and sons, walked back into the vestibule. I hoped they were leaving the building. One son had a firm grasp on his father's arm, and Barry seemed calmer. His eyes glazed over when he looked at us, as if he was reminding himself that George was not Alan. Then he saw Goddard Swerling, and chaos started anew.

Barry shook off his son's hand and pointed his arm, stabbing the air over and over again. "You! Of course you'd defend that killer. You're on everybody's side except my poor wife. Why do you hate her so?"

His choking up at the end of his rant sounded phony to me but I heard Regina actually breathe, "The poor man." And a deputy, who jumped in front of him before he could reach Swerling, raised his hand like a stop sign. "Tough times, Mr. Lipscome, but remember what the lieutenant said. We can't allow violence. It only causes more trouble."

Barry Lipscome raised his eyes to the ceiling and then he crumpled into an exhausted heap. He let his sons lead him out the front door and into the Florida sunshine without another word.

Goddard Swerling turned to us. Once again he gave us his most Cheshire cat–like grin, and he followed a deputy into the nether regions of the sheriff's station.

The last few minutes had taken its toll on the entire Mersky family. George was red-faced and sweating profusely. Regina was pale and leaning heavily against the wall as if she couldn't stand without support. O'Mally went digging in her sparkly oversized purse and came up with a protein bar, which she broke in half and forced her husband and sister-in-law to eat. She followed up with some wintergreen mints for dessert.

I was trying to get up the pluck to ask the deputy at the desk if there was a machine in the building where we could buy bottled water or other drinks, when Ryan Mantoni came into the room from a side door. I was never so happy to see a friendly face.

"Sassy, hey, what are you doing . . ." Ryan saw that I was

with folks unfamiliar to him and quickly put two and two together.

I introduced the Merskys and then asked Ryan if we could get bottled water anywhere in the building.

"No problem. Let me take care of it. Water okay for everyone?"

We were grateful for anything wet and cold. Ryan disappeared only to return in less than a minute with four ice-cold bottles of spring water.

When George tried to force some money on him, Ryan smiled and told him not to worry, he was merely trading the bottles of water for a piece of buttermilk pie the next time he stopped in the Read 'Em and Eat. Then he turned to me and said, "I'm sure glad Miss Ophelia shared her recipe with Miguel when he came back to work. I'd dearly miss buttermilk pie if it wasn't on the specials board now and again."

I had to smile as I remembered our "between chefs" transition. Ophie'd done a grand job filling in for Miguel until his broken leg healed. When he was healthy enough to come back, we all assumed Ophie would be eager to go home in Pinetta up near the Georgia border. Not so fast. As it turns out she'd fallen in love with Fort Myers Beach and was reluctant to leave. Bridgy and I were stunned when she announced she was selling her house in Pinetta and moving permanently to Fort Myers Beach. One thing was sure, there was no way meticulous Miguel and untidy Ophie could share a kitchen.

It was tough for us to wrestle the café kitchen away from Ophie until we realized that the town was short one very profitable consignment shop and there was a vacant storefront a few doors down from the Read 'Em and Eat. With her love of all things decorative, Ophie rented the store, started rounding up eclectic jewelry, trinkets, collectables and she opened the Treasure Trove, but not before negotiating recipes with Miguel. It took some time but she was able to get Miguel to trade the recipe for his fabulous *torrejas*, a sweet toast dish spiced with a drop of Cuban rum, for her delicious buttermilk pie recipe. And in the intervening months, they'd become great friends as long as Ophie stayed out of the kitchen. Lost in reverie, I missed Ryan's question. He asked again, "Do you want me to find a room where you could sit while you wait? Lawyer/client interview could take a while."

I knew everyone could use a few minutes off their feet, but George wouldn't hear of it. He fretted that if he wasn't standing in the same spot where he signed the papers for Goddard Swerling, the lawyer wouldn't bother to look for him and he could miss seeing Alan. Ryan explained that the lawyer could make the arrangement for a family visit but only a deputy could escort the family inside. Ryan offered to ask the deputy at the desk to make sure George was notified when Swerling appeared in the lobby. George wasn't having any, but it was evident he needed to rest. I got my clue when Ryan said that the lieutenant ordered him to make the Mersky family comfortable.

That's when I knew I'd owe Frank Anthony one. The solution was for me to stay in the lobby and Ryan to accompany the Merskys. "Ryan's a friend. He's on my speed dial." I held up my cell phone. "As soon as I see the first sign of Goddard Swerling, I'll call Ryan and delay Swerling until you get back here."

While George thought about it, he noticed his sister was nearly sliding down the wall, and, reluctantly, he agreed to the plan. As soon as Ryan and the Merskys disappeared through the doorway behind the desk, I punched speed dial two. Bridgy picked up on the first ring and didn't waste a minute.

"Sassy, Pastor John has called twice. Apparently he runs a post-traumatic stress disorder program at the church for veterans. Alan Mersky has been an on-again, off-again participant in the group. Pastor thinks that he and some of the other veterans can be of help to the family."

I felt a surge of relief. "George will be glad to hear that Alan has supporters. The family is so worried. They know Alan can't go through this all alone. And, truth be told, neither George nor his sister is holding up well under the stress."

Bridgy, always the sociable one, told me to make sure I brought the Merskys back to the café so we could smother them with well-cooked meals and warm companionship. She ended with, "I'll invite Aunt Ophie." And she hung up before I could question the wisdom of introducing Bridgy's flamboyant aunt to George's vibrant wife while we're all in the midst of the Mersky family chaos. I didn't have even a minute to call Bridgy back because I saw Goddard Swerling striding down the hallway as if he owned the building. I punched Ryan on speed dial and he answered even quicker than Bridgy.

"Lawyer out of the interview?"

When I said that he was, Ryan said, "Good, I'll bring the family right in. The lieutenant called five minutes ago. It's all arranged. Only waiting for the lawyer to leave. The brother, the sister, even the sister-in-law are cleared to visit. A deputy will be with them but it won't be me. And, Sassy"—he lowered his voice—"the prisoner is handcuffed and very agitated, so the visit won't be long." He clicked off before I could respond.

Goddard Swerling walked into the foyer. He swiveled his head and then looked directly at me, demanding, "Where is the Mersky family?"

I tried to explain that a deputy was bringing them in to see Alan, but Swerling brushed me off.

"You tell your friend Mersky that the fee is going to be a lot higher than first estimated. Alan has agreed to have me represent him but is extremely uncooperative. I'm not violating confidentiality when I tell you that the entire time we were together, he barely uttered a word. Have the brother with the money call my office for an appointment. We need a new strategy."

He glanced at his massive gold wristwatch. "I'm running late. Don't forget, if the Mersky family wants me to continue on this case, I'm going to need an increase in my retainer."

Goddard Swerling walked out the door and left me as the messenger. Bridgy's idea of food and company was sounding more like a great idea. It would provide a bit of solace before I had to tell the family the difficult news.

Chapter Eleven ‖‖‖‖‖‖‖‖

I paced back and forth, sipping my water, my eyes fixed on the oversized clock hanging above the front door. The second hand crept along but the minute hand seemed never to move. I increased the tempo of my steps and started to count each one to give me a focal point other than the clock. My anxiety was piling higher and deeper. I started marking off an imaginary rectangle—twelve steps forward, eight steps across, twelve steps back. Then close the rectangle with eight final steps across. Once more. And again.

What was wrong with me? George and Alan were reunited. I had a huge part in making that happen and instead of being pleased with myself, I was in total mental disarray. I needed to clear my mind.

I turned my back on all the activity going on around me; deputies working, telephones ringing and computer keys clacking. I stood still and closed my eyes. My favorite meditation spot had long been sitting on the beach with my mind focused on the horizon. When I couldn't make it to the beach, my meditations hadn't been as successful until I learned to close my eyes and visualize the horizon line, straight and true over the Gulf of Mexico. I had barely gotten completely immersed in my contemplation when I was startled by someone calling my name.

It was Ryan. "Sassy, the family will be out in a couple of minutes. I could hear some crying but no shouting. I think it was a good meeting. I don't know how close you are to these people but the perp, er, Alan Mersky, needs a doctor."

"Oh, no. Is he hurt?"

"Not that kind of hurt. Not that kind of doctor. He needs a psych eval—a psychiatric evaluation. I'm really surprised that Swerling didn't ask for one. Sloppy lawyering."

At the look on my face, Ryan patted my arm. "Don't worry, the prosecutor will probably request an eval before deciding on the exact charges. And the family can ask us to provide medical assistance."

Over Ryan's shoulder I saw Regina Mersky walking toward me. She was crying into a handful of tissues. I hurried toward her and stretched out my arms, grabbing her in a tight hug.

Sniffing back her tears, Regina's voice cracked. "I couldn't sit there anymore. Alan has no idea what is going on around him. He keeps asking when we're going to take him back to his hut. I don't even know what that is. Sassy, I didn't want him to see me lose control. But it's so sad. He'll never be able to defend himself in court."

When she realized Ryan was standing next to us listening to every word, Regina abruptly buried her face in the wad of tissues and began sobbing again. Ryan shifted from one foot to the other, looking uncomfortable, knowing he was adding to her stress. He offered to get us more water and vanished.

After a minute or two, Regina quieted down. She was wiping away her tears when she asked, "Can I wait out here with you? I can't go back in there. Alan mustn't see me like this. O'Mally says we have to be strong but . . . he's my baby brother."

Ryan came back into the room, handed me two bottles of water and fled. I was on my own with Regina.

I handed her a bottle of water. "Have a sip. You'll feel better."

She took a small sip. Then she sighed. I was afraid the tears would start again but she brushed the tissues across her eyes one last time, blew her nose and stuffed the tissues in her pocket.

She looked so dejected I was desperate to cheer her, so I told her, with far more confidence than I felt, that everything would work out. Regina asked if I truly believed that Alan would be exonerated and the real murderer would be caught. I doubled down, if only to make her feel better for the moment.

"Regina, here in Lee County we have the best sheriff's department in the state of Florida. They will absolutely solve this murder."

"I'm glad you have faith in us." Lieutenant Frank Anthony was right behind me. As always, when he caught me off guard, his eyes smiled no matter how serious he might otherwise look. He turned to Regina. "The sheriff's office is concerned about your brother's mental health. I have spoken to my superiors and as soon as your other family members are finished speaking to Alan, we are going to transport him to the hospital for a minimum twenty-four-hour period of observation—could be longer. They will check him out physically but the primary purpose will be to evaluate his mental state."

Regina's chin quivered and I was afraid she was going to begin to cry again, but she held the tears back and offered a brave smile. "You are very kind. Thank you. Could you . . . could you talk to my brother George? He'll be making the family decisions."

Frank agreed to talk to George and was kind enough not to tell Regina that it wouldn't be for George to decide, but I realized that nothing affecting Alan, other than hiring Goddard Swerling, would be the family's decision until this muddle was resolved.

Frank excused himself and I strived for small talk to distract Regina and keep her from crying again. We were already past, "Is this your first trip to Florida?" and "Hydration is really important in this climate" when George came down the hall. He had one arm around O'Mally and she seemed to be physically supporting him rather than offering comfort.

George was surprised not to find Goddard Swerling standing with us. I told them that Swerling left once he was assured the family would be allowed to see Alan. Nothing was further from the truth but I could see that the family couldn't take any more disappointing news, and sooner or later I'd have to deliver Swerling's message about the fee.

Regina wanted to know if anyone had asked George if it was okay to take Alan to the hospital. A sad smile flitted briefly across George's face. He took a step closer to his sister, put out his hand and chucked her under the chin.

"Gina, honey, a lieutenant *told* me that arrangements had been made to put Alan in the hospital for observation. I don't think we have much of a voice when it comes to Alan's care. I did tell them that he'd been treated at various Veterans Administration facilities and the lieutenant said they'd relay that information to the doctors who would be examining Alan. Don't you worry."

Regina reached up and patted George's cheek.

Watching brother and sister help each other cope was so touching, I felt tears begin to well in my own eyes. I brushed them away and suggested we head to the Read 'Em and Eat.

Regina protested. "Aren't there things we should be doing?"

Once more, her big brother offered a touch of realism. "Our job now is to wait. Wait for Alan to be evaluated at the hospital. Wait for the lawyer to do his job. Wait for the deputies to find the real killer." He heaved a massive sigh. "We may as well have something to eat. Could be a long wait."

The brief ride to the café was unnervingly quiet. Four people in the Heap-a-Jeep and no one said anything. I toyed with the idea of putting on the radio, but decided against it. Who knows what a newsbreak might dredge up?

When we got to the Read 'Em and Eat, I could see through the window that we had some customers. As soon as I opened the door I recognized Pastor John Kendall, husband of the always-irritating Jocelyn. I often wondered how such a kind and placid man could be married to a woman as petty and annoying as Jocelyn. For the most part, the marriage seemed amiable, so I guess the old adage about opposites attracting rang true. That reminded me once again how I'd often wondered about the pairing of docile George and high-spirited O'Mally. I guessed I'd just have to wait until my opposite number came along. I shook off the silliness floating in my head and concentrated on the present.

Pastor John was sitting with two men I didn't recognize. As soon as we walked in, all three men stood. Of course the Merskys had no idea that the men were clearly waiting for us. George asked where I wanted them to sit. Bridgy came rushing out of the kitchen and greeted everyone warmly. She'd met George and O'Mally in New York and I introduced Regina, who graciously thanked Bridgy for sharing me with them.

"I know you are doing the work of two people when Sassy is busy with us, so I want you to know we are grateful."

I was surprised to see Bridgy blush with pleasure at being recognized for doing her part. It occurred to me that we'd gotten used to covering for each other and shouldering as much as an entire shift when the other one had something to do outside the café. It was exhausting but it was how we'd always managed. It was time to take that next step. I was glad we'd decided to hire Elaine Tibor to fill in once in a while. I made a mental note to talk to Bridgy about that later. We should probably bring her in soon.

Bridgy looked directly at George. "Pastor John and his friends have been waiting for you." She indicated the three men standing by the Dashiell Hammett table. "They know your brother and they want to help."

The effect of her words on the Merskys was electric. All three brightened instantly. George murmured. "Alan's friends? He hasn't been alone all this time? Oh, thank goodness."

Pastor John and the two men came forward. John clasped George's hand warmly, identified himself and then introduced the two men at his side. The balding gray-haired man with a sun-mottled face and a wide scar on one arm was Mark Clamenta. Owen Reston was decades younger with longish blond hair and piercing green eyes. Even under the circumstances, neither Bridgy nor I failed to notice that he had an extremely well-toned body stretching against his muscleman tee shirt.

Bridgy and Owen moved the Barbara Cartland table alongside Hammett so everyone could sit together. Pastor John and his friends had been drinking coffee and nibbling on Robert Frost Apple and Blueberry Tartlets. Bridgy brought a tray of glasses and asked me to get a pitcher of sweet tea from behind the counter. While I poured the tea, Bridgy went into the kitchen and came out with a plate in each hand. One plate was piled high with Miguel's famous Cuban sandwiches stuffed with roast pork, cheese and thinly sliced dill pickles. The other was loaded with *Swiss Family Robinson* Cheeseburgers. She set the plates down and scrambled into the kitchen only to come back with an enormous bowl of *The Secret Garden* Salad. I grabbed lunch plates and salad bowls from behind the counter and set them out accordingly.

Bridgy and I hovered around until we were sure everyone had enough to eat, and then we sat at either end of the tables. By tacit agreement, no one mentioned the real reason we were all together. This meal break was a much-needed interlude of normalcy for the family, and everyone seemed to understand and respect that.

The conversation was light and mild. Pastor John asked if any of the Merskys enjoyed fishing. And when the talk of snapper, grouper and snook petered out of its own accord, Owen Reston told George that he taught an exercise class at the church twice a week and invited George to come along. George took one look at Owen's pectorals and biceps under the clingy tee shirt and laughed. "A half hour of exercise would probably kill me."

A sense of discomfort enveloped everyone at the table as soon as he said the word "kill." No one knew where to look or what to say. George looked stricken. "I'm sorry. It was nice being normal for a while, but well, there has been a killing, and my wife, my sister and I are here to prove my brother didn't do it."

He looked at the three men across the table. "You're Alan's friends. How can you help us?"

Chapter Twelve |||||||||||

"Truth be told"—Mark Clamenta broke the silence—"we're not sure how we can help. I can tell you that the night the woman was killed Alan attended a meeting at the church hall. It's not much of an alibi—a short meeting during a long night. As far as the, ah, incident goes, we only know what we read in the paper and saw on the television news. But we do know Alan and it doesn't seem likely . . ."

Pastor John latched on to Mark's wrist. "Let me."

Mark nodded.

Pastor looked directly at George and then widened his gaze to include Regina and O'Mally. Then he folded his hands on the table and began talking in the soothing tone I'd heard him use so often when someone needed to be comforted.

"Sometimes when people come home from war, the experience changes them." He paused. "More than a decade ago members of the local clergy council discussed their desire to help veterans returning home from the Iraq and Afghanistan wars. We wanted to provide definitive assistance for those suffering from the mental and emotional distress."

George interrupted. "My brother was fine after his first two tours. It was during the third tour that something happened."

Pastor John took a sip of sweet tea and continued. "The short version is that we met with experts from the Veterans Administration and other organizations, and those of us who have churches with room enough opened day programs where all vets would be welcomed. No questions asked."

Owen added, "Word spread and the vets living on the island stopped by. Some of us stayed to help or be helped. The retirees haven't forgotten, either." He tossed a hitch-hiker's thumb Mark's way. "Back in the Stone Age this old man spent some time in Vietnam."

Mark laughed and pushed Owen's arm away.

Regina took George's hand and squeezed tightly as if signaling she was ready to hear the worst. George threw back his shoulders and said, "Okay, tell us what you can. We know that Alan has spent time in mental hospitals but then he is off on his own again. We've never seen him at his most troubled. Is he capable of . . . Could he have done this?"

Pastor John wanted to comfort them but looked helpless as he tried to dredge up an answer.

Owen Reston had no such problem. "From what I saw on the news, Alan had a run-in with this woman, Mrs. Lip-scome, at the library. Based on that very public row, the deputies brought him in for questioning and then detained him. After any kind of confrontation, the Alan I know would have avoided that woman like the plague. He would mutter about her for days but he would never seek her out. Heck, according to the newspaper report, when they had the argument in the library, Mrs. Lipscome was the loud one. Alan never raised his voice."

I bounced in my chair excitedly. "That's true. I don't think he spoke to her at all. She was screaming but Alan walked out and was talking to himself under his breath."

Everyone looked at me like I had announced the winning lottery numbers.

"You were there?" Pastor John was incredulous.

"When you called me, it was because you saw Alan with this woman?" George looked like someone had blindsided him.

I felt terrible. I thought I'd explained it all clearly when I picked the Merskys up at the airport. Thinking back, perhaps I was more vague about Alan's arrest than I should have been. I guess I didn't want to give George any more bad news than necessary.

"Well, I wasn't *inside* the library . . ." And I recounted exactly what happened, ending with Alan being kind enough to pick up one of the books I dropped.

O'Mally, who'd been extra quiet since we arrived at the café, pinched George's cheek affectionately. "Didn't I tell you? He's still the old Alan?" She swung her head around, meeting everyone's eyes one by one. "Does that sound like the behavior of a killer to any of you?"

Pastor, Bridgy and I all spoke at once, assuring her that Alan's actions bore no resemblance to a homicidal fiend. I noticed that the veterans remained silent. I'm sure some of the things they lived through may have taught them that there is a speck of killer instinct in us all.

George turned the conversation around another bend. "The deputies have taken Alan to the hospital for observation."

Pastor rubbed his hands together. "Excellent news. A clinical evaluation will certainly confirm that Alan has no violent tendencies. Absolutely none. Do you know where he is? I can try to make a pastoral visit in the morning."

George took a scrap of paper out of his pocket and slid it across the table. Pastor glanced at it and passed the paper back to George, saying, "Fine place. Great care. I'm sure I'll be able to see Alan and perhaps I can make arrangements for you to speak with his doctor."

"I was wondering . . ." Regina began, stopped and began again. "I was wondering if any of you know where Alan lives."

Pastor stared at a spot somewhere high above Regina's head as though he was praying for guidance. The two veterans exchanged a look and then Owen sat back. Mark Clamenta cleared his throat. "You know that Alan is a real loner, right? Keeps to himself. He'll always pitch in to help another vet, but won't take help for himself. Just his way."

Regina nodded hesitantly, as if she wasn't sure exactly what she was agreeing to.

"If you read the newspapers anywhere in this country, it won't surprise you to learn that there are a lot of homeless veterans. When we came home from Nam, there were some soldiers, well, people would say they couldn't adjust to being home. There was no diagnosis of the problem. Post-traumatic stress wasn't recognized until the early 1980s. The war was long over. Thousands of guys went untreated. We're trying to make that different today."

George interrupted. "We know Alan has PTSD, we just don't know how to help him."

"Your brother gets nervous around people. There are a few vets who live in the woods down island. Not many, five or six. They built huts and lean-tos. Not really a social group, but I guess you could say communal. Alan lives near them. Not with them. He built his hut out of branches and palm leaves, about thirty, forty yards away from the group. He'll help out if asked but otherwise stays on his own."

"His hut. That's what he was talking about. He barely spoke to us, but when he did he kept asking to go back to his hut. We didn't know what he meant." George put his head in his hands. "Why is it so hard to understand my own brother?"

O'Mally put her arm around him and pulled him close.

I heard the word "branches" and had to ask. "Is that why Alan had that big tree limb in his car? Is he building another hut?"

Owen replied. "No. No. Alan is one of the finest wood carvers I've ever seen. His hut is filled with pieces of art. He has a beautiful hand-carved chess set. It must have taken him a year to make it but he won't play with anyone. Just sits in his hut staring at the board."

"Grandpa!" For the first time, Regina was animated. "Remember, George? Grandpa carved a chess set. We used to play chess with him all the time. He even showed us how to carve a pawn."

Now George was excited, too. "I remember. We had great times with Grandpa. What about the time he carved that flute? He played. We sang and danced. That summer in Maine. I was about eight. You and Alan were younger." He drifted back in time and no one said a word until he came back to the present.

"That might be it, you know. Alan is carving wood, staring at a chess set. He's looking for happier times so he can be happy again. Why didn't I see it sooner? We could have helped."

Pastor John leaned in and patted George's hand. "Be proud. You might have found a key that may help your brother get well again, but for now we have to deal with his present problem. Did he mention Tanya Lipscome? Did he say anything at all?"

"I can tell you he was amazed that we're here. He asked if it was Christmas. He seems not to know that he's in trouble. We did ask about the lady. The very mention of her made Alan wildly distressed. He kept mumbling and muttering. All I could understand were the words 'loud' and 'glittery.' Not sure of the context."

I got it immediately. "Well, she was so loud that I could hear her screaming through two sets of double doors while I was outside the library and she was inside. 'Glittery' would certainly describe Tanya Lipscome's expensive gold and diamond cigarette lighter. According to Sally Caldera"—I looked at the Merskys—"she's the librarian I mentioned. Well, according to Sally, Tanya carried the lighter everywhere, even in nonsmoking areas, and she flashed it every chance she got. Do you think that's what Alan meant?"

"Could easily be." I could see George was thinking about numerous possibilities.

O'Mally opened the clasp on her silver purse and started searching with great mock effort. She said, "I don't understand. There is no gold and diamond anything in my purse. That's what I get for marrying an accountant." And she heaved an exaggerated sigh.

Her knack for breaking the tension and easing the conversation back to social was, I'm sure, appreciated by one and all.

George started to stand up. "Listen, you folks have been great, but I really think I should get these two ladies back to our apartment for some rest. We have rough times ahead, no doubt."

"But no. Not yet." Miguel had come out of the kitchen holding a tray of mini cupcakes, decorated so lovingly that they were almost too pretty to eat.

George dropped back into his seat and laughed. "Well, I don't think any of us is so tired that we'd pass up the chance to taste one of your gorgeous creations."

Mark Clamenta said, "You'd have to drag me away from this table, kicking and screaming. I love cupcakes, especially minis—I can eat several different flavors and I don't feel like a pig, because they are so small."

The conversation turned to everyone's love of desserts. While Bridgy and I bussed the table and replenished the sweet tea, our guests voiced their opinions about favorite desserts. Carrot Cake. Banana cream pie. Any kind of ice cream.

O'Mally added, "Anything with chocolate" as she reached for a chocolate mini with mocha frosting.

The conversation had been so stressful, I was delighted to have everyone joking about sweet treats and expanding waistlines.

Eventually everyone exchanged phone numbers and got ready to leave. I went in the kitchen to get my purse so I could drive the Merskys home, but when I came out, Mark Clamenta had already offered and George had gratefully accepted. I had a twinge of guilt because I was so tired that I may have been more grateful than George.

When everyone left I sat down and drained my glass of sweet tea. Bridgy was cleaning around me and I guess I looked somewhat dejected, because she sat down next to me.

"You okay?"

"Tired." I pulled out my cell phone. "And I have to call Frank Anthony and 'confess' I inadvertently kept some information from him. That never goes well."

The lieutenant gave me some version of "you couldn't tell me this when I saw you earlier today?" and then told me not to leave the café until he got here.

When I hung up, Bridgy arched an eyebrow.

"That went well," I said with a grimace.

"Do I detect a soupçon of sarcasm?"

"I'm sure you do." I stood and grabbed a pile of dirty dishes that Bridgy had stacked and brought them into the kitchen.

"Your friends are gone?" Miguel looked up from his task of scrubbing the main work counter.

"Yes. One of the other veterans offered to drive them home."

Bridgy followed me into the kitchen and put another pile of dirty dishes in the sink.

Miguel cleared his throat. "While we are all together, we have to talk about that horrible snake. Yesterday it was seen on this side of the bay. It swam close to the mangroves at the end of Bayland Road. Many people saw it glide along."

Bridgy interrupted. "If we're going to all be in here, let me turn the lock on the front door. She was back in a flash. "No point locking the front door. A sheriff's car just pulled into the parking lot. Miguel, I think you have been trumped by an interview Sassy feels she has to give right this very minute so that she can stay on the good side of a certain lieutenant in the sheriff's department."

Miguel raised his eyebrows. "Now that surprises me. Sassy never strives to get on anyone's good side."

Chapter Thirteen

Bridgy and Miguel were both laughing at what he considered to be his witty comment but I decided to ignore them and walked into the dining room just as Frank Anthony and Ryan Mantoni came through the front door. Ryan started off giving me a little tough love about leaving the door unlocked when I was alone in the café, but the clatter from the kitchen of what sounded like dozens of pieces of cutlery hitting the floor corrected him before I had a chance to.

"Ah, not alone I see." Ryan grinned while pretending to duck. "Crash. Bam. Did you let Miss Ophelia back in the kitchen?"

"Don't be silly, that's Bridgy and Miguel cleaning up."

The lieutenant didn't find our chitchat the least bit interesting or amusing. He asked me to sit at the Emily Dickinson table and I countered by offering them coffee and a slice of pecan pie. Ryan was happy to accept but Frank settled for a glass of water.

I went to the kitchen for Ryan's pie and told Miguel and Bridgy that we did indeed have company. Miguel flashed a look of annoyance. This would further delay the conversation he was trying so hard to have with Bridgy and me about bringing his cat, Bow, to work to save her from the threat of the anaconda.

"What is so important that we must, once again, delay discussing how to best protect Bow from a fifteen-foot snake?"

I told him Ryan and Frank had come to speak to me on official business. I guess I sounded somewhat prissy because Miguel the Unflappable turned into Miguel the Excitable.

"Official business. I will give them official business. Every pet on this island is in danger and the sheriff's office does what? Nothing. Nada." Miguel took off his puffy white chef's hat, plopped it on the counter and marched out of the kitchen.

Bridgy and I looked at each other but said not a word. We could hear that Miguel was emphatic in explaining the dilemma as he saw it, but Frank responded in such a low voice that we both moved to the kitchen door so we could hear what he was saying.

". . . so Dr. Mays brought together a number of veterinarians from the communities surrounding the waterways from here to the Everglades and they meet with the law enforcement officials from the impacted towns and counties. The lead agency is, naturally, the Florida Fish and Wildlife Conservation Commission."

Miguel became calmer once he heard there was some

action being taken, but his goal was to protect Bow. "Fine, they are meeting, but tell me exactly what is being done to guard our pets. You know what that snake can do? He can wrap himself around a small sweet animal like my Bow and crush her. Then he will swallow her whole, in one big gulp."

Frank started to say, "If you keep the cat in the house . . ."

Ryan knew better and decided to move in a different direction. "Miguel, you know Dr. Mays. You and she volunteer together on the hurricane committee. You can be sure she will do everything she can to make sure that the small free-roaming animals are protected until the anaconda is removed from Estero Bay."

"Removed? No. There was a meeting at the community center last night and the overwhelming majority of people want that snake killed. *¡Dios mío!* There were men willing to take a boat out at first light and hunt the snake down. I've been here all day. Perhaps you heard? Did they succeed?"

"Why are we first hearing about this excursion now? We *are* only hearing about it now, correct?" Frank Anthony was reaching his boiling point.

I could almost hear Ryan snap to attention. "Absolutely, Lieutenant. This is the first whisper. If I'd heard, you'd know."

"Go check." Frank dismissed Ryan. "Miguel, I promise we are doing everything we can to assist in the capture of the anaconda. I know that's not what you want to hear but until our orders change, the multi-agency mission is to capture, not to kill. I suggest you talk to Dr. Mays and see what she can tell you.

"And now if Sassy would stop listening at doors and come back in here, I could ask her about her encounter with Alan Mersky."

Bridgy whispered, "How'd he know . . . ?"

I rolled my eyes at her. Of course he didn't *know*. But if I was behind the door, he wanted to get me rattled, hoping it would help his interview. We'd played these games before. The lieutenant's interview technique was to take charge quickly and keep the interviewee off balance by any available means. Accusing me of snooping would certainly work, *if* I heard him say so.

Miguel nearly hit us with the door when he came back into the kitchen. He laughed when he saw that Frank had been absolutely right, and then said, extra loudly. "Sassy, it is your turn now."

I gave Miguel a big smile and Bridgy started giggling uncontrollably. I knew I better get out of the kitchen before I wound up in fits of laughter, which would only make the interview more difficult. I pushed the door and walked into the dining room. I'd like to say I strode in like I was a million-dollar glamour girl, but I didn't have the energy. I'd need all my strength to verbally joust with the bound-to-be-annoying lieutenant.

Ryan was nowhere to be seen. I guessed he was tracking down information about the boaters who went looking for the anaconda this morning.

Frank was standing next to the Emily Dickinson table, and he immediately gestured for me to sit. I hesitated and then thought, *oh, why not*. I knew from previous experience that he was going to do his "stand tall and try to intimidate me" routine, which never worked. I don't intimidate.

Normally I would enjoy any conversation with a man as attractive as Frank Anthony. But his strong "take charge" attitude was a real turnoff. Then I reminded myself not to be confrontational. After all, he was the one with the badge. And this time I was smart enough to offer to talk to him before he found out I was "meddling" in his case.

He stood a few feet away from me and folded his arms across his chest, which made his biceps all the more prominent against the short sleeves of his uniform shirt. I steeled myself. The grilling was about to begin.

And then it didn't. He stood. I sat. No one said a word.

Ryan came back inside and told the lieutenant there was no report of any boaters finding or even searching for the anaconda. I realized that was going to annoy Miguel to no end, but he wasn't my immediate problem.

Ryan stood a few feet from Frank and looked from me to Frank and back again. It was like we were playing "who can stay silent the longest," and I was determined to win. Finally Frank said, "Okay, Sassy, we're here because you have information regarding the Tanya Lipscome case. Is that correct?"

"Almost." Obviously he hadn't listened carefully to me. "What I wanted you to know is that Alan Mersky has a support system here on the island. Pastor John and members of the veterans organization that meets at his church are willing to do anything they can to help prove that Alan is innocent."

"That's your urgent information? Mersky has friends. That's what you want us to know?"

Well when he put it like that . . .

"Of course not." I reached for the right words, words I hoped would help Alan. I decided to try for some flattery before I proceeded. "The family is so grateful for your decision to seek medical help for Alan."

Frank shook his head. "Sassy, a medical evaluation is

nowhere near the same as medical help. An evaluation tells us and the state attorney's office whether the accused is mentally aware enough to participate in his own defense should a case be brought forward."

Why couldn't he just smile and say, "Aw, shucks, I'm happy I made you happy"?

I tried again, deciding to start in agreement this time. "I appreciate the legal system is working to protect Alan's rights. And the family is pleased to no end that Alan will get medical attention of any sort. I think it is important for you to know that the Merskys are not alone in this fight."

Frank bristled at the word "fight" but didn't correct me, so I plunged on. "Pastor John has a very active veterans group at his church. Pastor and any number of vets are planning on working hard to help Alan in any way they can."

Now I had Frank's attention. "You aren't going to run amok with one of your fact-finding missions, are you? Look how that turned out the last time you tried. Almost got yourself killed. And who are you are recruiting now? The Estero Boulevard Irregulars?"

I was pleased to note that he read Sherlock Homes. Not so pleased that he adapted the Baker Street Irregulars to use as a dig at me.

"Don't be silly." He was acting like I was the Pied Piper, leading the innocents away. "We aren't going to go hunting for clues and criminals like Scooby-Doo and the gang. Our goal is to help the Mersky family take care of Alan. It's *your* job to catch the real killer."

Ryan shrank back as if I'd thrown a cup of cold water at him. Frank Anthony had no perceptible reaction. He let my words float away on the rays of afternoon sunshine streaming through the wide glass windows. Then he gave me a smile that was very close to a smirk, and said, "That's something we certainly agree on. You and your junior G-men stay out of our way and we'll solve this case sooner rather than later." He touched his brow with two fingers and tossed me a half salute as he turned and marched out the door with Ryan close on his heels.

Bridgy came out of the kitchen as soon as she heard the front door close.

"Were you listening at the kitchen door?" I teased.

"But, of course. Without listening at the door how could I be sure that the deputies hadn't dragged you off in handcuffs?" She giggled, plopped down in a chair next to me and asked, "So?"

"What?"

"Did he do that whole 'stand over you with his arms folded while he asked the questions' routine?"

I nodded.

Bridgy shrugged. "What a waste. Good-looking guy. If only he wasn't so officious. If he had a sense of humor and was less bossy, we could all be friends."

Miguel came out of the kitchen, ready to leave for the day. "I am going to visit Cynthia Mays. If this big snake is not on the 'endangered' or the 'threatened' list I see no reason why it cannot be killed to save my Bow and the other pets."

Neither of us knew quite how to respond, so I told him we'd see him in the morning. Bridgy sighed and waved.

"Did you change your mind about asking Ophie to come over and meet Alan's family? It's not like her to miss a gathering of any sort or size."

"No, she had a client scheduled. I guess this one showed

up." Bridgy pulled a piece of paper from her pocket. "I had a few minutes so I made up a list of things we need from the restaurant supply house: dish towels, disposable gloves, twelve-ounce glasses. We might want to try a different glass; the ones we have now chip too easily."

"Can't we just call in an order and have it sent?" I was too tired to drive over to the mainland and back.

"We could, but the real problem is that our ice machine stopped working today. I plugged and unplugged and then jiggled the switch and it came back. I know it's a big-ticket item but I thought we should take a look at what's out there, then we can decide on the value of repair versus purchase."

Sensible. I agreed to take a quick ride provided Bridgy drove. We agreed to stop in and tell Ophie about Alan's family and the veterans. Otherwise it wouldn't be long before she started haunting our every move to make sure she had up-to-the-minute news.

"It's not like she'll have gotten any information on her own." As usual, I'd underestimated Bridgy's aunt Ophelia.

Chapter Fourteen

Ophie was awash in self-satisfaction when she welcomed us at the Treasure Trove door. "I'm more than sorry that I didn't get to meet your friends but because I put business before pleasure y'all are going to be happier than an old dog lying in the sun and gnawing on a hambone."

Then she gave us a big grin, folded her hands demurely and waited for us to ask. Naturally, Bridgy did.

"Aunt Ophie, darlin', what are you talking about? Have you made the sale of a lifetime? Is it thanks to you that we can now retire and spend each and every day lounging on the beach?"

"I only wish that were true, honey chile, but my news is darn near as good. I have it on the best authority that your murder victim may have had a fancy man."

Bridgy and I exchanged questioning looks, then I remembered an old song by the Rolling Stones. I hummed the tune until the lyric floated across my mind. *"You've got a fancy man on the side."*

I nudged Bridgy. "Boyfriend. Tanya Trouble had a boyfriend." I looked to Ophie for confirmation. "Am I right?"

"Quite possibly. Come sit down and I'll tell you what I heard." She led us to the delicately plaited wrought iron patio set where she conducted business with her clients, usually while plying them with pastries and sweet tea from the Read 'Em and Eat.

"Just as I was getting ready to come on over and meet the Merskys—is that their name?—why y'all won't believe who walked in as bold as the morning sun after a week of rain. And pretending she never missed so much as one appointment, never mind two. Frederica, the designer for Lipscome Builders."

Ophie bobbed her head and waited for us to take in the fact that the source of her gossip was well credentialed.

I couldn't resist pretending that I didn't get the connection so I asked if Frederica had bought some of Ophie's more expensive decorative pieces.

"Why, yes she did but that is the least interesting bit of the story." Ophie leaned across the table and motioned us to lean in as well. If there were hidden microphones in the Treasure Trove, Ophie was making certain they didn't pick up a word. She spoke in the tiniest of whispers. "Frederica told me"—here Ophie actually glanced around to make sure no one was sneaking up on us—"well, she told me that Mr. Barry Lipscome, y'all know, husband of the deceased, wasn't so sure where his wife was spending her time before she met her unfortunate end. He pushed her to sign up for volunteer jobs and charity endeavors so he could go on working his hundred-hour weeks and not be worried about where she was, who she was with."

"Makes sense to me. Tanya Trouble no more wanted to be volunteering in the library than I want to backpack the Appalachian Trail."

Always easily sidetracked, Ophie started telling us that hiking the trail is an exhilarating experience and she ought to know, since she'd hiked it several times and she was much older than we are now, so what were we waiting for?

With wide eyes and a slight tilt of her head, Bridgy gave me the "you sent her astray now bring her back" look. I tried. "I didn't see that Tanya was the least bit interested in the stacks or the patrons or the research material or anything else the library has to offer. If that was one of the projects her husband suggested to keep her busy, very likely it increased her boredom."

"From what Frederica said, the husband was very sure that Tanya's extracurricular activities involved men, not books."

"Men? Plural?" Bridgy was aghast. "How many could she handle at once?"

Ophie smiled. "Honey chile, I could tell you stories . . . But of course well-mannered ladies never kiss and tell." And she preened just enough to let us know she still had what it takes.

I almost choked. Now it was Bridgy who'd gotten Ophie off track and on to something neither of us wanted to hear. I jumped in superfast, lest Ophie thought we'd try to wheedle information about her romantic past. "Does Frederica have any idea who Tanya was, ah, interested in?"

"Well, it seems that Frederica has lunch at least once a week with Lipscome Builders' head of security, a retired police detective from New York. I got the impression that

Frederica would like to move past lunch but so far . . . zippo. Anyway, the security man told Frederica that Barry Lipscome wanted him to hire a private investigator to follow Mrs. Lipscome for a while. Of course Lipscome wanted to remain at arm's length and the investigator would never know who the real client was."

I was perplexed. "Why would the security boss risk his job by telling Frederica all this?"

Ophie smoothed her oat-colored hair. "He said he was conflicted. Needed advice."

"And what advice did Frederica give, pray tell?" I was getting tired of this pointless story dragging on and on, all speculation, nothing concrete. I had to remind myself that was how conversations with Ophie often went.

"What advice could she give to a colleague about their mutual boss? She told him to follow Lipscome's directive and hire an investigator."

Bridgy started tapping the tabletop with her fingertips, clearly restless. "Wait, if there was a PI following Tanya Trouble, then shouldn't he have seen the murder? Or maybe tried to stop it, or at least tell the sheriff's deputies who the killer is?"

"Mr. Lipscome was too slow in coming up with the idea, and the head of security was even slower in finding an investigator, so Mrs. Lipscome was murdered without a soul to witness it. An investigator could have stopped the murder entirely but no investigator was ever contracted." Ophie threw up her hands.

We sat for a moment reflecting on what might have been if a private investigator had been on the scene when Tanya Trouble was attacked.

Then I realized it wouldn't have made a difference. "She was in her own backyard sitting in the hot tub. If an investigator was following her, he'd have to stay out of sight and probably couldn't see the yard from the street."

Bridgy gave me a look. "Sassy. Stop it. There was no investigator. The deed is done. Now let's get to the restaurant supply house."

We invited Ophie to come along for the ride, but she already had plans for the evening and wanted to go home and "buff up" as she liked to call it. "It's Blondie Quinlin's birthday and we're having a little celebration. I thought dinner would be in order, but some of the girls from the environmental group thought we should cut loose with a little wine and a little gambling. And of course a cake. Augusta Maddox is making the cake. Can't say I trust her cooking, but she did volunteer."

"Aunt Ophie!" Bridgy pretended to be shocked. "I can't believe you are going to spend the evening gambling. What has gotten into you? And what kind of gambling? Roulette? Baccarat? Wait 'til I tell Mom."

"You leave your mother out of this. It's only playing cards. What is that game the girls here like to play? A canasta game of sorts. Hoof and Mouth? No. No. Hand and Foot. That's it. So much fun. We laugh all night. I'll have to teach you." Ophie took a peek at the starfish-shaped clock hung high on the wall and said, "Well if y'all are heading to the mainland, you better move along. But tell me, did Charmaine do right by that poor fellow's family? How is the rental she arranged?"

After telling Ophie how happy the Merskys were with their apartment, Bridgy and I walked over to our cars. Since

I'd spent much of the day driving the Merskys hither and yon, I was thankful that Bridgy offered to drive to Royal Restaurant Supply. We piled into her shiny red Escort ZX2.While she was pulling out of the parking lot, Bridgy asked, "You met this Mrs. Lipscome. What do you think? Was she the type to have a—don't you love Ophie's phrase—*fancy man*?"

Talk about being put on the spot to make a judgment call. "I didn't exactly meet her. I only saw her walk by me at the library."

"Well, what was your impression? Did she look like a woman that would make herself, ah, easily available?"

I sunk back in my seat and stifled a yawn. "Really? In this day and age we gauge a woman's morality by how she looks? Seriously?"

I glanced at the iPod dock on her dashboard and tried to change the subject. "And where is your iPod?" I tapped the radio on. Instead of music we heard an announcer raving about a furniture sale in Bonita Springs.

Bridgy shrugged. "Not sure. I guess I left it at home. Anyway, don't change the subject. Do you think Mrs. Lipscome had a boyfriend?"

"We have no way of knowing. All we know is that somebody told somebody else that her husband *thought* Tanya Trouble was fooling around."

"But if it's true," Bridgy persisted, "if she had a fancy man, maybe they had a lovers' quarrel and he killed her in a fit of jealous rage."

When I refused to answer, Bridgy scoffed. "You really don't want to speculate about this, do you?"

"Speculation won't get Alan out of the mess he's in. We need facts and so does the sheriff."

Not one to give up, Bridgy said, "Well we can be sure of one fact. If she had a lover, it sure wasn't Alan Mersky."

Well, she had a point there. A lover would certainly increase the suspect pool. If the lover wasn't a suspect, maybe he had a wife, or a jealous ex.

While I was lost in thought, the latest cut by Florida Georgia Line came on the radio and the duo, one Georgian and one Floridian, sang us right into the parking lot of Royal Restaurant Supply.

Royal is like a Toys"R"Us for cooks and foodies. You name it, they have it and in dozens of styles. A few months ago, Miguel asked us to pick up a new basting brush. There were so many to choose from that I wound up snapping pictures with my phone and sending them to him until he decided on a snazzy long-handled model with natural bristles. Although the café side of the business was more Bridgy's domain, I still loved to wander up and down the aisles looking at all the gadgets and the totally upscale service items.

A section of finely woven tablecloths and napkins caught my eye. I was selecting colors for imaginary holiday parties when Bridgy called me over to aisle three. She was with Patsy, our favorite salesperson, and they were discussing ice machines of various sizes and capabilities. I zoned out immediately. What does an ice maker have to do besides make the ice and keep it frozen? Well, according to Patsy, size matters. Did we want ice cubes, ice nuggets or crushed ice? All three? I stifled another yawn but snapped back to attention when they started talking price. Talk about sticker shock. Every machine, even the most compact, cost thousands of dollars. I didn't think those little yellow energy-efficiency stickers that indicated a reduction in electrical use would save us enough money to warrant such an expensive purchase. I was relieved when Bridgy took all the brochures that Patsy gave her and said we'd make a decision soon. Sure we would. Right after we won the Powerball lottery.

Bridgy gave Patsy our list, arranged for six dozen of the glasses we picked out to be delivered to the café tomorrow, and in short order we were carrying two sturdy boxes of straws, plastic gloves, dish towels and assorted supplies across the parking lot.

"Should we go straight home or do you want to go to the café? We could drop off the supplies and you could pick up the Heap-a-Jeep at the same time."

I barely heard Bridgy's question. Two men came out of the sporting goods shop a few doors down the walkway. They were heading in our direction and the closer they got, the more certain I was that Bridgy and I were about to cross paths with Barry Lipscome's sons.

Chapter Fifteen

I elbowed Bridgy. "You see these two fellows heading our way?"

"If you mean the handsome dude in the blue golf shirt and his tag-a-long friend, how could I miss them? Do you want to drop a box and play damsel in distress? Fine with me, but if they invite us for coffee or a drink, you have to take the young one."

Always one for a little harmless flirtation, Bridgy leaped at any opportunity to increase her social circle. I rolled my eyes. "This isn't a pickup. Those are Barry Lipscome's sons. Too old to be Tanya's. Probably her stepsons."

My response was enough to make Bridgy nearly drop the box she was carrying, but it would have been a genuine accident and not a flirtation technique. "You're kidding," she said under her breath, although the Lipscomes were still yards away. "Let's talk to them. Put your package on that bench. Quickly."

We put our boxes on the nearby bench as though it were a rest stop. I only had to take two steps to the right to be directly in the Lipscome brothers' way. The older one moved to walk around me but stopped when I addressed him by name.

"Mr. Lipscome?"

"Yes?"

I put on my serious face. "I'm Sassy Cabot and this is my business partner, Bridgy Mayfield. We own the Read 'Em and Eat café in Fort Myers Beach. I knew your stepmother and I want to say how sorry I am." Bridgy tapped me on the back. "How sorry we both are for your sad and sudden loss."

He nodded and tried, once again, to move around me but I took another side step, blocking his way, and stuck out my hand, holding it deliberately straight until he was forced to acknowledge me and shake my hand. "I'm Abbott Lipscome. This is my brother Ellison."

I said I was pleased to meet him although the circumstances could have been better, then I asked, "How is your father doing? It broke my heart to see how stressed he was this morning."

That's when he took a good look at me. "This morning. You were at the sheriff's office. You a deputy?"

It would have been so easy to bob my head in agreement and continue talking but honesty took over. "No."

Bridgy stepped a little closer to me as if my answer gave us a reason to close ranks, and said, "She was visiting her boyfriend. He left his watch at her place last night. He's a deputy."

I gulped and quickly shifted away from my imaginary love life. "Actually, I knew Tanya from her volunteer work in the library. She was always helpful."

Ellison raised one eyebrow and gnarled his lips. "Maybe

she was all sweetness at the library but you didn't have to live with the—"

Abbot put his arm around his younger brother. "If you'll excuse us. The entire family is upset."

But Ellison refused to be quieted. "The murder is so disruptive. We have to deal with the constant inconvenience of deputies, technicians trooping through the house and reporters showing up all over the place. And why? Because of Tanya. I know Dad was going to get rid of her. I know it was a matter of time 'til he would force her to sign the divorce papers."

From the look on Abbott's face, I would not have been surprised to witness another murder right then and there. He tightened his grip on Ellison's shoulder until he amended, "Well, I'm sorry Tanya is dead." But he couldn't quite let go. "Even though it makes me happy that Dad is rid of her, period."

I was aghast at Ellison's callousness but Bridgy took no notice and inquired as to the wake and funeral arrangements.

That's when Abbot exploded. "What is wrong with this town? Perfect strangers accosting us in a shopping mall to ask about the arrangements for someone they barely knew. I wish I could say you were the first nosy nellies we've heard from, but the house phone has been ringing off the hook. Is it the goriness of the murder or the chance at being around my father's money that you ghouls find so attractive?"

He yanked his brother's arm and dragged him into the parking lot. They were about ten feet away when Ellison threw over his shoulder, "The service is private. Invitations have already gone out. If you show up without one, we'll have you arrested for trespassing."

It took a few seconds for me to shake off my stunned silence. "Talk about overreacting! I never saw anything like that."

Bridgy was always able to laugh off awkward social scenes more easily than I could. She dismissed the Lipscomes with a flap of her hand. "At least he acknowledged we're perfect."

I accused Bridgy of not hearing a word Ellison Lipscome said, to which she replied, "I heard the one word that mattered. He said we were 'perfect' strangers. Now let's get these boxes into the car."

Once again I turned on the car radio and this time was happy to hear Jimmy Buffett's voice singing about what he liked on his cheeseburgers. Personally, I was only with him as far as "*lettuce and tomato*." All the rest of the stuff he craved was fine for him but too much for me.

Still, Bridgy and I, foodies that we are, knew every word and sang along like dutiful Parrotheads.

During the commercial for a sneaker sale at the Reebok in the Tanger Outlets, we decided to bring the supplies to the café so we could get everything put away neat and tidy for the morning. After two or three more commercials, we were singing along to one of our favorite girls'-night-out songs. All those years practicing voice in the church choir when I was growing up back in Brooklyn and I still couldn't belt lyrics out like Carrie Underwood. It was so much fun to sing along with her anyway. The song was over but we were still dragging out "*I don't even know my last name,*" putting about ten syllables into the final "*name.*"

Carrie gave way to Billy Currington, as if we needed a song to remind us that "People Are Crazy." I was glad the music made such a radical shift. I was afraid another girls'-night-out song would remind Bridgy of her fabulous bachelorette party in Las Vegas. The party was a blast. Unfortunately, the marriage was less successful. It was bad enough Bridgy caught her ex-husband—the Bonehead—cheating. His paramour had enough Botox and plastic surgery that she didn't look quite as Mrs. Robinson-ish as she seemed. Unless you took a really close look at the old lady's face.

The Bonehead was half of the reason we fled Brooklyn. Howard Accounting, where George works and I worked, moved to Connecticut, too long a commute from Brooklyn for me. So we packed up and here we are.

Bridgy brought my thoughts back to Tanya Trouble.

"Oh, about the funeral. Call Cady."

"And ask him what?"

"Don't ask him anything. *Tell* him that if he brings all the information he can scrape up abut Tanya Lipscome's "private" funeral to the café before lunch tomorrow, breakfast is on me. And that includes dessert."

We normally don't serve dessert with breakfast, but Bridgy knew how to get the attention of Cady's sweet tooth, which brought the rest of him right along.

He answered before the second ring. "Sassy. I was going to call you in a while. How are the Merskys doing? Did they get in to visit Alan? How did that go?"

Actually, he didn't rat-tat-tat the questions. Like the great news reporter that he is, Cady asked, I answered and then he asked another question. And so on. As soon as he assured me that he was strictly a friend inquiring about my other friends, not, at this moment, a reporter hunting down a story, I didn't mind answering any of his questions.

As soon as I pressed the "End" button on my cell, Bridgy asked what I thought of the young Lipscomes.

"Arrogant comes to mind. And obnoxious. You'd think

they'd at least pretend to be sorry their stepmother is dead. I mean, if their father's net worth is as large as the boys imply, Tanya's death increases their inheritance, doesn't it?"

"You've seen the father. Is he tottering at death's door?"

"Nope. He looks healthy enough, but the Menendez brothers spring to mind."

Bridgy was shocked. "You mean those brothers who killed their parents for their fortune when we were, like, babies? I saw the story on some sort of 'where are they now' television show. Maybe *Larry King Live* before it went off the air."

"We studied the case in my family psych course junior year. Really creepy. Not that I think the Lipscomes are Menendez weird, but money is a strong motive and they disliked their stepmother so much that they can't even put on a show of being sorry she's dead."

Bridgy parked the car in front of the Read 'Em and Eat, and the Lipscomes were largely forgotten until we'd unloaded and stored our supplies. The supply room was stuffed to the gills, but I knew within a week we'd use up a third of what we'd dragged home. Bridgy opened a bottle of root beer and waved it at me. I nodded and she filled two glasses with ice and led me into the dining room. When we're closed and the cleanup was finished, we often sat and enjoyed the silence around us. Both Bridgy and I were still astonished by how much our lives had improved in the three-plus years we'd been the proud owners of the Read 'Em and Eat. We liked to sit quietly and look around at our domain. The thrill never got old.

Bridgy took a sip of her root beer and started rummaging in her sea green cross-body purse. She'd added a dolphin pin to the clasp and every time she opened the bag, the dolphin wobbled, but he never fell off. Bridgy pulled out a stack of papers and pushed them across the table.

"I know you don't have much interest in kitchen supplies, but we really have to talk about the ice machine. We've had it repaired twice and it is puddling again. It's time to invest in a new one."

I nervously traced the edges of the picture of Dickinson's house, which, along with a picture of the poet and copies of several of her poems, sat under layers of lamination on the tabletop. I hated when we had to talk about money. After expenses, the Read 'Em and Eat was providing just enough income for Bridgy and me to survive. As long as we continued to share the apartment we liked to call the Turret, because it was five stories high overlooking the beach and had miles of gorgeous views, we were fine.

I made a show of thumbing through the papers and then set them down. "Honestly, have you looked at these prices? How can we afford . . . ?"

"We can't afford not to. We serve cold drinks all day long. Do you realize how many customers order sweet tea rather than coffee for breakfast? And nearly everyone wants a glass of ice water with their meals. We have to have good-quality ice."

As our bookkeeper, or "resident money guru" as Bridgy liked to call me, I knew the purchase would crimp our budget for a few months. But the café wouldn't survive if we suddenly stopped serving ice. I caved gracefully.

"Okay, how about this. Have Miguel look these over with you. Pick two or three you think would suit our needs. Call a couple of the restaurants our size, you know, like the Sandwich Shack and Estelle's Eatery. See what kind of machines they use. I'll find the money for whatever model you think is best. Royal gives us a ninety-day line of credit, right?"

Bridgy jumped up. "Oh, I thought this conversation was going to be a lot tougher. That accountant's mind of yours puts everything in order lickety-split." She leaned in and gave me a hug.

Bridgy's use of the word "accountant" reminded that I couldn't go home without checking in to find out how the Mersky clan was managing. While Bridgy gathered up all the ice machine papers, I pulled out my cell phone and began searching for George's number.

Chapter Sixteen

O'Mally answered George's phone on the first ring and she was whispering. Before I had a chance to think how strange both those things were, O'Mally said George was asleep. She raised her voice to normal. "Sorry, Sassy. I would have turned his iPhone off after he went to bed, but he ordered me to leave it on. Ordered! Can you imagine George ordering me to do anything? I tell you, Sassy, this entire situation is taking a toll on my poor Georgie. Anyway, he had a gut-wrenching conversation with that shyster lawyer. Gave George a headache. Are you sure that Swerling is the best around because, personally, I'd fire him for insolence or impudence or one of those things."

She finally stopped for a breath, allowing me a chance to talk. "I wanted to check and make sure you are all right. What is on the agenda for tonight? Tomorrow? Anything I can do to help?"

"Well, George is hoping that by some time tonight the sheriff's office will be able to give us a contact person at the hospital. We need to know who will be observing Alan so George can follow up with them and maybe cross-refer Alan's VA records."

"Perhaps Pastor John could help with that."

"Great idea. Do you have his number? I know he and George exchanged phone numbers but I don't want to search around. Anyway, I'd rather use my phone. Keep George's free for incoming."

I could certainly see the wisdom of that, so I rattled off cell numbers for me, Bridgy and Pastor John, plus our home number in the Turret. I took a quick look in a local directory we kept under the front counter and found the number for Pastor John's church.

I hung up and looked at Bridgy. "Boy, for all her 'nutty as a fruitcake' demeanor, O'Mally is one tough gal when it comes to taking care of George."

"Obvi. All you have to do is see the way she looks at him when he's busy doing something else. It's totes adorb."

I raised my eyebrows.

"Okay. Okay. I'm practicing. Next time the Teen Book Club comes in, I want to sound 'with it' when I serve the refreshments."

"A suggestion here. If you want to relate to the kids, the first thing you should do is stop saying 'with it.' Makes you sound like you're ancient. Isn't that from like the disco age or something? Next you'll be saying 'my bad.'"

We spun into one of our giggle sessions and, before we knew it, Bridgy passed me a napkin and we were wiping tears from our eyes.

She looked at me and said, "Man, we needed that. Oops. Another hokey saying, right?"

"Ah, but totes appropriate. And you know what would also be appropriate—an hour at the beach."

"Great idea. Let's lock up and I'll race you home." Bridgy turned off the light switch. "You know what would also be a great idea? We should start keeping bathing suits and beach towels in the office so we could go for a swim after closing once in a while."

I gave my head a "why didn't I think of that" smack and we locked up for the day.

It only took a few minutes to drive both cars home and change into swimsuits. We wandered through the rear deck of our building, fancifully named the Beausoleil, although no one could argue with the fact that we basked in the beautiful sun most days of the year.

We plopped on towels we'd spread on the sand and looked up and down the beach. It was nearly dinner hour for everyone. Even tourists have to eat, thank goodness, or we'd be out of a job.

"Do you want to swim first, or do your meditation?"

Bridgy's question had startled me, so I realized that I'd probably begun my "look at the horizon" meditation as soon as I sat down.

"Meditate first."

"Great. I'm going shelling along the shore. Back in twenty."

Bridgy walked along the shoreline carrying the mesh cosmetics bag she used for her shell collecting. She bent down a time or two but nothing she examined made it into the bag. I watched her for a couple of minutes before shifting my eyes to a mother standing at the water's edge with two toddlers. Each time the Gulf tide washed up on the sand, the little girl shrieked gleefully and splashed with her hands and feet, while her brother took any number of steps backward until the water retreated once again.

Finally, I turned to the horizon, calmly sitting at the distant edge of the Gulf, waiting for me. I shifted into the butterfly pose that Maggie had taught me in my first yoga class. I brought my knees in to my chest and then dropped them out to each side. I slid my feet together and leaned forward slightly until I was comfortable. I began to breathe deeply, never allowing my eyes to leave the horizon. When the occasional thought slipped into my mind, I mentally swatted it away, keeping my mind open and focused on the exact spot where sky meets sea.

After a while, I closed my eyes and let the events of the recent days reemerge in a finer semblance of order. I looked around and Bridgy was only a few feet away, using her hand as a visor and staring up at the sky. I twisted my head and followed her gaze. She was gawking at the bright red canopy of a parasail pulled through the air by a towline attached to a speedboat.

"Get anything good?" I was referring to the shells.

But Bridgy was captivated by the parasail. She pointed skyward. "We should try that. And soon."

"Not a chance. Now let me see the shells you found."

She fell to her knees beside me and unzipped the shell bag. She lifted out two shells that looked like tiny ice cream cones. "I found two flawlessly shaped Florida Cones. Almost identical. Aren't they perfect? I have one like them at home but the beige is a little darker and it doesn't have as many yellow stripes. If I put these two on either side of the one I have, they'll make a gorgeous necklace."

She tucked the shell bag into her beach tote, and we ran into the water for a brief but invigorating swim.

The café was super busy the next morning. There was a continuous line on the benches outside the door of people waiting for tables. Three separate groups of fisherfolk came in to have their thermoses filled with coffee or sweet tea to go along with the takeout meals or boxes of pastry they wanted packed for later in the day. Bridgy and I couldn't have moved any faster if we had ridden around on skateboards. At one point I reached over for the water pitcher that sat at Bridgy's elbow as she was filling thermoses with fresh coffee. I couldn't help but observe, "We are going to have to get that young woman. Elaine, was it? We have to get her in here for a trial run as waitstaff. We need help."

Bridgy nodded but I flew off to fill water glasses before she had a chance to answer me. We were less pressured once the takeout crowd was gone. And within a half hour, there were no more customers enjoying the salty aroma of the breeze coming in off the Gulf of Mexico while they sat outside our front door awaiting a breakfast table.

I was bussing Robert Louis Stevenson—piling the dirty dishes and cutlery in a plastic bin—when I realized there were no customers hovering to jump in the seats as soon as I finished the scrub down. I glanced at the clock. It was nearly a quarter to eleven. The breakfast crowd was slowing to a drizzle and the lunch crowd had yet to begin. I was deciding to use our break time to talk to Bridgy about bringing on part-time help, at least for breakfast, when I heard the front door open.

I gave the Stevenson tabletop a final swipe and turned to invite the customers to sit, but it was only Cady Stanton. I smiled whenever I thought of him by his full name or saw it as a byline in the *Fort Myers Beach News*. I am sure her friends and family were surprised when Cady's radically feminist mother had voluntarily taken her husband's last name. But of course she married a man whose last name was Stanton, so she was able to name her children Cady and Elizabeth after the founding feminist Elizabeth Cady Stanton, one of the authors of the "Declaration of Sentiments" that came out of the Seneca Falls Convention held long before the Civil War. If she'd fallen in love with a man named Smith or Jones, I wonder if she'd taken his last name.

Cady marched over, stood in front of me rubbing his hands together and said, "Okay, I did my part. Bring on the breakfast, and—" He stopped to look at the specials board. "Great, Miguel made Ophie's buttermilk pie. I'll have a piece."

He had pulled out a chair and sat down before I realized that he was talking about Tanya Trouble's funeral arrangements. I kept my voice low so as not to bring our exchange to the attention of the other breakfasters. I wasn't going to have a repeat of the chaos that occurred when Ryan and Ophie talked in the dining room about the murder. The victim's funeral would be no less sensational. "You found out the arrangements for, er, Tanya?"

He nodded. "Bridgy asked me to, remember? And offered free breakfast. With pie." He looked around. "Where is she?"

"The kitchen. Come on, we can talk there."

I saw the reluctance spreading across his freckled face and added, "It's where great breakfasts are made."

He followed me into the kitchen, but of course as we

walked in, Bridgy walked out with an armful of food-laden dishes. "Tell Sassy," she directed as she moved passed us. Miguel gave Cady a wave but kept his cooking on track. No interruptions tolerated.

As a reporter, Cady was nothing if not concise. He listed facts in descending order of importance. "Tanya Lipscome's funeral will be held tomorrow morning at ten o'clock in the Peace of Heart Chapel in Fort Myers. Invited guests only. No flowers, please. Donations may be made to the American Cancer Society. Her mother was a victim."

Cady checked off the mental list in his head and decided he told me all he knew or at least all he thought I needed to know.

Bridgy came into the kitchen, put a handful of dishes in the rinse sink and gave me an inquiring glance.

I nodded and gave Cady an "atta boy" pat on the shoulder. "Feed the man, Bridgy. He brought all the information we need."

Cady looked perplexed. "Why would you need the funeral information? Didn't you hear me? Invitation only. Oh, Sassy, you aren't going to snoop again, are you? Don't you remember what happened the last time you decided to do a bit of investigating on your own? Nearly got yourself killed."

Definitely not a conversation I wanted to have, so I cut him off. "We have empty tables if you'd like something to eat."

Bridgy intervened. "Sassy, be nice. Cady is helping us. Oh, and I called Elaine Tibor. She is going to help out with the lunch shift. Sort of a trial run."

I gave Cady my widest smile and head-nodded toward the dining room. "Go sit down and I'll bring you some hot corn bread and honey butter while you decide what you want for breakfast." And I started putting together a plate.

Miguel looked up from the vegetables he was chopping. "Cady, you want the veggie omelet, *sí*? With all that corn bread, you need veggies to be healthy."

"Never argue with the chef," Cady said with a smile. "Veggie omelet, it is."

I followed him into the dining room. He took a seat at Robert Frost and motioned for me to sit. I put the corn bread platter in front of him and took a quick look around the room. Everything seemed under control, so I sat opposite him.

"Sassy, I meant what I said. Everyone remembers what happened the last time we had a murder in town. I know you are friends with Alan Mersky's family but you cannot get involved any further than you already are. And for goodness' sake, no sleuthing."

I intended to humor him. I really did, but instead I wound up telling him that while I thanked him for getting the information requested, I was a grown woman and would do as I pleased. "Besides, I'm too busy to sit and listen to one of your lectures. We have a new employee coming in for training and I have the Potluck Book Club this afternoon."

I pushed back my chair and stood straight up.

Then Cady said, "You do know that Tanya Lipscome was the woman in the lawsuit, right? You heard about that, didn't you?" And he flashed a gotcha grin when I sat right back down in my chair.

Chapter Seventeen |||||||||||

"What lawsuit?"

Cady pointed to the copies of his employer's newspaper, the *Fort Myers Beach News*, stacked by the cash register. "Don't you read the *News*? Folks don't buy the paper, then I'm out of a job." He patted my hand. "Only kidding. I'm not the reporter following it so I don't know the story in its entirety but . . . our murder victim, Tanya Lipscome, and her husband own a big house just around the bayside curve of Moon Shell Drive. You know, it's one of those streets that goes straight east off Estero Boulevard and then juts to the south and runs along Estero Bay.

"They own a wide expanse of bay-front property and apparently the original builder, for the Lipscomes or somebody else, I don't know, decided to put the house on the extreme south end of the property to give the homeowners maximum privacy. You know, kept it away from the houses before the curve."

I was tapping my toes with frustration. Would he never get to the point? "What has this got to do with anything?"

Cady held up a hand. "Honestly, Sassy, you have no patience at all. I'm telling you what led up to the lawsuit. In my business, background information is extremely important." He sat silently waiting for me to agree.

Instead I leaned in and jabbed my index finger in the air directly in front of his face. "Don't give me any more of your 'I have the floor and I'll take as much time as I please.' In my business, I have to be on my feet and serving customers. And I may have to start serving again at any moment. Now get to the lawsuit."

He ripped a piece of corn bread in two, then saw the look on my face and thought the better of testing my tolerance any further. He put both pieces back on the plate.

"Okay, the bottom line is that the Lipscomes—although from what I hear it was her pushing the idea, not him—decided they wanted to build one of those elevated swimming pools. You know what I mean. It's a ten-foot-high concrete enclosure where they can build a six-foot-deep pool above ground because the water table is too high to put it in the ground."

I rolled my eyes. "Is there a bottom line?"

"Okay I'll skip to the end. The Lipscomes filed for permits and the neighbors on the eastbound part of Moon Shell Drive filed a lawsuit trying to prevent the Lipscomes from building the pool on their property that sits on the top of the curve. The pool would block the neighbors' view of Estero Bay and the shoreline foliage."

Now he had my interest. "Who are these neighbors? Any homicidal maniacs among them?"

"Sassy, you really should read the *News*. One of the

neighbors is a former pro wrestler named Otto Ertz. He's been so confrontational with Tanya that the sheriff's deputies had to be called. Twice. No one seemed to fight with Barry about it. I don't know if he cared whether they built the swimming pool or not. It's like it was Tanya's pet project."

The door opened and I started to get up, ready to move into waitress mode. But instead of customers, it was Elaine Tibor, our potential part-time waitress. Once again she was wearing a black knee-length skirt. This time her white man-tailored shirt had short sleeves. I looked down at my denim shorts and green tank top covered by a white bib apron and realized we forgot to tell her how informal we are here at the Read 'Em and Eat.

I greeted her warmly but was grateful when Bridgy offered to show her around. I volunteered to watch the dining room. I made the rounds of the few occupied tables with a coffeepot and a pitcher of sweet tea and offers of "Can I get you anything else?" Then I returned to Cady.

"What else do you know about the lawsuit? How dangerous is this wrestler? And who else is involved?"

Cady swallowed a mouthful of corn bread and leaned back in his chair. "Well, Goddard Swerling is the lawyer representing the neighbors. Although how that works along with him representing Alan Mersky, I have no idea. I don't know why you're asking me all these questions; your book club and yoga pal, Maggie Latimer, is one of the plaintiffs in the suit. She'd know more than I do. Can I have my omelet now?"

I had a lot more questions but we'd run out of time. Customers were coming through the door and I had to get back to work. I seated a couple at Dashiell Hammett, gave them menus and then went into the kitchen to get Cady's omelet.

Miguel gave me a broad wink. "Ay, *chica*, I thought you would never let the poor man eat. Are you pumping him for information about the murder?"

I noticed Elaine watching us from where she and Bridgy were standing near the office door. I didn't want to have her think we were morbid gossips, so I laughed off Miguel's remark and told a complete lie. "Actually, we were talking about taking a trip to St. Augustine sometime in the next few weeks. Historical Florida, you know." I grabbed Cady's omelet off the steam table and fled.

Lunch patrons began surging through the door. I led them to seats and poked my head in the kitchen pass-through to let Bridgy know we had a crowd building. She and I had agreed that for this trial period, Elaine would work the dining room for the entire lunch shift. Bridgy would stay in the kitchen with Miguel instead of running back and forth as she usually did. I'd handle the dining room and keep an eye on Elaine. Later on Bridgy and I would switch. This way we could both evaluate Elaine and, as the lunch crowd dwindled, I could focus on getting ready for the Potluck Book Club. This month's book, *Fictitious Dishes* by Dinah Fried, was so different from anything we'd read before so I was extremely curious to hear how the clubbies interpreted the author's concept.

Elaine was a quick learner. When she had a question, she asked it, took in the answer and retained it. She never asked the same question twice. And she was a meticulous server, which is a trait I knew would make a good impression on the patrons. The early lunch crowd ate briskly and rushed out again, anxious to get on with whatever plans they had for the rest of the day. The folks who came in later were more casual about their meals and tended to linger over dessert or a second cup of coffee.

Bridgy and I switched places about an hour before book club was due to start. She asked me what I thought of Elaine, and I told her that this could work out well for us. "In fact, see if she can come in tomorrow morning around nine so we can go to Tanya Trouble's funeral."

Bridgy looked surprised. "Did you wangle an invitation?"

"Don't be silly. We don't need an invitation to watch who comes and goes." And I shooed her out of the kitchen.

I filled the dishwasher and washed down the work counter Miguel wasn't using. He asked me to chop and slice onions and celery for his famous *Old Man and the Sea* Chowder. While I cut the vegetables, I watched him move from the counter to the stove top and back again, effortlessly putting together a meal and then placing it on the steamer tray or in the pass-through and immediately moving on to the next meal and the next. Within an hour there were few requests for new meals, and I guessed the lunch rush had subsided to a near halt.

I went into the office and took my copy of *Fictitious Dishes* from the shelf next to our tiny desk. There were bookmarks stuck in several places. Miguel was busy bagging and refrigerating the chopped vegetables. I waved the book in front of him. "I see you've been marking pages. Have you decided which fabulous treat you are going to make for the book club meeting this afternoon?"

"*Sí*, but you must not be nosy. I am preparing a surprise that you will all enjoy. You will see it when I bring it to the dining room near the end of your meeting."

Miguel loved to whip up special dishes now and again for our book club meetings. As much as he reveled in the praise he received from the book club members, he also enjoyed the opportunity to be more creative than our café menu generally allowed.

I went into the dining room to begin setting up the chairs for the Potluck Book Club meeting and saw that there were customers lingering at two tables. Bridgy was doing a quick all-purpose tidy-up. I looked around.

"Where's Elaine?"

Bridgy looked up from washing the countertop. "We're not busy. I told her she could leave. She was professional, wasn't she? Having her help out once in a while would benefit us and she can make a couple of tuition bucks. Win-win."

"Sure is. Did you ask her if she can work tomorrow?"

"Oh, I forgot." Bridgy dropped her cleaning cloth on the counter. "She walked out the door two seconds ago. Maybe I can catch her in the parking lot." And Bridgy hurried out the door.

I checked with the folks at the two occupied tables and when they didn't need anything, I went back to setting up the book corner—chairs in a circle, extra copies of *Fictitious Dishes* under my chair, pencils and paper on the bookcase ledge in case anyone wanted to take notes.

I looked up when the door opened, half expecting it to be Bridgy, but it was Sally Caldera waving a copy of *Fictitious Dishes*. "Extraordinary book. Really extraordinary. I didn't want to hear secondhand what the book club members have to say about it, so here I am."

She came and sat in the book club circle. "How are you doing? Sassy, I'm really sorry that I had to give your name to the deputies, but they wanted a list of who was in the library when Tanya and Alan had their . . . flare-up. And, well, I knew you'd shine a sympathetic light on Alan. But I didn't know you are friends with his family. That was a complete surprise. I heard you brought them to town."

I was saved by Lisette Ortiz from having a conversation that was bound to take up the tiny bit of time left before book club started. Lisette came in carrying a bright red bowl. She popped the lid and gave us a peek at the heap of fresh blueberries inside.

"I soooo had to bring some berries in a red bowl. Life imitating art. I know the picture in the book was really a red pail but I needed a bowl with a top for the car ride." Her dimples were playing hide-and-seek on her cheeks as her joyful enthusiasm got the best of her. "*Blueberries for Sal* has been one of my all-time favorite books since I was a toddler. I have bought a copy for each of my nieces and nephews as a present on their second birthday, and every year I donate a few copies to the Children's Toy Fund, as you well know because you order them for me."

Sally and I were relishing Lisette's joy as she continued to beam while marveling at the fact that the author had included some children's books in *Fictitious Dishes*.

Bridgy finally came back into the café and signaled that we needed to talk. I started to walk over to her but a customer at one of the still-occupied tables stopped me.

"Miss, could I ask what is going on back there? Oh, and could we have our check?"

I explained about the book club meetings that we hosted in the café and gave her a book club flier along with her check. By the time she settled her bill, Bridgy was busy filling a takeaway order for two young girls who had walked in a minute earlier. I stood by the counter and asked what was up.

"Elaine can't work tomorrow." Bridgy put the finishing touches on tying the pastry box shut. "And there's plenty more you need to know, but not now." She nodded toward Maggie Latimer and her sister, Karen, who'd just walked through the café door chatting animatedly with Augusta Maddox and Blondie Quinlin.

It sounded like they were talking about the anaconda snake swimming in Estero Bay.

I smiled and ushered them back to the book corner, all the while wondering what had Bridgy so peeved and how I was going to separate Maggie from her sister long enough to glean information about her lawsuit against Tanya Trouble. Fair to say, it was going to be difficult for me to concentrate on book club with all this whirling around in my head.

Chapter Eighteen

As everyone was settling in their chairs, Maggie introduced her sister, Karen, to any clubbies she hadn't already met.

Lisette pulled small paper cups and a large spoon out of her bag. "Would anyone like some blueberries? I thought we could nibble while we talk."

Only Sally didn't take a cup of berries. As the rest began munching, I asked a starter question. "What did you think of the concept of *Fictitious Dishes* and the layout?"

Augusta Maddox boomed her response. "When we talked about picking this 'un, I wasn't inclined but I went along with the group." She stopped, looked at the other clubbies for a beat or two and then smiled. "Mighty glad I did. Top-notch idea, taking snippets about food from other books and then doing a fancy picture to show what the food might look like."

Maggie nodded in agreement. "And the array of books!

When we first spoke about this book, it never occurred to me that the assortment would include children's books like *Bread and Jam for Frances*, and go all the way to classics like *On the Road* by Jack Kerouac and *One Hundred Years of Solitude* by Gabriel García Márquez."

Lisette agreed. "The variety was stunning. I have to admit that I read this on my e-reader, and I was wondering if, later, I could borrow someone's book so that I could see the pictures. I'm sure they are larger, more detailed than on the e-reader."

Blondie Quinlin handed hers over immediately. "Keep it for a while. With Augusta's copy right next door, I can holler over the fence if I want to look at something again. Speaking about rereading"— she looked at Sally—"I'll be coming down to the library in the next day or so to check out a copy of *To Kill a Mockingbird*. The scene we have here"—she pointed to the book she'd just given away—"is so touching. Sums up the whole story, the Finch family eating a breakfast including the chicken Tom Robinson's father sent as payment for services." She sighed. "I need to read that book again."

Karen noted that she had never read *East of Eden* but was intrigued enough by the piece in *Fictitious Dishes* to try it. "I was never a fan of John Steinbeck, but the description of the relationship between the Trasks . . . well, I might give the book a try."

I could see how excited Sally was getting. Anything that encouraged people to read more books warmed her librarian soul.

Conversation flew around the group with ladies laughing and turning pages to take another look at a passage from a particular novel and the accompanying picture. I couldn't help but think how much nicer book club meetings were when Jocelyn Kendall wasn't among us.

Thinking of Jocelyn reminded me of Pastor John, which led me directly to Alan Mersky. I glanced at the wall clock. As soon as this meeting was over, I needed to talk to Maggie about the lawsuit, then call George to see how his day was going and, oh, what were we going to do about Tanya Lipscome's funeral? I had a long afternoon ahead.

The conversation was moving along without me so I looked around for Bridgy, wondering if I might slip away for a few moments and find out what had upset her when she went to look for Elaine. A couple, mid-fifties, and their inquisitive grandson were sitting at Robert Frost. The grandfather was patiently reading "The Road Not Taken" from the laminated tabletop, and the child kept stopping him to ask questions like "Why was the wood yellow?" and "What is 'undergrowth'?"

Honestly! They should have sat at Dr. Seuss. It gave me a good excuse to leave the book corner. Bridgy came out of the kitchen with a plate of black bean dip and crackers, and I was able to stop her before she reached the family. "Did you suggest Seuss?"

She sighed. "I did, but according to Grandpa, sonny boy is too advanced for such childish things."

I gawked at them and pivoted back to Bridgy. "The boy can't be more than six or seven. How is that too old for Dr. Seuss? *I* still love to read Seuss."

"You also wear Winnie the Pooh footie pajamas, and I bet they wouldn't let the kid have those, either."

While I had her attention, I decided to ask. "Elaine? You looked, I don't know, disturbed."

As she shook her head, her golden hair circled into a halo and then fell back into place. "Later. But I warn you, it's a long story."

I slid back into my seat, wondering how long the story could really be. Bridgy was only outside for a few minutes. I was drawn back into the conversation when Sally asked how we enjoyed the footnote-ish sentences about each author, book and food that fell between the quote from the book and the picture of the food.

Lisette said she loved the section on Beverly Cleary's *Beezus and Ramona*. She had no idea that there were eight Ramona books spanning Ramona's age from four to ten. "More books to entertain the nieces and nephews."

Completely switching topics, Lisette continued. "Am I the only one who didn't know that Patricia Highsmith referred to her Tom Ripley books as the 'Ripliad'? How many Ripley books were there, anyway?"

We all knew *The Talented Mr. Ripley*. Then it got dicey. I seemed to remember a title where Ripley was under something. Out loud I tried "under trees" and "under rocks" but nothing sounded right.

Sally, ever prepared, did a quick search on her phone and read off all five titles. I was pleased that Highsmith wrote both *Ripley Under Ground* and *Ripley Under Water*. I felt like quite a smart book maven.

Maggie was still interested in why Highsmith called the collection of Ripley novels the "Ripliad." "Do you think she started out thinking she'd write a trilogy and merged the word 'triad' with Tom Ripley's last name, and then when the public clamored for more, well by then she'd already coined 'Ripliad'?"

We were murmuring about the possibility when Bridgy came and leaned over my shoulder. "Excuse me, ladies, it sounds like you're having a grand time. I hate to interrupt but Miguel has made a delicacy based on one of the foods in the book and he sent me out to take orders for drinks."

Augusta and Karen opted for water while the rest of us asked for sweet tea.

Blondie looked directly at me. "What did he make?"

I shrugged. "Miguel never said a word and I didn't see any signs of anything out of the ordinary when I was in the kitchen earlier."

"Well, I'll be happy as long as it ain't that gruel from *Oliver Twist*."

Maggie shuddered. "So true. Even the picture of the bowl of gruel was depressing." Then she glanced toward the kitchen door and whispered, "Well, if Miguel chose to cook the gruel, we should all be polite about it."

That set us into gales of laughter.

Bridgy served the water and sweet tea and Miguel, his *toque blanche* sitting on his head at a rakish angle, came out of the kitchen carrying a tray of avocado halves stuffed with crab salad. Each avocado half was plated on a large lettuce leaf with sliced cucumbers and a sliver of orange, exactly as pictured in *Fictitious Dishes*.

Sally clapped her hands in delight. "*The Bell Jar*. Oh Miguel, this is so wonderful. That was the one book that I was determined we would speak about and then we got swept away in other books, other issues and well, now you've reminded me."

I got up and helped Bridgy serve while Miguel stepped to

the side and waited for the clubbies' responses after they tasted his surprise. I was pleased that he'd made enough so that Bridgy and I could each have one. I loved trying his "off menu" specialties, any one of which could easily become "on menu" stars.

I nibbled on the crab salad and it was tangy and delicious. Then I took a bit of smooth, cool avocado on my fork along with a dab of salad and oh, the melding of flavor was delightful.

The clubbies were silent for a bite or two and then Augusta Maddox spoke for all of us when, in her deep baritone, even louder than usual, she said, "This is the best danged crab concoction I ever ate. Only thing that could make it better would be a couple of fingers of corn likker."

Everyone laughed. Augusta's fondness for Buffalo Trace was well known among her friends and acquaintances.

"Mmmm. Augusta is right. This crabmeat is outrageous. So fresh." Maggie swooned in mock ecstasy. "Where did you get it?"

"Pine Island, of course. I had it delivered this morning." Miguel tried to look modest but he was beaming at all the praise being heaped on his newest recipe.

His answer took me back. "How did you sneak it in?" I waggled a finger between Bridgy and me. "We were here all morning."

Now it was Miguel's turn to laugh. "*Chica*, my morning starts much earlier than your morning. And the fishermen, they are early birds, too. I called in the order yesterday and it was delivered a few minutes past six A.M."

One more example of why Miguel was such a treasure. He could and did handle anything to do with the kitchen. I wondered if he and Bridgy had reached any agreement about which ice machine to buy. I'd check later.

There were no more diners in the café, only the book club members and they, along with Bridgy and Miguel, were having a rip-roaring good time talking about ingredients and passing open books around, having jocular arguments about which book had the most exotic-looking food, the most gorgeous picture and the most mind-grabbing story.

Blondie Quinlin was arguing strongly for *Gone with the Wind*, while Augusta Maddox was a big supporter of *Robinson Crusoe*, which she considered a "seafaring" book. Everyone jumped into the fray and another twenty minutes passed by.

Finally, Sally stood. "It's been grand, ladies. I am always glad to join any of the book club meetings, but duty beckons and I really must get back to work."

There was a large chorus of "Thanks for coming" and "See you soon."

"Library lady is right. Time to go. Things to do." Augusta shoved her book back into the denim tote she carried, a sure sign that, for her at least, the meeting was over.

"Okay then, has anyone an idea of what we should read for our next meeting?"

Sally was halfway to the front door but stopped to see if anyone had suggestions.

Lisette turned her palms up to the group. "How could we possibly find a book that we'll all enjoy as much as this one?"

The clubbies looked at one another but no one had a suggestion.

Sally walked back to us. "I know I'm not a regular, but

if I may make a suggestion . . ." She fiddled with her iPhone and held up a picture of a bright red book cover titled with large yellow letters. "It's called *A Fork in the Road* and was published by Lonely Planet. Chefs and writers got together and each wrote a few pages about a fabulous foodie experience, often to do with travel. I think it would make a nice follow-up. Sassy?"

By then I was looking at the book on the screen of my cell phone. It was reasonably priced and not overly long. "Looks good to me. Ladies?"

Nods all around. Sally said the library had two copies, which she would put on hold for the club members as soon as she got back to the library. I said I'd order copies for the bookshelves later in the afternoon. Settled in a snap.

Each clubbie stopped to personally thank Miguel for his marvelous avocado stuffed with crab salad and then they left in twos and threes. When Maggie Latimer and her sister Karen stopped to say good-bye to Miguel, Maggie asked if we'd see the stuffed avocado on the menu soon. Miguel looked at me. I was quick to answer, "The kitchen is Miguel's domain with an assist from Bridgy. Whatever they do is fine with me."

Bridgy responded immediately. "You can expect to see the avocado dish on the specials board once a week for the next month. Then we'll decide whether to make it a regular menu item during crab season."

I touched Maggie's elbow. "Do you have a minute? I'd like to talk to you."

Karen immediately stepped back. "If this is private . . ."

Maggie sent me a questioning look.

"The Lipscome lawsuit," I said quietly.

147

Maggie took Karen by the arm and led her back to the book corner. "Come, little sister. Sassy and I have to talk, but it's nothing you can't hear."

As we arranged ourselves in a small circle, I accepted that the fun had gone out of the day. For now, we would focus on the lawsuit filed by one of my good friends against a woman who was now a murder victim. Could that make Maggie a suspect, too?

Chapter Nineteen

"Honestly, I didn't want to sue," Maggie began, "but there didn't seem to be anything left to do. Some of us tried to talk sense to Mrs. Lipscome but she was opposed to even the tiniest compromise. Still, her husband had little to say and we thought he might persuade her to come around. After all, he's a builder and, I would think, used to compromising on these land issues. Some of us thought the lawsuit would get his attention."

Noticing that Karen was looking perplexed, Maggie gave her sister a brief summary of what led up to the lawsuit between the residents of Moon Shell Drive and the Lipscome family, and then turned back to me. "Cordelia Ramer, rabid environmentalist and flame-throwing gossip, is the one who got the neighbors all riled up."

I interrupted. "I thought Otto Ertz was the ringleader."

Maggie rubbed her hands together and folded them on

the table like a prim schoolmarm in an old western movie. "Otto is the muscle but Cordelia is the mouth. I sometimes think that if the block had another spokesperson, we might have reached an amicable solution long before now, but Cordelia is fixated on saving every mangrove tree, every sea grape bush and every bog white violet on the entire island. She is determined that there will be no construction on Moon Shell Drive, period. And now that poor Mrs. Lipscome is dead, it's likely Cordelia will get her way."

Maggie's hand flew to cover her mouth. "Oh, I didn't mean Cordelia would kill . . ."

"Of course not, but perhaps you should talk to Ryan about the neighborhood group."

She gave a slight head bob. "I will. The deputies knocked on everyone's door. I wasn't home. They left a phone number but, well, I've been out and about. I taught double classes yesterday and Holly is in a play in school. Yesterday I had to pick her up after rehearsal. I assumed the deputies would come back. Maybe they have. I'm still not home."

Maggie seemed so distressed that her sister started to rub her shoulders. I knew I'd led her to feel bad, so I quickly changed the subject straight to Tanya Trouble. "You know, I only saw Mrs. Lipscome once and, frankly, she wasn't at her best. What was she like as a neighbor?"

Maggie's eyes pleaded with me not to take her down that path.

"Maggie, the woman is dead. If there is anything that could help us figure out why, well, you really should let everyone know."

Karen's head popped up when I said "help us figure out why," and I realized I might not have used the best phrasing.

I tried again. "Perhaps talking about her will jog loose a memory that we can tell the deputies and it will lead them to solve her murder."

I could see both sisters were happier with that line of reasoning. I waited a full minute and prodded gently. "So, Maggie, how would you describe Tanya Lipscome?"

"I really don't like to gossip but . . . well, to be honest, Tanya was brash and loud. She was flashy and, more than anything, she loved to throw her husband's money around. That's why she had a cigarette lighter that cost more than some of the condos on the island."

"I know. I saw it. Talk about flashy. I wondered if it was real gold and diamonds or if she was playing—"

Maggie cut me off. "Oh, it was real enough. Remember Reba Whalen? She moved to Sarasota a few years back? Well, anyway, she was great friends with Tanya Lipscome. They went everywhere together. And when Barry bought Tanya the lighter, Reba went with her to get the appraisal for the insurance. I always thought Tanya really brought Reba along as a witness for the island chatterboxes. That lighter appraised for, are you ready? More than seventy thousand dollars."

That knocked the wind right out of me. "Wow. I never dreamed . . . I thought by expensive, we were talking in the few-thousand-dollar range."

Maggie laughed. "That *would* be expensive for us. Not for the Lipscomes. Barry is rolling in money and Tanya reveled in it. Although to tell the truth . . ."

Her hesitation made me nervous. I was hoping Maggie had a golden nugget of information that she didn't realize was important. She was just getting comfortable talking when she stopped. Still, I didn't want to push for fear of damaging our friendship. And, of course, I didn't want her sister to think that I was a buttinski pumping Maggie for all the gossip I could get. That description did feel uncomfortably close to the truth. Still, I sat silently, hoping Maggie would fill the void. At long last she did.

"Well, I don't know how to say it so I'll say it right out. I think Barry was getting tired of her shenanigans."

That piqued Karen's curiosity. "Why would you think that? How well do you know the husband? Did he say something? Do something?"

"A few months ago he started coming home very late in the evenings. And they would have fights. Not, you know, 'you forgot to take out the garbage again' or 'how could you buy another dress after I told you money was tight this month' kind of skirmishes. Raucous battles, voices getting higher and higher." She heaved a great sigh. "Just when I'd decide to call 911, they'd go silent, as if they'd abruptly realized that they could probably be heard up and down the beach."

"And the night Tanya died?"

"Not a peep. A normal quiet night. For a while we sat on the patio. All I heard was the murmured conversation of people out for a stroll, the sandpapery sound of someone scraping his barbeque, and of course, the croaking and squealing of the egrets as they finished their dinner and got ready for bed.

"Then Karen, Holly and I went into the kitchen and played Apples to Apples, so you know we were laughing long and loud. We were too noisy to hear anything but each other. But tell me about this veteran and how you know his family."

"I'd seen Alan once at the library and he reminded me

of my old boss, so I gave George a call and sure enough they're brothers." I shared a bit of what George told me about Alan's history and then mentioned that Pastor John and the veterans filled us in on Alan's present way of life.

Maggie was genuinely surprised. "How could I not know about Pastor John's veterans program? We attend services at his church. Even if we were parishioners elsewhere, John's church is only a couple of blocks from my house. You'd think I'd know."

"Well, it's possible word didn't spread outside the veteran community."

"Oh, but I could help. Yoga is being used in a number of places around the country to help combat PTSD. I've read about it in training manuals and magazines. I'll talk to Pastor John. Perhaps we could set up a program." Her green eyes flashed joy at the prospect of assisting the veterans.

Karen added, "You could hold the class right in the church, since that is a place already familiar to the vets. They wouldn't even have to come to the studio."

I agreed it was a fine idea and then pulled back to the topic that was of most concern to me at the moment. "Maggie, do you know much about Barry Lipscome's sons? Did they have anything to do with the neighbors?"

"Oh, you mean 'spoiled' and 'spoiled-er'? That's what Holly calls them. Can you believe the younger one began driving slowly past our house in that fancy convertible of his, and if Holly was outside, he'd ask her if she wanted to go for a ride? She's fifteen years old!"

I couldn't help but smile. Holly may be fifteen, but she is sharp as a whip and quite able to hold her own in adult conversation. I had to ask, "How did Holly respond?"

"You know Holly is the last person on earth to be intimidated. Afterward, she was elated. It's not often she gets a chance to tell off an adult. You had to see her dancing around the house singing that line from the Katy Perry song. Oh what is it? Something like '*I am a champion and you're gonna hear me roar.*' She told me she 'slagged him proper'—in teen talk that means she made fun of him. But you know, another girl, one less sure of herself, might have been persuaded to get in the car. Who knows what could have happened?"

I was shocked that a twentysomething-year-old-man would invite Holly to hop in his car. Showed his lack of character. Made me really want Maggie's impression of how the Lipscome sons got along with their stepmother.

I asked the question and Maggie answered. "Anyone will tell you neither of the sons could stand Tanya. They were barely civil when their father was around and downright rude when he wasn't."

I was hoping for examples but Maggie's cell phone rang. She answered, hung up and turned to Karen. "Want to take a ride? Holly missed the school bus. Insert enormous sigh by overworked mother here." She rolled her eyes, grabbed her purse and the sisters hurried out the door.

Bridgy was standing at the specials board, erasing today's tasty menu additions and writing tomorrow's. She looked around at the door as it closed behind Maggie and Karen and sang out, "Alone at last!" She sounded for all the world like an actress in a cloche hat and beaver-trimmed coat from a mid-1930s romantic comedy.

I went behind the counter and picked up the water pitcher, and in the vein of a tuxedoed lothario, waved the pitcher toward Bridgy and asked in as deep a voice as I could muster, "Can I interest you in a drink, my fair maiden?"

We both laughed long and loud. I had to set the pitcher on the counter for fear I'd break it. Bridgy dropped her marker and it rolled across the floor.

I twirled an invisible mustache. "See, this is when we need those mustaches we wore at the Food Pantry fund-raising party last month. If I had one, I could have slapped it on my upper lip and twirled away. Really looked the part." And we broke into peals of laughter again.

Acting goofy with a bestie is the greatest stress reliever known to womankind. And with all the chaos of the past couple of days, we needed to detox. I was wiping my eyes with a napkin and Bridgy was looking on the floor for the marker she'd dropped, when the front door opened. As soon as I heard the sound, I was annoyed with myself for not locking it when Maggie and Karen left, but when I turned, I was happy to see it was Mark Clamenta. He'd promised that the veterans would rally to help Alan and I hoped he had some good news.

When Mark saw that the café was empty he apologized for interrupting our break time. I got him a glass of sweet tea and beckoned him toward Robert Frost. He took a deep drink and set the glass on the table. "Ladies, I need a favor. I tried to get in to see Alan at the hospital but the regulations are 'family only' for the first three days. Psych ward. Special rules. Could you put me in touch with his brother? I know he exchanged phone numbers with Pastor John, but, accord-ing to his wife, the pastor is out on parish business and I'd like to arrange to visit Alan with the family if I can. I am at a loss to find a way to help, but maybe seeing Alan will trigger something.

I ripped a page from my order pad and scribbled George's phone number. I also wrote O'Mally's number in the hope that sooner or later she'd succeed in turning off George's phone so he could have a chance to rest. When I passed the paper to Mark, I said, "Bridgy and I have a plan that might be useful. Perhaps you'd like to help."

He folded the paper and tucked it in his shirt pocket, and without even asking what we had in mind, gave me a thumbs-up. "I'm in."

Chapter Twenty

I explained our idea to become funeral watchers rather than mourners, and Mark thought it was a practical strategy. "I've lived in Fort Myers Beach for more than thirty years. It's where I came to start my new life after I was discharged from the army. I'm bound to recognize folks you might not know. And, hey, no one can stop us from looking."

We decided to meet at the café an hour before the funeral. As soon as Mark left, Bridgy ran to lock the door behind him and turned back to me. "Okay, no more interruptions. When I went out to the parking lot looking for Elaine, she was leaning over the driver's side of an expensive-looking convertible. Guess who was driving? Never mind. I'll tell you. Ellison Lipscome. And Elaine was all flirty and giggly."

My mouth dropped open but Bridgy was far from done. "So I waited until the car pulled away and then I approached Elaine. She dismissed Ellison with a flap of her hand as one of the 'many' students she tutors. Looked to me like more than a tutoring job."

I shook my head. "Honestly you are getting like Ophie—seeing romance everywhere."

Bridgy protested. "I didn't say there is a romance, but they were sure acting as if they'd both like there to be a romance. And soon. So, without saying why we wanted help, I asked if she could work tomorrow morning. She was very sorry but—she will be attending Mrs. Lipscome's funeral. Threw me the big eyes and a sappy smile and said, 'She was Ellison's stepmom, you know.' And away she walked."

I was sunk. "What are we going to do about tomorrow? I already asked Mark to help out at the funeral. I really think it would help us to know who the Lipscome family's close friends are."

"Oh, easy peasy, you're more the wannabe Miss Marple than I am. You go with Mark to spy on the funeral guests and I'll stay here."

We heard the doorknob rattle and a pounding on the door. "I can see y'all sitting in there lounging. I could sure use a tall glass of your sweet tea. Open up."

Bridgy got up to unlock the door for her aunt while I went to pour another glass of tea. Ophie spun into the room like a Miss America contestant making her first grand entrance the final night of the competition. Her flowered skirt did a little twirl of its own and then fell back into place with soft folds draping from her extra-wide pink patent leather belt and landing softly at the top of her knee. She glanced behind her and said, "No sense locking the door. Here comes Pastor John, and he has some folks with him, overdressed for this climate, I'd say."

"The Merskys?" I'd been wondering all day how George

and his family were doing. I hoped to call but things kept happening. Busy day.

Ophie gave me big owl eyes. "I wouldn't know. I haven't met them yet, poor souls. Still and all, a cold drink and a bite to eat might raise their flagging spirits, leastwise if their spirits match their faces." She tut-tutted." Draggy, draggy."

I ran to the window and sure enough, the Merskys were trailing across the parking lot behind Pastor John, who was on his cell phone, no doubt getting an earful from Jocelyn if he'd been out of her sight for any length of time.

I held the door open and welcomed them all. As if this was a festive social occasion, Ophie used her most Southern charm to introduce herself. She fluttered among the Merskys, and I was pleased to see she made an extra fuss of Regina, who was the most bedraggled. "You come over here and have a seat, honey chile. Can I get y'all a cold drink?"

Ophie looked slightly shocked when Regina asked for coffee on such a warm day, but then her penchant for hospitality won over. "I'll make a fresh pot. Y'all just get comfortable."

Miguel came through the kitchen door. "*¿Qué pasa?*" He stopped, clearly surprised to see everyone, but sized up the situation instantly. "Ah, we have guests. Welcome." He walked over and shook George's hand. "I am sorry you are having these problems. I hope it is over soon. In the meantime, can I fix you something to eat? And what about a snack for the ladies?"

All three Merskys shook their heads, but Miguel went back into the kitchen and I was sure he'd be out with a platter soon. Pastor John and I pushed the Hemingway table up against the Emily Dickinson while Bridgy and Ophie flapped around like hens rounding up the chicks until everyone was seated. I noticed that George was listless and his face had a pasty sheen. I could understand why O'Mally was worried about him. I served water and sweet tea. Ophie was a minute behind me, coffeepot in hand. Bridgy disappeared into the kitchen and came out again with a tray covered with bowls of *Old Man and the Sea* Chowder paired with sides of crackers and corn bread.

I helped her set the plates in front of our visitors. It didn't do any good for George and Regina to wave us away. Bridgy and I were determined, and, ultimately, the Merskys were gracious. Pastor John reached for George's hand on one side and motioned Bridgy to sit and hold his hand on the other. We all bowed our heads and Pastor led us in a prayer that was part "grace before meals" and part "help us in our hour of need." It was a short, much-needed conversation with the Lord, and although I got misty eyed, I know I felt better for it and I hoped the others did as well.

Miguel came out of the kitchen with his long white apron tied over his tank top and denim shorts. He fussed around George and his family as though they were as special to him as his beloved Maine Coon, Bow. "Eat. Eat up. Now tell me, when do you visit your brother again?"

George obediently took a spoonful of chowder. "This is delicious. Thank you so much. Well, the hospital asked that we leave for a while. I hope we'll be allowed to see Alan again in a few hours. Mark, I can't remember his last name, but he is one of the fellows from your program, Pastor John. Anyway, he called a few minutes ago. He wants to visit Alan and I said he was welcome to come along."

"Excellent. I will make you a package of tasty treats that will charm the hospital staff into stopping by to check on your brother frequently." Miguel rubbed his hands together and as he bounded back into the kitchen, someone banged at the front door. Who on earth could it be now? We should have been closed an hour ago, yet the café was busier than a political party headquarters on election night. I looked through the glass and Cady Stanton was peering back at me. Here we go. Another county heard from.

I unlocked the door but put my finger to my lips in case Cady hadn't looked through the glass panels and noticed the crowd gathered in the dining room. He seemed taken aback but relaxed when I introduced him to the Merskys and didn't mention his job. I knew Cady well enough to know that he wasn't a sneaky reporter. If he needed to question the Merskys, he would tell them exactly who he is and what he does for a living.

I told him to pull over a chair, but he surprised me when he asked to speak with Miguel, who, at that moment, walked through the kitchen door carrying a plate of muffins, tarts and scones. "Here is a sampling of the treats I have packed up for your brother." He set the plate on the table and stood watching the Mersky family enjoy their soup. I knew he would wait patiently until they began eating the pastries. Then he would be satisfied he had done his best.

Cady cleared his throat. "Ah, Miguel, about the green anaconda."

Miguel turned. "Did they find him? Is he dead?"

Cady shook his head. "No. There's a problem. It seems he came ashore by the Mound House. A couple of tourists spotted him but by the time they could raise the alarm, he had disappeared."

Miguel shuddered. "So now he is here. Right on the same

island as my sweet Bow, and she could be his dinner tonight. I will not stand for this. I am calling those Wildlife people Lieutenant Anthony spoke about."

I tried to soften things. "Miguel, maybe tomorrow you could bring Bow to work with you. If she stays in her carrier . . ."

"You want me to keep her locked up all day? No. That is not right. The big snake—he should be locked up, not my beautiful little kitty."

I hadn't noticed Aunt Ophie get up and come around to where we were talking. She rested her hand on Miguel's shoulder. "Miguel, do you think Bow would like to stay in the Treasure Trove with me? I wouldn't keep the darlin' girl in her carrier and I can lock the front door. When a client rings the bell, I can pick up the little honey and hold her safe as can be so she can't run out. What do y'all think?"

Miguel hesitated, and then his face nearly split in half when he burst out with a huge grin. He threw his arms around Ophie and planted a big kiss on her cheek. "*Tu eres una verdadera amiga*. You are a true friend, not just to me, but to my Bow."

Rarely one to get flustered by male attention, Ophie colored slightly and covered her confusion by asking Regina if she wanted more coffee. I breathed a sigh of relief that at least one crisis was averted. We had so much going on, and as if on cue, there was a knock on the door.

Bridgy walked over, took a quick look and opened the door. Jocelyn Kendall pushed the door aside and fumed, "Is my husband still here? It's been hours"—then she stopped in mid-sentence when she realized that there were more than half a dozen people in the room and we were all staring at her. She absentmindedly pushed at a lock of her straw-colored hair that hung down over one side of her face. Then right before our eyes, she morphed from strident shrew to helpful spouse. She walked directly to the Merskys, introduced herself as Pastor John's wife and offered to do whatever the family might need to make their time in Fort Myers Beach as comfortable as possible.

As often as I'd seen Jocelyn pull off this transformation, I was always amazed. It was as though she alternated her personality by flipping a switch and moved back and forth between being the Wicked Witch of the West and the Good Witch of the South.

The Merskys seemed charmed by the Jocelyn they were meeting. The rest of us knew better. Pastor John was standing by his chair. He began checking his pockets for the odds and ends he carried around. I'd watched him do it a hundred times. Cell phone, pocket Bible, notebook, pen. All present and accounted for. Feeling obliged by her presence to go home, the pastor told Jocelyn he was ready to leave. She gave him a sad smile. "John, I'm here to help. But if you're tired, poor dear, then I guess we should go." And she triumphantly marched him out of the café.

George said, "Well she seems like a nice woman."

O'Mally gave his cheek a pinch and said, "Don't kid yourself, honey. She's a tigress and that poor man is a lamb. Oh well, every wife can't be as wonderful as yours."

The laughter was spontaneous. Once again, O'Mally had snipped off a little chunk of tension while the rest of us were totally stressed, wondering what was going to happen next.

Chapter Twenty-one ‖‖‖‖‖‖‖‖‖

George looked at our big round wall clock, took out his cell phone and in keeping with O'Mally's jest said, "Dear wonderful wife, do you have that piece of paper with the phone number the doctor gave us?"

O'Mally passed him a paper that she drew from the pocket of her billowing chartreuse blouse, and George excused himself from the table and walked back to the book corner. Cady signaled me with a head nod toward the kitchen. When we got inside he told me that the *Fort Myers News* had assigned him to write a story about the veterans program at Pastor John's church. "I didn't want to bring it up with Alan Mersky's family sitting there, but I want you to know that I'll be talking to Pastor John as soon as I can, and then I'll be talking to as many vets as will talk to me."

I curved slightly away from him so I could think without him staring in my face, but Cady was having none of it. He put his hands on my shoulders and turned me until I was standing straight in front of him and we were less than shoulder length apart. "Sassy, it's my job. I have to do this."

From the doorway Miguel said, "So sorry, my friends, I didn't mean to interrupt."

I slid out from under Cady's hands. "You're not interrupting, Miguel. Cady was telling me that he is going to write a story for the paper about the program that Pastor John runs for the vets."

Miguel gave me an odd look. "But that's a good thing, no?"

I could see how Miguel might think publicity could help gain support for the program from folks who didn't know it existed. But I feared some of the veterans would become anxious or upset by what they considered an invasion of privacy. When I said that out loud, Cady shook his head. Then he automatically smoothed his hair from front to back, a frequent gesture, especially when his mind was scrambling.

"Sassy, my editor is a Vietnam veteran. He wants a story that will help, not hurt the vets. Trust us. Trust *me* to be careful not to stir up problems for people who, quite frankly, may already have far more than their share."

I looked to Miguel, who kept his head down at the work counter. He was busy pretending we weren't in the room.

"Well, it's not like I can stop you. I hate to see George's brother and the other veterans used to sell newspapers."

Cady gave me a look that said I was clearly missing the point. Then he stomped out of the kitchen without another word. But Miguel had two cents he decided I should hear. "You know Cady likes you and is a good friend to you, yet you treat him like yesterday's ham sandwich. Don't push him too far away, *chica*, or someday you may be sorry."

When I turned to stare him down, he raised his hands in surrender and went back to kneading dough for whatever sure-to-be-delicious thing he was making.

Everyone in the dining room was in motion. George had finished his phone call and was walking back toward the tables. O'Mally hurried over to put an arm around him and give him a little squeeze. Bridgy and Ophie were taking Regina on a tour of the bookshelves, and I was delighted to hear Bridgy say, "Go ahead. Take a couple. Our treat."

I knew from experience that when life hands you lemons, reading a good book makes the lemonade sweeter. I was happy that after wavering for a few minutes, Regina gave in and graciously thanked Bridgy for two books with such cheerful covers that they could only be cozy mysteries.

Cady was nowhere to be seen.

George looked happier and much more energetic than he had when he slouched through the café door a while ago. I was pleased that a small break with friends and good food had lifted his spirits.

"Okay, ladies, we are on the move. The hospital will allow us a longer visit with Alan this afternoon. And we can bring all the pastries Miguel will provide. Alan has no food restrictions right now. That's a great sign because some of his hospitalizations, well, the food was terrible and outside food wasn't allowed." George demonstrated his exuberance by reaching over and giving O'Mally a playful smack on the butt.

We shouldn't have been surprised when she squatted and wiggled a twerk, saying, "Once more for good luck."

George obliged and while we were all laughing, he turned to me. "I called that fellow Mark from the veteran's group. He'll meet us right outside in your parking lot. Sassy, I can't thank you enough for all you've done."

I gave him an impulsive hug. "Come on, I'll wait for Mark with you."

Ophie walked out with us and was her most flirtatious self when Mark Clamenta drove up and got out of the car to say hi and round up the Merskys. We waved good-bye as they pulled out of the driveway, then Ophie headed to the Treasure Trove. I was walking back to the café when a sheriff's car pulled in the driveway. Frank Anthony was in the passenger seat. Ryan Mantoni rolled down the driver's window. "Is the family here?"

No need to say which family. There was only one family he'd be looking for at the café.

"Nope. You missed them by minutes. Drove off to the hospital. Can I offer you some pie?"

Ryan turned to Frank, who surprised me by nodding. If he wants to stop for pie, he's got something to say or questions to ask. I reminded myself to carefully check every word that came out of my mouth. No sense adding more fuel to the lieutenant's fire.

The deputies sat at Robert Frost. Bridgy brought a sweet tea for Ryan and a coffee for Frank. I became even more suspicious of their motives for stopping by when Frank declined a piece of peach pie. He was here on business no matter how casual he tried to make it appear.

I brought Ryan his pie topped with whipped cream and then began to move deliberately away. Frank politely asked me to sit, but I had a sense that it was more an order than a question. I glanced at Bridgy, who had begun steam cleaning the floor. The cleaner wasn't overly noisy but it was distracting. She clicked it off and came to sit with us.

Ryan dug into his pie like a kid on the beach with a new pail and shovel. Frank, on the other hand, took a sip of coffee and then pushed his cup across the table and sat ramrod straight and dove right into questions without preamble. "Was there any particular reason you chose to recommend Goddard Swerling as the attorney for Alan Mersky?"

Never saw that one coming. Well let's hope my answer would rattle him. "You. You were the one who said 'Tell the family to hire a lawyer.' I didn't want to pass along that message without a name or two."

He raised his eyebrows and folded his arms. Neither was a good sign. "Let's try again. Why, with a broad choice of hundreds of lawyers in Lee County, did you decide to recommend Swerling?"

"I asked Cady, and that was the name he gave me. Why are you questioning me about this? You didn't say a peep when we were all together at your office. Never questioned how Goddard Swerling became Alan's lawyer. What changed?"

He leaned back in his chair and clasped his hands behind his head. "There's a lawsuit about a swimming pool. Swerling is the attorney for a group of plaintiffs in a suit against the Lipscomes, and suddenly he's the defense attorney for a man accused of her murder. Didn't that strike you as some sort of conflict when you foisted him on the family?"

Foisted? Really? I bit my tongue. "Until Alan was arrested and *you* told me to advise George to hire a lawyer, I'd never heard of Goddard Swerling in my life."

"And yet you recommended him to the family. You can't blame that on me."

I reminded Frank that I was blame free. That one was on Cady.

Frank ran one hand over his hair, ruffling back and forth until it looked like a mini Mohawk. That hand-on-hair thing was a trait he and Cady had in common. Frank ruffled, Cady smoothed, either way it meant their brains were in gear.

Frank started muttering, almost to himself. "He should know better. He covers the crime beat for the paper and if he reads his own paper, he knows about the lawsuit. The whole town knows about the lawsuit."

He shot me a look that was somewhere between a glare and a frown. "Except, of course, for you. Don't you ever read?"

I tossed a tougher scowl right back at him and pointed to the book corner. "Seriously? You're asking me if I read."

He heaved an exaggerated sigh. "I meant 'read the newspaper.' How else do you follow what goes on in town?" Then he looked around and said, "Or did I forget that this is gossip central? Oops. Did your gossip mill miss a beat?"

He pushed his chair back and signaled Ryan, who said a quick "Thanks for the pie," and followed the lieutenant out the door.

I folded my arms on the tabletop and rested my head right there between our copy of "The Road Not Taken" and Frost's fruit poems. I needed a minute to collect myself before I helped clean and close the café.

But Bridgy didn't seem to realize I was totally spent. "Honestly, Sassy, does a reasonably young, reasonably attractive man ever come through our door without you winding up in an argument with whoever it is? What is up with you?"

She had her hand on her hips, with her shoulders held high—a pose that spelled doom for whoever had ticked her off. I wasn't quite sure why but apparently it was me.

"What did I do? Cady expects me to be the bridge to the vets for his story. Frank came in, all full of 'whys' and 'why nots.' Now you're calling *me* a troublemaker? I don't think so."

Normally when Bridgy moved into tantrum mode I ignored her until she calmed down, a process that rarely took longer than ten minutes. Today, however, I was done with people pushing me around. First Cady and his editor, then Lieutenant Frank Anthony. Now Bridgy had the nerve to tell me I'm the rabble-rouser.

Miguel came out of the kitchen, took one look at the two of us and said, "I'm leaving. If you're going to have a fight there is ice cream in the freezer. You can eat it when you make up." And with a wave he was gone.

I looked at Bridgy. "I wonder what flavors we have."

"Vanilla, for sure. Miguel has apple pie a la mode on the specials tomorrow. Probably chocolate and strawberry, too. The basics. Let's skip the fight. You sit. I'll serve."

Ice cream. The one thing guaranteed to nip any potential skirmish in the bud. In a flash Bridgy was back with two glass bowls each holding scoops of all three flavors. "I assumed you want whipped cream and chocolate sauce?"

"But of course."

She sat down and we both savored the cool and creamy treat. When we'd scraped the last bit of sweetness from the bottom of our bowls, Bridgy laughed. "Miguel sure knows how to get us to do what he thinks is the right thing."

"Food. Duh. He's got our number. Bridgy, I'm sorry I snapped."

She dismissed my apology with a flap of her hand. "I listened, you know, when you were, shall we call it, 'talking' with Frank Anthony. What do you think the concern is? Is there a connection between the lawsuit and the murder?"

"I have no idea, but I know one thing. Before I go home today I am going to visit the scene of the crime."

Bridgy, who is usually hesitant about anything to do with sneaking around, especially when it comes to gathering information we have no business collecting, shocked me by shouting, "Field trip."

Chapter Twenty-two

I had driven us to work this morning, so we piled into my Heap-a-Jeep. I pulled out of the parking lot and headed for Moon Shell Drive. Bridgy was impressed I knew exactly where it was. "There are so many tiny streets on the island, some with only a house or two. How do you happen to know this one?"

"I've dropped books at Maggie's house more than a few times. I had no idea that the road curved. I thought it ended in the foliage leading to the bay."

"Sassy, what are we looking for?"

"Nothing, really. It's just, well, if the Lipscomes' house is so close to Maggie's, how come I don't know it? I've been on the road. It's the first turn off Estero Boulevard south of Pastor John's church. The Lipscome house must really be hidden for it not to come to mind. I guess I'm curious."

"Yes, well, remember what curiosity did to the cat." Bridgy

was always quick to remind me of the potential consequences of my weaknesses. "Speaking of cats . . ."

"I know what you're thinking. Ophie's offer to keep Bow in the Treasure Trove during the day is a temporary solution at best. Miguel is at work before the crack of dawn while Ophie . . ."

"She's my aunt and I love her, but Ophie saunters to work whenever she feels like it, unless she has an appointment, and she rarely schedules those before ten in the morning. What is Miguel supposed to do with Bow until Ophie shows up in the midst of the late breakfast rush? We can't allow Bow to roam around the café. The Board of Health would never allow it."

"Maybe we could set up a fenced-in area for her in the book corner . . ." But even as the words came out of my mouth, I was shaking my head. Bow is used to being free, wandering as she pleases, which is why when her previous owner passed suddenly, Bridgy and I couldn't take her to live in the Turret with us. A fifth-floor apartment is no place for a cat who likes to luxuriate in the sunny spot on a patio and chase small critters around and about the mangrove roots. Miguel's house had been a regular stop on Bow's daily walk-about and when she needed a new home, she settled in with Miguel without much difficulty. But now we had a problem.

I turned onto Moon Shell Drive and drove slowly past Maggie's house on the right and two bungalows on the left. Straight ahead there was nothing but scrub pines and mangroves leading directly to the bay. I slowed to a crawl and we drove past the houses. I was thinking we were better off in the Heap-a-Jeep than in Bridgy's Ford Escort ZX2, because there was a good chance we'd land in a mud patch and the Heap-a-Jeep would manage to get out again. I wasn't sure the Escort could do the same.

We were about ten yards past Maggie's driveway and nearing what looked like the end of the street when the road took a sharp right turn and dead-ended in front of a three-story villa of epic proportions. It could easily have been an upscale waterfront hotel. When Bridgy finished oohing and aahing, she said, "Aunt Ophie did say the Lipscomes have lots of money."

I pulled over to the side of the road. "This house screams 'lots and lots and lots' of money. Want to get out? We'll get the lay of the land. Whatever happened back there"—I gestured toward the house and its lush surroundings—"certainly couldn't be seen from here." I looked behind me. "Or from any of the houses around the curve."

Bridgy made fun of me in her spookiest voice, while rubbing her hands together with great exaggeration. "Aye, dearie, 'tis the perfect spot for murrrderrr."

I smacked her hands and started to cross the street to the bay side, when a flamboyant cobalt car came tearing down the driveway from the Lipscome house. It screeched to a halt. Uh-oh. Barry Lipscome. I pushed Bridgy forward while whispering in her ear, "He knows me from the day I brought George to visit Alan." I was glad I had my big wire-rimmed Ray-Ban aviators on. Still, I dropped my head for good measure. Maybe he wouldn't remember me.

"You're trespassing. This is private property. If you are with the press, get out now." He stood with legs spread and folded his arms like a stern father. He must have realized that the arm fold would wrinkle his blue linen blazer, because he suddenly dropped his arms to his sides. But he didn't lose the stern look. He knitted his eyebrows and glared as if he could make us disappear by sheer force of will.

Bridgy decided to go with her "I'm too adorable for you to stay mad at me" routine, while I stayed behind her, looking at the ground, kicking pebbles in the road and trying to become invisible.

She lifted a hand and started twirling her blond curls. Even though I was behind her, I knew she was raising her big blue eyes to heaven. I'd seen this act before.

"I'm so glad you're here. We've been on every road on this island. We are sooo lost."

Barry Lipscome snarled. "Well, whatever you are looking for, it isn't around here."

Bridgy must have widened her eyes to the max because by the end of the sentence, his snarl was gone.

Then she took a half step forward and dusted a piece of imaginary lint off the lapel of his blazer. "Perhaps you could direct us to the country club. We'll never find it on our own."

"The country club?" His tone was skeptical. He gave us the once-over but was more interested in our shorts and tank tops than what was underneath them. "You can't go the country club dressed like that. Oh wait, are you new staff? Kitchen help, huh? Well, didn't you have to go for an interview?"

As fascinated as I was by his desire to protect the country club from riffraff like us, I was more concerned that our story was wearing thin.

Bridgy saved the day. She looked down as if realizing for the first time that rather than a ball gown, she was wearing striped shorts and a salmon-colored tank decorated with, what else, dozens of leaping salmon. "Oh, no, no, no. We're not going to the country club. We're picking up someone.

His car is in the shop. He rode over with friends, but they are staying for dinner. He has to get home. Family from up north driving down. They called to say they're in Tampa."

Lipscome nodded as if all Bridgy's fictitious drivel made perfect sense. And in a Florida beachy way, it did. Everyone on the island was used to being called to help out a friend who had company already here or about to arrive. All the wonderful things that made Fort Myers Beach such a delightful place to live was exactly what made it a magnet for visitors, especially folks who knew they could get free bed and board because they were related to you, had been your neighbor when you lived up north, or sat behind you in fourth grade. That's one of the reasons I'm careful whose Facebook friend request I accept. Facebook friend today, houseguest tomorrow.

My mind stopped wandering when Bridgy grabbed my arm and said, "We're in luck. This nice gentleman is going to lead us to the country club. Let's get going. "

We tumbled into the Heap-a-Jeep while Barry Lipscome glided into the plush driver's seat of his fully loaded gazillion-dollar-bill on four wheels. As soon as he started his engine, I said to Bridgy, "The country club? Seriously. And that story! I can't believe he fell for it. Apparently even a widower whose wife is barely cold can't resist your big blue eyes."

Not the least bit miffed, Bridgy tossed her head. "And don't forget my curly blond hair." She turned the rearview mirror and started to fuss with her hair. "I think my blond is starting to fade. Should I do something about it?"

"Do what?" I pushed the mirror back in position. "What you have to do now is figure out what happens when we get to the country club and no one is waiting for a ride. Or do you want me to peel off into the next mini-mall lot and hope he doesn't notice we're not behind him?"

"Oh, please. Have you no imagination? I'll make this all go away like that." And she emphasized "that" with a snap of her fingers. She tapped her cell phone a few times. "Ah, there it is." She dialed a number and then spoke in a voice I'd never heard before. It had no trace of her Brooklyn roots and none of the southernisms she'd picked up from Ophie. "Yes, good afternoon. A Ms. Bridget Mayfield will be inquiring at the front desk for Mr. Atwell. Please tell her that her services are not required today. We are sorry for any inconvenience." She listened for a minute. "I'm Ms. Cabot, Mr. Atwell's personal assistant. Thank you."

We were stopped for a red light right behind Barry Lipscome. His car looked so expensive and yet vaguely familiar. Then I saw it. A silver shape, like the pilot's wings a flight attendant gave me on my first airplane trip when I was seven. But this one had "ASTON MARTIN" emblazoned in the center. James Bond. I smacked Bridgy's arm. "Look. Look at the car."

"What about it?"

"It's the car Pierce Brosnan drove in . . . which movie was it? The one when you fell in love with him?"

"*Die Another Day*. Years ago, but wow, you're right. Though, Pierce had the classic taste to drive a silver Aston Martin Vanquish, not this gaudy blue. Do you have any idea what a car like that costs?"

"Forget the cost of the car. You can Google it when we get home. For now, tell me how you're going to pull off this country club stunt. Do you even know that anyone named Atwell belongs to the club?"

"Sassy, stop obsessing. If someone called the Read 'Em and Eat and left that message, would you say, 'Sorry, I don't know anyone named Atwell'? Would you? No. You would not. You'd take the message and if no one claimed it, you'd toss it in the recycle bin during cleanup."

"But this is a country club. The staff should know the members' names."

"And who said we were picking up a member?"

Barry Lipscome pulled up the circular driveway and when the valet opened his car door, we saw Lipscome point to the Heap-a-Jeep, which was looking dingier by its proximity to highly buffed Lincolns and Porches. The valet nodded and came directly to my door, holding out a red and white valet ticket as I watched Barry Lipscome step up on the sidewalk.

"Oh, I won't be getting out. Just my friend. We'll only be here a minute." The valet pointed to a spot a few feet past Lipscome's Aston Martin and told me I could pull in and wait for no longer than ten minutes. He ended with, "club rules" as if that explained everything.

Lipscome was walking slowly toward us, so Bridgy hopped out of the Heap-a-Jeep before he could get a good look at me. I was starting to feel like I was in the witness protection program. I heard him say, "I thought I'd escort you inside. Perhaps I know your friend." He held out his arm and Bridgy hooked it with her hand. They walked into the country club side by side. I moved the jeep to its assigned spot and sat in my seat, hand hovering over the ignition key while I waited for Bridgy to come running out yelling, "They're right behind me. Gun it."

And I pictured the parade behind her: Lipscome, a couple of brawny club security men, an elderly well-uniformed concierge and perhaps even a chef with a toque like Miguel's. I kept my eye on the clock. With nearly two minutes left in the ten-minute countdown, Bridgy strolled out of the club's front door, smiled at the doorman and waved to the valet. The country club posse I imagined to be following her was nowhere to be seen.

She opened her door and before she was even in her seat she was giving me that "How cool am I?" smile.

I wasn't falling for it. "So you got away with fooling Lipscome. Big deal."

"Oh, that was nothing." She made Mr. Atwell and his fake assistant disappear with a flap of her hand. She clearly had something more significant to reveal.

I leaned back in my seat. "What? Don't keep me in suspense."

"It's the 'on a need to know basis' conversation that I didn't need to know but heard anyway that is important. Now let's get out of here." She pointed to the clock. "Our ten minutes are up."

Chapter Twenty-three

I kept quiet until we drove off the country club property, then I said, "So? Am I going to have to beg?"

"Of course not. I'm organizing my thoughts. I want to get this right." She left me hanging for another fraction of a minute. "Okay, so I walked up to the desk with 'Barry Baby'—"

"Barry Baby? Seriously?" I raised my eyebrows.

Bridgy giggled. "As in 'call me Barry, baby.' He'll be Barry Baby to me forevermore. Anyway, he was hovering over me like one of those helicopter moms. Does he know your name? I was nervous, wondering if he'd pick up on the name Cabot if the young guy at the desk recited the message word for word. I needn't have worried. Just as the desk clerk asked if he could help us, a voice louder than Miss Augusta could ever manage thundered, 'Barry Lipscome, is that you? Last person I expected to see here tonight.' Lipscome muttered good-bye to me and practically sprinted over to a man with a wide handlebar moustache and a cowboy hat. Oh, I never looked at his feet. I should have checked for western boots. You know how I love outlandish footwear.

"Anyway, I had to talk to the desk clerk. He didn't doubt who I was or that Mr. Atwell existed. I thanked him for the message and headed to the corner where Barry Baby and the cowboy were jawing. I was hoping to get an earful before I said my thank-yous and good-byes. Did I ever."

She was preening because she knew something that I didn't. The look of delight on her face was every bit as annoying as if she were shouting, "Na, na, na, na, na." I slid to a stop at a red light and turned to her. "Bridgy, tell me right now, or you can get out here and walk home."

"You take all the fun out of everything. Okay, so . . . Barry Lipscome filed for divorce a few days before his wife was murdered. She didn't even know. Hadn't been served with the papers before . . . before she was conked on the head and out for the count."

I was glad Ophie wasn't around. That line would have earned a well-mannered-ladies lecture for sure. "How did Cowboy Hat know about this if Tanya Trouble didn't?"

"Cowboy Hat is named Glenn something or other and he is Barry Lipscome's lawyer. I heard him say, 'As your personal attorney, I am advising you to allow me to withdraw the papers before anyone discovers you were planning to discard your wife a few days before she wound up dead.' Shook Barry Baby up. I knew that because his face blanched like boiled almonds.

"Then he said, 'Good point. Do you need me to sign anything?'

"Glenn said he wanted permission but he didn't want a

paper trail back to Barry Baby. That way if the lawyer is ever asked, he'd say the petition became moot so he withdrew it. What with clogged calendars and all.

"They were so wrapped up in their talk that neither of them noticed me, so I tiptoed away without saying good-bye."

My mind was doing somersaults. A man wealthy enough to own a palatial house and vain enough to drive an Aston Martin Vanquish might not be willing to share a fortune by divorcing his ex-wife, when he could keep it all if she conveniently died.

Never one to be ignored, especially when she'd discovered a fascinating nugget of information, Bridgy was bouncing in her seat and pressing me to share my thoughts. At that exact moment the thought consuming me was that Ellison Lipscome sure knew his father. Made me wonder what else he knew.

"Maybe you'll find out when you 'spy' on the guests at the funeral service. Be interesting to watch the tension between the father and his sons."

That made me think of the suspicions we had after meeting the sons. With Tanya dead, Ellison and Abbot Lipscome had no one standing between them and their father's money—except their father.

"Are you cray-cray?" Bridgy squealed. "Why are we turning here?"

But her complaint was too late. We were back on Moon Shell Drive. I drove up the road, made the quick right and parked in the same spot we'd been in less than an hour ago. I hopped out of the Heap-a-Jeep, went around to the passenger side and opened Bridgy's door. "Come on. You know you don't want me to go exploring alone."

Bridgy made a face that, loosely translated, said, "Meanie, meanie, tangerine-y" and then slid off her seat. "Okay. We're here. Now what?"

I threw my hands in the air. "I don't know. It's not like I have a plan. I want to see the place. Get a feel for it."

"We'll get more than a feel if Barry Baby comes back. We'll be spending the rest of the evening explaining to some deputy why we're trespassing on a crime scene."

"Crime scene?" I snapped back at her. "Do you see any yellow tape? We're on a public street, for pity's sake. No harm in that."

Bridgy ignored me as she is wont to do. "Well, if we get in trouble with the law, I hope the deputy who nabs us is Ryan Mantoni. He'll go easy. That Frank Anthony—he's as rigid as he is good-looking." She babbled along but I wasn't paying attention.

I'd moved over to the woods on the bay side of the road and peered at the ground, which was alive with several turtles resting in their shells, a couple of frogs hopping around sea grapes and more salamanders than I could count skittering around. I kept a sharp eye out for snakes. If the fifteen-or-so-foot-long anaconda was around, he'd be easy to spot. It was the smaller snakes that worried me. I saw something light stuck in the gnarled roots of a mangrove. The way it fluttered in the soft bay breeze made me think it was some sort of paper. My first step into the woods caused all the creatures to hide or flee, except the turtles. I guess they were resigned to the fact that anything as big and noisy as I was could clearly outrun them. So, what was the point? They slept on.

I took another step and felt something on my shoulder. Ew. Maybe a snake hanging from a branch? I jumped back and crashed into Bridgy, who proceeded to scold me in a hoarse whisper. "What is wrong with you? Do you think I'd let you roam around in the woods at dusk with a killer on the loose? Of course I'm right behind you."

No point in mentioning that I wouldn't have to worry about a killer on a loose if I died of fright from her sneaking up behind me, so I took a few more steps and picked up the paper. I recognized it instantly. It was a valet parking ticket from the country club. I elbowed Bridgy back to the road. "Look at this. It's from the country club. A valet ticket. I hit my iPhone for light and peered. Holy moly. Date stamped the day of the murder."

If I was expecting an enthusiastic reaction from Bridgy, I didn't get it. "Big deal. We know the Lipscomes belong to the country club. Except for Maggie, who I am pretty sure isn't the country club type, everyone on this block could be club members. Or that little scrap could have blown in from a boat skimming along the bay, which, if I might remind you, is right there, maybe thirty yards away."

I knew Bridgy was likely to be right. But I thought it was too much of a coincidence that the only piece of litter to be found on Moon Shell Drive was a valet parking receipt from the day of the murder. I shoved the ticket into my pocket and moved along the edge of the woods, getting closer to the house.

Bridgy followed along reluctantly. When I reached Lipscome's driveway, she pulled me back. "Sassy, there are lights on in the house. Barry Baby could come back any second and we have no idea where the sons are. Could we get out of here?"

I stepped on a tree root that made me six to eight inches taller. I leaned on the trunk, stood on my toes, craned my neck and gawked at every inch of the Lipscome property that was visible. Finally, I stepped down and gave up. Bridgy seemed surprised when I started walking back to the Heap-a-Jeep but she tagged along, happy to be getting away from Moon Shell Drive.

I made the right onto Estero Boulevard, discontented and heading for home, when Bridgy asked what was bothering me.

I heaved a sigh. "Tanya Trouble was clobbered while sitting in the hot tub. Try as I might, I couldn't see it from the road or the woods. Seeing the site might give me clarity into what happened. The hot tub obviously had more privacy than I imagined."

Bridgy agreed. "More privacy than most of the hot tubs on the island, except those that are fenced in. Did you see a fence?"

"No. Not even a screened-in patio. All their outdoor living must be done on the part of the property not visible from the road."

"I bet it's visible from the water. Who in their right mind would own a house on bay-front property and not include a view of the bay? It they can see the bay from a patio or hot tub, boaters on the bay can see them."

I could see where she was going with this. A while back, Bridgy and I had gone kayaking looking for a canoe and its owner. It was the first time we were on the water completely on our own. No estuary tour, no certified boating teachers, only the two of us. It was such an awesome experience that we'd gone out every now and again just for fun. "Don't start. The Lipscome house is way south of Tony's rental pier. We're not experienced enough to paddle a kayak all these miles. Tony would have to send the Coast Guard to find us."

She shocked me with a quick bob of her head. "You're right. A boat ride would be silly. Probably couldn't see much anyway." She dismissed the topic of Lipscome's hot tub as a petty annoyance and turned on the car radio.

I got an idea about something guaranteed to take my mind off the killing. I made a quick turn into a mini-mart parking lot and stopped. "While we're out, what about Dr. Mays?"

Bridgy thought for a few seconds. "What about her?"

"Remember Frank Anthony said that she'd been working with all the government agencies to keep control of the big snakes?"

Bridgy nodded.

"Miguel trusts her with Bow more than he trusts anyone else. Why don't we see if the veterinary hospital is still open? Maybe she could give us a few minutes of her time and some suggestions as to what Miguel could do with Bow until the anaconda is captured."

I pulled back out onto the boulevard and headed south once again. If we couldn't help George solve Alan's problem, perhaps we could help Miguel.

We were little more than a block away from the veterinary hospital when Bridgy pointed. "Look. Dr. Mays's office is lit up like a Christmas tree. Someone is definitely there. This was a great idea. I've been so worried about Miguel. Goodness forbid anything happens to Bow."

I made a sharp left into the lot. "What is going on here?"

Among the half dozen cars in the parking lot was one sheriff's marked car and Miguel's SUV.

I slipped into a parking spot and we both jumped out in a great hurry to find out exactly what had brought so many people together.

Chapter Twenty-four

Two more cars pulled into the lot while we were doing a heel-toe quickstep toward the animal hospital. We opened the front door and there was so much commotion, we could have been in any Bealls Outlet store on senior citizen discount day.

Inga, Dr. Mays's competent jack-of-all-trades, was standing behind the counter with a phone glued to her ear. She waved us in and gestured toward a clipboard on the counter. Confused but curious, we played along. Then a voice from the reception area stopped us.

"*Chicas.* Have you come to help?" Miguel was standing with an older gentleman holding the leash of a cottony snow-white dog with a face like a snowball. "Come meet Mr. Gerrity and his magnificent bichon frise. Her name is Countess Aurelia but she answers to Tess." Miguel turned from us to the pup and gave her fluffy head a brief pat. "Aren't you a good girl? Yes. You are a good girl." And he slipped her a dog treat.

"Miguel, what will Bow say when she discovers you are stepping out on her? And with a dog, no less?" I shook my finger at him and we all enjoyed the joke.

Mr. Gerrity had a deep, hearty laugh that made his belly shake like Santa Claus. "Actually, young miss, Bow and Tess, well, I can't say they're friends but they do tolerate each other as neighbors, sort of like me and Miguel here. Say, where are your pets?"

I shook my head. "Apartment dwellers. We thought about it but it wouldn't work out. With a fifth-floor patio, I'd be a nervous wreck every time we opened the patio door."

"For which I am so grateful. If Sassy and Bridgy—" Miguel indicated to Mr. Gerrity who was who. "If they were able to have a pet, they would have given my Bow a loving home and I would be without my *corazón*, my beloved kitty."

"Is that why you are here? Is Bow getting a checkup? I didn't know Dr. Mays had such late office hours."

"No. I thought you knew. I thought you are here to help. Dr. Mays, fine woman that she is, has decided that until the anaconda is gone, we will run a pet-sitting service for the animals who usually roam free on the island. When the animal's family is at work or church or shopping, the animal can stay here. There will be volunteers on call to help out as needed."

"So Bow can stay here while you work?"

"*Sí.* And for part of that time, Mr. Gerrity and Tess will come and watch over her. It is all nicely arranged. So far twenty-two animals will reside here safely for some part of the day. It's like a cooperative. When I'm not working, Bow and I will come here for a few hours to help keep the other pets safe and happy."

Mr. Gerrity told us that he was on his way to meet friends

for supper. "Tess isn't much of an out-of-doors dog. Sits around the side yard for a while during the day. Barks at the occasional egret. That's about her speed outdoors. But Miguel and I thought it would be a good idea if I brought her in for a bit tonight so she gets used to the place. When we come back tomorrow to help out with the other dogs and visit with Bow, Tess will be comfy."

He bade us good night.

I had to ask. "Miguel, when did all this happen?"

"It was Lieutenant Anthony's idea. He spoke with Dr. Mays and then called me. We three met and decided we could provide safety for the pets until the snake is . . . resolved."

"Frank Anthony? Really?" I was having trouble under-standing that he would be concerned enough to worry about the small animals. Didn't the sheriff's department have other things to do? Like solve a murder? Still, I was overjoyed. Miguel was not the only pet owner who was alarmed about the anaconda. No matter who had the idea, it was a good one.

"*Ay, sí.* This is so much better than the old days. During Hurricane Charley, no one would help with pets. Islanders were told to go to shelters on the mainland. No pets allowed. Can you imagine? That is when I met Dr. Mays. I was work-ing in the big hotel, the one down on the beach, and the sous chef decided he would not leave his cats behind. I invited him to come with me, cats and all, to stay with my relatives in Orlando. We were ready to leave when he heard that Dr. Mays had rented a vacant restaurant on the mainland for animals and their owners if they wished to ride out the storm together. That is where he decided to go. I went along to help with the animals. It is how I met Dr. Mays."

The door to the examining room opened, and Ryan Mantoni

and Frank Anthony came out deep in conversation. I heard Frank say, "And see that a car stops by every hour that this facility is open. The deputy is to park and stop to see if there is anything we can do to help. And make sure the front desk has the doctor's cell number."

Ryan nodded and then turned around and practically bumped into us. "Oh, hey, are you two here to help?"

Since everyone seemed to think so, I found it easier to smile and nod.

Frank gave us a quick salute and they hustled toward the door as though they were expecting a busy night.

The few times I'd met Cynthia Mays she was dressed in the most professional suits and dresses with a long white medical coat on top. So when a tall, attractive African American woman dressed in cutoffs and a white tee shirt emblazoned with the colorful emblem of the most recent Fort Myers Beach Shrimp Festival appeared, it took me a minute to recognize Dr. Mays.

She came over and welcomed us warmly. "Nice to see you again. Thanks so much for joining our little crusade. We're covered for the rest of today and early tomorrow, but Inga can fit you into a convenient volunteer slot."

Frank Anthony interrupted. "Doctor, I have to get back but Ryan is arranging for you to have the watchful eyes of the Lee County Sheriff's Department on your office at all times. Anything you need, just call one of those phone numbers I gave you, someone will be at your service."

He gave us all that "two fingers to the eyebrow" salute that he is so fond of and walked out the door with Ryan right behind him.

"Everyone has been so helpful. Miguel, did you tell the ladies about Publix?"

"Oh, I stopped in at Publix to pick up some distilled water—I won't allow my Bow to drink tap water—and Rhonda was on the register. I mentioned that Dr. Mays was running a temporary shelter to protect the small animals from the big snake. Before I could walk across the parking lot, the manager was calling me. He asked that I bring my car to the curb and he had two clerks load up animal food and treats, and even more distilled water."

That is the way of life on Estero Island. Neighbors help neighbors no matter what the crisis. I thought of George and wondered how his visit with Alan went. I'd have to call as soon as we were done signing up as volunteer pet-sitters.

Bridgy and I decided we'd alternate late afternoon, early evening and cover each other's tour of duty if something came up. She signed up for the following day and I was on tap for the day after that.

Dr. Mays thanked us profusely and then moved off to greet two women who came in with a small pet carrier. I was wondering if the occupant was a cat or a dog when I heard an angry meow from inside the carrier and that question was answered.

My cell phone rang. As I pulled it out of my pocket, I felt something drop to the floor. The valet ticket. Darn. I could have given it to Ryan but it never crossed my mind. I was busy being charmed by Mr. Gerrity and Tess. And the two deputies were there and gone. All too quick for me. I decided to call Ryan first thing in the morning. First thing after the funeral service, that is.

The caller was Pastor John. I feared bad news but I chirped a cheery hello.

"Sassy, so glad I found you. I'm home. Owen and Mark are here. I know you're going to see Mark in the morning but they were wondering if you could meet with them tonight. We could come to the café."

"No problem. Stay where you are. Bridgy and I are right down the street at the animal hospital. We'll see you in a few."

I hung up and told Bridgy we had another mission. We waved good-bye to Dr. Mays and as we were walking to the car, Bridgy said, "What a great person. Do you think we could hang out with Cynthia Mays sometime?"

"I'd love to, but I doubt we'll have the chance to before the big green anaconda is permanently removed from Estero Bay."

And we headed from one crisis to the other.

The three men were sitting on the patio, and Jocelyn was being the perfect pastor's wife serving cold drinks and a tray of droopy vegetables with a grayish-looking dip. Miguel would not approve. I decided to pass.

Bridgy and I sat on a love seat of white wicker covered by pillows decorated with a motif of brightly colored birds-of-paradise. The chairs the men occupied were an exact match. The grouping surrounded a glass-topped green wrought iron coffee table. Once we were seated, Mark Clamenta got right to the point. It had been such a long day that I appreciated his directness.

"I went to the hospital with Alan's family and we were able to see him this afternoon. I gave them privacy for a while but then all five of us spent the rest of the visit together." He shifted to the right and the left edge of the seat cushion popped on an angle when he crossed his legs.

"First off, Alan knew who they were and he knew who I was. He was inclined only to have small, polite conversations. No matter what you asked—how did he feel, how were they treating him, how was the food—Alan answered 'fine.' That seemed to unnerve the family. I think they expected more.

"When George was outside talking to the doctor, the sister pressed Alan about the murder. She asked Alan if he hurt the woman. He got agitated, started fussing with his blankets, pulling at his restraints."

"Restraints?" I was horrified.

"Apparently there was an incident earlier in the day. He threw something at the woman who came in to mop the floor. No one knows what triggered it. The doctor prescribed restraints until his meds are more effective.

"The thing is, the lawyer showed up. I'm not sure why they let him in. Anyway, he was loud and arrogant and demanded more money. George held his ground but the sister, Regina, is it? She got upset, started crying. That got Alan and George upset."

He let us imagine the scene before he continued. "I figured the best thing to do was to ring the nurse's bell. The two that rushed in were very take-charge, as nurses tend to be. One was a take-no-prisoners gal about my age and the younger one was a burly guy, so when they told us all to leave, even the lawyer didn't give them any guff. We hustled out of the room and they directed us off the floor."

He stopped talking just long enough to be sure he had all of our attention.

"As I see it, we have two problems. Number one, the

lawyer has to be put in his place. He has to stop browbeating the family for more money. Far as I can see, he hasn't done a lick of work. We're not going to let him bleed the family dry."

He looked to Owen, who nodded forcefully.

"Next problem, and this is where you two come in." He gestured to Bridgy and me. "The sister is emotionally frail. Even with O'Mally's support, George is going to be crushed under the weight of his brother and his sister. Whenever you can, try to distract her. Keep her away from her brothers. Less stress for Alan and it'll give George some room to breathe. What do you say?"

Of course we agreed. The only problem was how.

Chapter Twenty-five

The next morning, through the café window, I saw Mark Clamenta walking across the parking lot toward the front door of the Read 'Em and Eat. I took off my apron and went behind the counter to grab my purse. I checked the time and realized he was a few minutes early. Ophie hadn't arrived to help Bridgy while I was gone, but I was sure she'd turn up soon.

The door opened and I heard Mark say, "After you, pretty lady."

And Ophie pranced into the café like a nominee on Oscar night. She actually did that "index finger on her chin while batting her eyelashes" thing that the southern belles perfected decades ago in black-and-white movies. "Why thank you, sir. It's delicious to know there are still some gentlemen left in the world."

Bridgy came through from the kitchen with a hot breakfast plate in her hand. I could tell by the look on her face she'd heard her dramatic aunt. I raised my eyebrows and telegraphed my thoughts. Delicious? Really? I mean, who talks like that? The answer to my question was standing in front of me.

"Sassy, honey chile, don't y'all keep this handsome man a-waitin'." She sounded exactly like a character in the classic *Gone with the Wind*.

Before I could say whatever joke came to mind at Ophie's expense, Bridgy rushed in to do the rescue with a little Scarlett O'Hara of her own. "My darlin' aunt Ophie, thank you for always being here in my hour of need. Now let's get an apron to cover that pretty dress. Blue is such a becoming color for you. Can't be having it ruined." She dragged her aunt toward the kitchen but not before Ophie pitched what I thought was a rather steamy gaze directly at Mark Clamenta. He must have picked up on her intent because he colored a lovely shade of pink right to the roots of his thinning silver hair. He stood stock-still and watched her disappear into the kitchen.

Finally, he remembered why he was here. Turning to me, he clapped his hands. "Are we ready?"

Mark volunteered to drive, which pleased me to no end. I was content to sit in the passenger seat as beachgoers crossed over to the Gulf side of the island with all their paraphernalia, books and e-readers for the grown-ups, sand pails for the kids and broad-brimmed hats for everyone. As we turned up San Carlos Boulevard and drove across the bridge, I watched the ospreys and blue herons circle lazily, silhouetted against a cloudless sky. Occasionally, one would dive-bomb into the bay and come up with a prize. We crossed San Carlos Island and drove onto the mainland.

Mark told me he'd scouted out the unitarian church earlier in the morning. "A small street ends right opposite the church. I'll park there and we can watch for a while. If we decide to get out and mingle, we can cross over in a jiffy."

He parked curbside under a stately royal palm. We were directly opposite the front entrance to the church, which was a fairly new and exceptionally aesthetic stucco and glass building. There was a large parking lot on one side and a tastefully landscaped lawn on the other. Two men in navy blue suits and somber ties were standing on either side of the main entrance. With their aviator sunglasses they could easily be mistaken for Secret Service agents. The few mourners who had arrived early were mingling in the parking lot. They chatted softly, perhaps not wanting to be first to go inside.

The sun was moving higher in the sky and there was less of a breeze than we'd had the past few days. I was glad I'd worn a beige cotton blouse and tan linen skirt. It was worth getting up extra early to iron so I could be comfortable. Sitting in the car for any length of time could get sticky.

Mark was silent and watchful, his eyes darting from face to face, his spine stiffening with every new car that entered the parking lot. He leaned forward, as if to verify what he was seeing and said, "Okay, now watch her." He pointed. "The lady in yellow."

Sure enough a woman in a pale yellow sundress wearing a wide-brimmed straw hat was walking purposefully past the mourners and toward the front door. She grabbed onto the handrail but only got to the second step before one of the blue suits held up a hand indicating she should stop. When she ignored him and proceeded to the third step, both suits moved to the center of the wide doorway and stood shoulder to shoulder, preventing her from going any farther. The lady in yellow became agitated and was screeching loud enough that we could hear her tone if not her words.

Mark clapped his hands and chortled. "This is getting good. Want to go over?"

"Why not? Who is she?"

"One of the kooky neighbors."

By the time we crossed the tiny street, everyone in the parking lot was drawn to the staircase. The woman was flapping her arms and ducking back and forth like a boxer trying to find an opening. Her shrill "I have a right to pay my respects," didn't sound one bit respectful.

The suits crossed their arms. There was no way she had a chance of getting past them. From behind me I heard a familiar voice. "Excuse me. Thank you. Excuse me." Cady Stanton maneuvered his way through the crowd and stood at the bottom of the stairs. In his quiet, controlled voice he approached the woman. "Mrs. Ramer, I'm Cady Stanton from the *Fort Myers Beach News*. Do you have time for a short interview?"

The woman went dead quiet, so Cady pressed on. "I won't take much of your time. I promise."

She turned her head and then her full body. She took off her hat and held it high to shield her eyes from the sun while she took in Cady's full measure. "Why, I believe I can spare you a few minutes." She tossed a cantankerous "You two haven't defeated me" look over her shoulder and walked back down the steps. Cady extended his arm and escorted her to a shady spot on the edge of the parking lot. The men in blue relaxed. They moved back into position on either side of the door, their mission fulfilled. A number of mourners decided it was better to enter the church now before the path was blocked again by someone else. Men slipped their hands into jacket pockets and women opened purses. They retrieved buff envelopes and drew out stiff cream-colored cards. When shown to the suits, the cards were a magical entrance key.

"The husband is a builder, right?"

It took a second for me to realize Mark was asking the question of me. "Oh, yes. According to Ophie, he is a regular Daddy Warbucks. Money to burn. His car backs that up."

"His car?"

"He drives one of those James Bond Aston Martins. Very showy."

"Yeah, well he must have a thriving business to support the car because every general construction contractor, electrician, plumber and landscape architect from up and down the west coast of Florida is milling around this parking lot or already inside the church. Guess they want to stay on the husband's good side."

I started to agree, and then it dawned on me. "The construction guys may be here sucking up to Barry Lipscome for business reasons, but if they are getting into the church, they were sent invitations. Look around; everyone here has an invitation. Perhaps Lipscome is using his wife's funeral service as a business event instead of the other way around."

Mark gave me a look of appreciation. "I'll have to be careful around you. You're a sharp cookie."

Two things happened at the same time. To my left, Sally Caldera stepped out of her car, while to my right, there was a loud commotion in the shady spot where Cady and the woman in yellow had been talking quietly just moments before. I gave

Sally a quick wave but moved away from her and toward Cady. Whatever was going on, I didn't want to miss it.

A bulbous man with a grizzled beard, whose surfer shorts hung past his knees to reveal hairy, spindly calves, was shaking his finger rapidly in the face of the lady in yellow.

"Ah, terrific. I've been waiting for him," Mark said. He looked delighted that the man was here, regardless of the chaos he was causing.

Perplexed I asked, "Who are these people?"

Immediately contrite, Mark answered, "Sorry, I thought you knew. They are the Lipscomes' neighbors. The plaintiffs in the lawsuit. Cordelia Ramer, rabid environmentalist, and her next-door neighbor Otto Ertz, former wrestler, and not above episodes of 'roid rage. Quite a pair."

A semicircle of gawkers was gathering around them as Cady tried unsuccessfully to calm Otto Ertz down. Mark Clamenta simply walked up and put his hand on the back of the wrestler's neck and gave it a pat. "Otto, how's it going? Woman giving you grief?" Mark laughed and swiveled his head as though he was looking for some agreement that the situation was amusing. Cady and I both caught on and let out a few "hee-hees."

Ertz calmed down immediately. He shook hands with Mark, said he was pleased to meet me and generally acted as though his tantrum in the previous couple of minutes hadn't happened. While Mark was making small talk and Cady was trying to swing the conversation back to whatever aspect of the funeral his news story would cover, I spotted Elaine Tibor walking across the parking lot. She was dressed to the nines in an expensive-looking grey sheath dress and high heels that Ophie would envy. What were surely fourteen-karat-gold pendants graced her neck and ears. It was a heck of a look for a graduate student who waits tables for a living. I watched as she displayed her invitation to one of the men in blue. Then she sashayed through the double doors and into the church.

"That's interesting," I said to no one in particular. "Why would anyone invite the tutor and not the neighbors?"

"That's the most galling part of it all. Who was physically closer than we were? Us just down the road?" Cordelia Ramer spread her hands in appeal to the small group around her. "I mean, if a tragedy occurs, neighbors are the first on the scene . . ."

Her face crashed to stricken and she couldn't pull back either the words or the look. A tragedy had occurred. No one was around to help. And who knows whether or not a neighbor might have caused it.

Otto pushed her hands downward. "What difference does it make now? I don't care who got invited. I'm only here to make sure that Miss Rich Witch is dead and will soon be buried. The woman gave us nothing but grief." He assumed a high-pitched chalk-on-blackboard kind of voice. "Your trash can is too close to the edge of the road. Don't mow your lawn so early in the morning. Leave your outside light on at night." His voice returned to normal. "Orders. All the time, orders. I'm glad she's dead."

Cordelia gasped. "Otto, please."

"Come on, Cordy. Life will be happier on the block and you know it. As for the pool . . ."

"Oh, that. The pool issue is over and we won." She nodded confidently.

Cady, ever the newsman, went after the scoop. "Really? Congratulations. When did the court decide?"

Cordelia gave him a look as if she was a teacher, and a martinet at that, and he had failed his fourth-grade spelling test for the third time. "Sonny, we don't need judges or courts to win this one. Barry Lipscome is a high-flying business man who is rarely home. Why would he go through the fuss and bother of a lawsuit to build a pool he doesn't have time to use? The pool issue is dead."

"Dead as Mrs. Lipscome," Otto chimed in.

No one else said a word. But I'm sure I wasn't the only one thinking that these two were flush with motive and opportunity.

Chapter Twenty-six

On the ride back to the island, I was feeling discouraged that we hadn't come up with a longer list of suspects. But I supposed finding two was better than finding none at all. I wondered what Mark thought. "Between those two neighbors, there are certainly plenty of motives for murder, don't you think?"

"I don't know. They're both crackpots, that's for certain, but killers . . . I don't see it. Loud and pushy, sure. You can see Otto took steroids for years. Never sure exactly how he'll respond to things. Then again, I'm not a deputy. I expect the deputies are taking a look."

When we got to the café, I invited Mark in for an on-the-house lunch but he said he had to stop by the church for a group session and then hoped to spend some more time with George and Alan. "You haven't forgotten to try to get the sister out of the mix, have you?" When I shook my head he said, "Good. That one's a fragile bird. Not at all like Bridgy's aunt. Now there's a gal who can fend for herself."

I got out of the car thinking he didn't know the half of it.

The café was quiet with only two occupied tables, but a quick look at the clock told me the early lunch rush was about to start. Bridgy was taking a pile of tableware and cutlery from the soaking sink and loading it into the dishwasher when I walked through the kitchen to our tiny office to change into my usual work uniform of shorts and a tee shirt. When I came out she'd disappeared. I poked my head through the dining room door and saw she was pouring coffee for the folks at Robert Louis Stevenson, so I decided I'd finish loading the dishwasher. I was nearly done when Bridgy pushed through the kitchen door and immediately grabbed her stomach and doubled over. Miguel looked at me in alarm and we both ran to help her. Then we realized she was laughing hysterically but trying to do so as quietly as she could. She looked up, her face wet with tears. "N . . . n . . . napkin. P . . . please." And went right back to stifling her laughter.

Miguel handed her a napkin and I half led, half dragged her to the back of the kitchen. "Bridgy, what? And why are you hiding in here?"

She stood still for a moment wiping her face, trying to gain control. She wheezed out, "Ophie," and pointed to the door. "You have to see it to believe it." And her irrepressible giggles started all over again.

Miguel had had enough. "I'll go and report back. Then perhaps I can have some sanity in my kitchen, *sì*?"

Bridgy reached out to pull him back. "No. I mean yes

you can have sanity in the kitchen but let Sassy deal with Ophie. She's dressed oddly is all."

Miguel picked up his black-handled pastry blender and went back to cutting the butter into his piecrust dough. I looked at Bridgy, who gave me the universal double-handed shooing motion to rush me out of the room.

Bridgy should have prepared me. Then I realized nothing could have prepared me. Ophie was standing in the middle of the room dressed in white capri pants with wide silver buckles at the cuffs. On top she wore an oversized white tee shirt, imprinted with a huge green snake. The snake's head covered Ophie's considerable bosom, and the snake's body curled around the tee shirt front to back, back to front, over and over. Ophie spun like a top several times so that I could follow the snake's "natural beauty" from head to tail until I was totally dizzy.

Then I looked at her feet. She of the "well-mannered ladies always dress their feet properly" persuasion was wearing sneakers, and not just any sneakers like rubber-soled backless slide-ins with pretty little bows on the front, or even the sensible deck shoes that she refused to wear the one time we all went out on Cady's boat. Ophie was wearing hardcore sneakers. Thick firm soles and a toe box wide enough for an actual foot. These on the feet of a woman who wore sandals with mini heels to the beach. Amazing. Before I had a chance to recover from the outfit and the sneakers, Ophie had one last thing to show me. Her picket signs. Each one was colorfully printed and neatly attached to wooden sticks about four feet long. One read:

FRIENDS DON'T LET FRIENDS KILL SNAKES

The next:

DO YOU WANT YOUR GRANDCHILDREN TO LIVE
IN A SNAKE-FREE SOCIETY?

And finally:

ST. PATRICK DIDN'T KILL THE SNAKES
HE DROVE THEM OUT OF IRELAND

That one had a picture of a bearded man wearing a bish-op's miter behind the wheel of a convertible, the backseat overflowing with snakes.

Now I knew why Bridgy didn't want Miguel to cross Ophie's path today. The longer we could delay that, the better off we'd all be. I've seen what happens when there is a cranky Miguel in the kitchen, and it isn't pretty.

"Ophie, why don't you sit down and let me pour you some sweet tea." She settled in at Emily Dickinson and I tucked her signs, upside down, in the back corner behind the counter. She started to object but I said, "We can't have anyone trip over the sticks. Take a long time to sort that lawsuit out."

The word "lawsuit" put the brakes on Ophie in a hurry.

Ophie took a sip of the glass of tea I'd set in front of her. Then she looked me straight in the eye. "I don't know what's wrong with folks 'round here. Snake hasn't done anything and y'all are ready to kill him for just showing up. The members of the Guy Bradley Environmental Action League are not going to stand for it. We're having a protest today in Bowditch Point Park. I'm waiting on Augusta and Blondie. We're meeting here so we can leave our medicines with you, that way you can have Ryan or that handsome lieutenant smuggle them in to us if we wind up in the hoosegow."

Oh, good Lord. I took a deep breath. "What league? And how did you get involved?"

"Honey chile, Guy Bradley is a martyr for the cause. He was a deputy sheriff and game warden in the Everglades during the Plume Wars."

Never smart enough to keep my mouth shut, I said I'd never heard of the Plume Wars.

"You know how we admire the ladies' hats in those pictures from about a hundred years ago. The hats with gorgeous feathers flying high. Where do y'all think the feathers came from? Right here in south Florida. Our herons and egrets and other plumed birds. It was Guy Bradley's job to stop the plunder and he got shot for his troubles back in 1905."

Like pulling teeth. "Okay, I get who Guy Bradley was but how did you get involved and what has it got to do with the anaconda?"

"Well, over at the community center, Cordy was handing out fliers, looking for volunteers . . ."

Clang. Clang. Clang. Lights and sirens went off in my brain. "Cordy? Cordelia Ramer?"

Ophie nodded. "Sure. You know her? She's president of the Action League. She's the one got this demonstration all set up. And this is just the beginning. Cordy says that all living beings have a right to live out their natural life, even the snakes among us."

Well that was food for thought. Unless Cordelia Ramer believed that Tanya Trouble was lower than a snake, she might fall off my suspect list. I decided to switch topics. "Ophelia, I can see that you are very busy but I need a favor.

You remember Regina Mersky? You were so kind to her yesterday. She needs more of your down-home kindness." ›

"Whatever that poor darlin' needs, just tell me."

I tried to phrase it as delicately as I could. No telling what Ophie would repeat, or who she'd repeat it to, including Regina. "She is tired, stressed, and who wouldn't be, given the situation. I was thinking that a little time away from her brothers might clear her head."

Ophie caught on immediately. "I'll tell you what. If we don't get arrested at this afternoon's protest, I'll give her a call and ask her to supper. She needs a friend, poor thing."

The door opened and in came Miss Augusta Maddox and Blondie Quinlin. They were wearing the same big-snake tee shirt as Ophie. On tiny Augusta the shirt hung so close to her ankles that I could barely see her ever-present jeans straggling below, while on Blondie the shirt was a better fit, even snug in some places. The diners who'd been sitting in the back of the dining room were just leaving, and I met them at the cash register. After they paid their bill, they gave the ladies a wide berth, probably afraid they were environmental terrorists, given the ferocity of the snakes emblazoned on their chests.

Augusta handed me a bottle of baby aspirin. "I don't hold with medicines but Doc says it's time I started taking one of these each day. Good for the ticker."

Blondie was right behind her with a daily pillbox. "I'm not as fortunate. Hang on to these for me please. In case."

I poured them all a round of sweet tea and went inside to ask Miguel to put some cookies in three sandwich bags. I heard the front door open and when I walked into the dining room there were two sets of customers waiting for tables. By the time I sat them and gave them menus, the three environmentalists were on their feet and ready to go. I carried the signs outside for them, careful that our customers couldn't see the slogans. Augusta and Blondie were duly impressed with Ophie's graphics, especially the convertible full of snakes.

I gave them each a bag of cookies and a hug before I sent them on their way. By the time I got inside, Bridgy was taking orders from the folks who had just come in. I pulled out my phone to call George but the front door opened again. Lunch rush had begun.

Sally Caldera came in and stood at the counter for take-away service. Always a healthy eater, she ordered a double house salad and one hardboiled egg. I dropped her order on the pass-through.

Bridgy was walking around the dining room, checking in at each table. I took the moment of downtime to ask Sally about Tanya Lipscome's funeral.

She replied, "I saw you in the parking lot. You never made it inside?"

I explained that I hadn't been invited and was there more on a "scouting" mission, to use Mark Clamenta's phrase.

"Snooping again, huh? Don't let Lieutenant Anthony find out. I think it was because of your last escapade that he asked us to let the deputies use our conference room for a series of talks on how to tell the sheriff's office every little thing."

I couldn't help but laugh. "I had no idea. He wants to know every little thing?"

Sally pushed her eyeglasses atop her abundant russet curls. "Well he didn't use that term but the speakers were so comprehensive, I gave it my own interpretation. Anyway the funeral was plain, simple and peaceful—all the things that Tanya was not. She would have hated it."

"Do you think that's why her husband went with ordinary? Some private little joke?"

Sally grimaced. "Never know with those two. I mean just look at the invitation list. I understand why I got invited, but the church was filled with off-islanders. If someone lives here, I might not know them well, but I'd know them by sight. Everyone on the island comes into the library at least once in a while to get a book or a movie, or to participate in a program."

I told her what Mark said about Barry inviting any number of business acquaintances.

She nodded. "That makes sense. Then there was that grad student, Elaine. You know who I mean. She was waitressing here the other day when I picked up my yogurt and tea."

"Elaine Tibor. Why wouldn't she be there? She tutors one of the stepsons."

"Perhaps. But I can tell you for a fact Tanya couldn't stand her. Elaine spent a lot of her research time in the library. You saw how Alan affected Tanya. Elaine got her just as riled but Tanya responded in a more subtle, passive-aggressive way. Books Elaine reserved suddenly went missing. If she left her notes on her worktable unattended for a few minutes, when she came back, some pages would be gone. And Tanya bad-mouthed her at every opportunity."

I was sorting out a variety of issues that would cause hostility between Tanya and Elaine but I still managed to be attentive enough to give Sally her lunch and take her money.

She got as far as the front door and turned around to tell me that I had company fast approaching. I knew who it was as soon as she said, "Be sure to tell them every little thing."

Chapter Twenty-seven

I was glad the café was nearly full of customers so I'd have an excuse not to be available for a long conversation with Ryan and Frank. As soon as I saw they were wearing civvies, I realized what I should have known all along. They were at the funeral. And they knew I was there, too. I sighed. This wasn't going to be fun.

I led them to Dashiell Hammett in the rear of the dining room so that our conversation couldn't be easily overheard and asked if they'd like anything. They both ordered coffee, and Ryan asked if we had any Harper Lee Hush Puppies, a menu item that Ophie had introduced and Miguel enjoyed making.

I brought a heaping plateful along with their coffee.

Frank Anthony looked around. "I see you're busy but I'd appreciate it if you could find a few minutes to sit with us."

He was so nice about it that I started to fear they wanted

to talk about something more serious than my sticking my nose in where it doesn't belong. I said a silent prayer as I went to ask Bridgy to cover the dining room for a few minutes.

I sat at the table and folded my hands primly in my lap, expecting a barrage of questions. When it didn't come, I knew something was very wrong.

Ryan put down his coffee cup and looked at Frank, who gave a slight nod. Then Ryan cleared his throat. "I know you're good friends with the Mersky family. Things aren't going well for them right now."

I interrupted. "If this is about Regina, I know she's fragile and I'm working on getting help."

By the looks on both their faces, I knew I was completely off track.

Frank spoke in the gentlest voice I'd ever heard him use. "Listen to Ryan." In that moment I was sure someone was dead.

Ryan started again. "A lot of the forensic test results are complete now. We can say with certainty that the branch that crushed Tanya Lipscome's skull is a perfect match to the tree limb found in Alan Mersky's car."

He sat back and his shoulders relaxed a little, the worst part of his job done.

"The one time I saw Alan's car, the windows were wide open and the doors were unlocked. Anyone could have . . . And what about fingerprints?"

Frank answered. "The bark isn't conducive to lifting prints. The techs tried all the modern stuff including alternate light sources, various glues, even magnetic powder. Trouble is, after the crime, the perp dropped the branch into the hot tub. Techs dried out the branch before it was tested, but the chlorinated water had more than done its job."

"Why are you telling me all this?"

"Well, first off, we are preparing to arrest Alan Mersky. A lawyer from the state attorney's office and I are going to meet with his doctor later today to discuss how best to proceed."

Goddard Swerling popped into my head. "What about Alan's lawyer?"

"The assistant state attorney will contact him as soon as we're sure . . . I'm telling you this because the family is from out of town and you're their only friend here. We thought you should be prepared to help them get through what is coming."

I couldn't think of a response and then I remembered something I could contribute. I excused myself and came right back with the valet parking ticket I found in the woods by the Lipscome house. To Frank Anthony's credit, he didn't berate me immediately for withholding evidence, although his face indicated storm clouds were brewing.

He looked at the ticket, turned it over and back again. Then he passed it to Ryan, who pulled a baggy from somewhere and dropped the red and white receipt inside. Ryan wouldn't make eye contact with me, another bad sign.

Frank asked me to repeat my story of how I found the receipt. And then he made me repeat it again.

When I finished the third telling, I said, "Look we're really swamped. I have to help Bridgy."

Frank nodded and I assumed we were done. I started to stand but he signaled me to stay in my seat. "I just want to be sure I have this right. You saw something you thought might help exonerate your friend and point us toward someone else. So you picked it up. You and Bridgy both handled it. You never thought to surrender it when you met us last night at the animal hospital. And now you present it to me as a saving grace because its date stamp matches the date of the murder?"

When he put it like that, I sounded like a complete dolt. In for a penny . . . I nodded in agreement.

He tilted his chair back and then leaned forward until we were practically nose to nose. "I did really hope you learned your lesson the last time you interfered in a murder case but I can see you didn't. Let me be clear. You are not to touch anything you think is involved in this case. Other than the Mersky family you are not to speak to anyone you think is involved in this case. Have I made myself clear?"

I allowed myself one extremely meek head bob.

"Good." He sat back, giving me the impression that the worst was over, but then he hammered me again. "Now tell me what you and your reporter pal were doing talking to the neighbors at the funeral this morning."

"I wasn't *with* Cady. We were both there, but not together, at least at not at first. Cordelia Ramer caused a scene. Cady talked her down. Then while my friend Mark and I were observing the mourners, Otto Ertz came along and started another hubbub. Mark calmed him down. Then we left."

"Observing the mourners, huh? And what did you observe?" Frank's voice was dripping with sarcasm.

"I observed oddities." I ticked them off on my fingers. "The newly minted widower was mindful enough of future profits that he invited every business acquaintance in a fifty-mile radius. The son's tutor was invited but the neighbors were not, and there didn't seem to be any local friends."

That last one was Sally's but I decided to throw it on my pile. Neither of them said a word. Ryan still looked like he wanted to be any place else but here. Frank was completely blank-faced until he finally thanked me for my time.

I forced myself to get up slowly and move away from the deputies rather than run screaming from the room, which would have reflected my true feelings.

I started at Barbara Cartland and was reciting the specials for a woman who left her eyeglasses home, so she couldn't read the daily board. When I looked over at Dashiell Hammett, the table was empty save two coffee cups and a few Harper Lee Hush Puppies.

We were super busy for a while longer, and then the late lunch crowd dwindled. A couple sat at Dr. Seuss with a toddler and a baby both asleep in their double stroller. I brought them a piece of Miguel's apple pie a la mode with two forks. I started cleaning the back of the dining room when I noticed that someone had been browsing the bookshelves and left some books askew. I was just getting them back in order when I heard the front door open and turned to see Mark Clamenta and George Mersky. I panicked for the moment. Should I tell George what I had just learned from the deputies? They hadn't sworn me to secrecy; still, I had a sense I was being forewarned, not given the go-ahead to repeat the conversation all over Fort Myers Beach.

Mark and George sat at Robert Louis Stevenson. I brought over two cups of coffee. "You look like you could use these."

George nodded his thanks. "Sassy, do you have a minute?"

He was so glum that I knew he needed a pal. I sat down instantly, ready to hear whatever he might have to say.

"We dropped O'Mally and Regina at the condo. I told them to get some rest, but I really wanted to hash this out with friends but not, well, worry them, especially Regina. She's not handling all this very well."

That reminded me that Ophie agreed to try to distract Regina. When I mentioned it, George didn't hold much hope but gave me Regina's cell number to pass along. "Anything that might pull her out of her funk."

When he didn't say anything else, I offered to get something to eat for him and Mark. George just shook his head. "Thanks, but I don't think I can eat." Then he blurted, "Sassy, they're going to arrest Alan for murder. I'm not sure he can handle the process, much less a trial."

I was floored. At least I didn't have to decide whether or not to tell George. But how did he know? I asked quietly, "George, are you sure?"

"Quite sure. Some kind of government lawyer and representatives from the sheriff's office are going to meet with Alan's doctor and line up the protocols. Got to be all legal without putting Alan in deeper medical jeopardy."

"What about Alan's lawyer?"

George deflated completely. "I don't know what to do with the guy. He claims that Alan is uncooperative so it's going to cost more money than we originally agreed. He's not just looking for an increase. He's talking double. We're not a rich family . . ."

Mark took a deep breath as if doing so could make his words more forceful. "I told you. Don't worry about the shyster. Owen will take care of him."

Always a bit cynical, George laughed. "If you want to sell me that particular rainbow, Owen better come up with a pot of gold to go with it."

Mark tented his hands, fingertips touching. "Owen

doesn't spread it around but he is a lawyer. Licensed to practice in the state of Florida."

A tiny spark of hope came into George's eyes. "Maybe he can represent Alan. Owen understands what Alan is going through and—"

"George, Owen isn't a criminal attorney. He works for a veteran's rights organization. He and another representative of the group are meeting with Swerling and going to put their very large cards on the table. My bet is the last thing any lawyer wants is a lawsuit against him, especially a suit that alleges he's taking unfair advantage of our military heroes." Mark gave me a wink. "Think your young newspaper friend would be willing to cover that story?"

"Not only would he, his boss is a Vietnam vet. The story would probably be front page all the way." I managed a big grin and watched George relax ever so slightly. I leaned in and patted his hand. "Now, how about some apple pie a la mode? Today's special. Homemade pie."

George's smile was tiny but genuine. "I believe I will."

I was serving the pie when the circus came to town, bringing the ringleader along for good measure.

Ophie burst through the door, her head twisted as she spoke to those who followed behind. "Don't be silly, my niece and her friend will be overjoyed to meet y'all. And I just know there will be sweet tea and snacks a plenty."

Even wearing her sturdy sneakers, Ophie managed to spin into the room like a rock star taking center stage. In addition to Augusta and Blondie, three other women straggled along behind, all wearing the symbolic green anaconda tee shirt. The last one through the door was Cordelia Ramer. And, oh Lord, Miguel was still in the kitchen. This wasn't going to go well.

Ophie shepherded her little flock over to Emily Dickinson and urged them to push the Robert Frost table closer so they could sit as a group. As soon as she had them properly distracted she walked over to me, but her eyes never left Mark Clamenta.

"Honey chile, I am so sorry to interrupt your, ah, conversation with these handsome gentlemen, but y'all don't mind if I help myself to some treats from the kitchen." She was so busy batting her eyelashes at Mark that she nearly didn't notice me jump from my seat.

"Ophie, you've had a busy day. Why not unwind with your friends. Bridgy and I will be happy to serve." I could keep her out of the kitchen for the moment, but I knew chaos would ensue the minute Miguel spotted those shirts. I went into the kitchen hoping I could feed the demonstrators and get them out of the dining room before Miguel and Bridgy finished cleaning the kitchen.

But I knew I was in trouble when I saw that Miguel had already removed his chef's jacket and Bridgy was carrying her purse. She saw the question on my face and said, "We're off to help Dr. Mays. Remember? Today's my day. And Miguel has to pick up Bow."

But first they had to wade through the crowd of snake savers in the dining room. That should be fun.

Chapter Twenty-eight ⅢⅢⅢⅢⅢ

"Ophie and her friends popped in for a snack after their, er, excursion to Bowditch Point Park." Bridgy got the message. We were both wishing there was a back door so she and Miguel could leave through the kitchen and never cross paths with the Guy Bradley contingent.

In the meantime, Miguel, totally oblivious to our panic, was rummaging in the refrigerator. "Here you go. I made a few dozen donuts for the morning. I could spare two or three. We can cut them in thirds." He brought a platter to the counter. "We have fruit and cookies . . . What?"

The fact that Bridgy and I were rooted to the floor was not lost on him. Bridgy looked at me, but I backed away, saying, "She's your aunt." And mentally I wished her good luck.

Miguel repeated his question, this time in Spanish. *"¿Qué pasa?"*

Bridgy gave a little nervous giggle. "It's Ophie . . . don't get upset but she and her friends have joined an environmentalist group."

When she stopped there, Miguel gave a "so what" shrug and patiently waited for the rest of the story.

Bridgy blurted out. "They're trying to save the green anaconda."

Miguel was confused. "Save it from what? Is there a bigger predator in the waters?"

"Not that I know of."

Bridgy was floundering, so I decided to go the direct route. "Ophie and her friends are opposed to the wildlife agencies killing the anaconda if it is captured alive."

Miguel knitted his eyebrows, always a sign of deep thought, and then his brow straightened, decision made. "We'll see about that. You can feed the environmentalists. Bridgy and I are going to see Dr. Mays and help protect the pets living on the island."

Bridgy looked at me, threw up her hands in confusion and hurried out the kitchen door behind him. I grabbed the platter Miguel had set on the counter. Of course he hadn't yet cut the donuts. I was reaching for a knife when the yelling started. Platter in one hand, knife in the other, I pushed through the kitchen door.

Miguel was speaking in the gentlemanly tone he always used. "I said the safety of all animals is important but sometimes predators need to be removed."

Cordelia Ramer was directly in front of him and stabbing the air with her index finger. "You don't get to decide. No one can pick and choose which animals live and which animals are mercilessly killed."

I wasn't worried about Miguel; he was always a gentleman

even in the worst of circumstances, but I wasn't so sure that the ladies would remain ladies.

Ophie stepped in between them. She adopted the wide stance, hands-on-hips body language that I always see on Bridgy when I annoy her. Ophie swung around to Cordelia. "Y'all have no cause to be insolent to my friend Miguel. His darlin' Bow is in danger and he has a right to be concerned. You apologize at once, hear? Well-mannered ladies do not use an abusive tone when speaking to a fine gentleman."

Cordelia's shoulders hunched and she reared up like a horse who'd been spooked. Then she relaxed and turned away, not willing to apologize but not willing to fight, either.

Bridgy grabbed Miguel's arm and waved good-bye to me, and they headed off to the animal hospital.

I stood in the middle of the floor, a platter of donuts in one hand and a knife in the other. I decided to cut the donuts on the counter and leave the knife tucked safely out of the way of the environmentalists should another skirmish break out. As I was dividing the donuts into portion size I heard Mark say to George, "That Ophelia—she's something else."

I smiled to myself. Ophie may have made a conquest.

I set out the donuts for the ladies, brought them a pitcher of sweet tea and went over to see if Mark and George wanted anything else. Mark shook his head. "No, we're going to find Owen and see what his vets group can do before Alan is formally arrested."

I wished them luck and began my final cleaning of the day. Bridgy had finished the kitchen before she left and I had most of the dining room sparkling in very short order.

I listened as Ophie and her friends planned a trip to Ding Darling Refuge on our neighboring island of Sanibel. One of my favorite places, Ding Darling is where I first heard the phrase "a park is for people, a refuge is for animals." Whenever people visit a refuge, they are guests. It was a bit of a surprise to learn that open spaces had different purposes.

Miss Augusta Maddox waved me over and asked for her bottle of baby aspirin. I went behind the counter and pulled out her tiny orange and white bottle and Blondie Quinlin's bright green pill counter. "When are you going to Ding Darling?"

"Tomorrow," Miss Augusta boomed. "Pretty place. Reminds me of the old days when these islands weren't so cluttered with houses and such."

Blondie Quinlin tilted her head toward me. "Would you like to join us? Weather forecast is perfect."

"When isn't it?" asked one of the ladies I'd never met. And five of the women laughed. Not Cordelia, though.

She rapped her knuckles on the table as if she were the teacher in a room filled with errant third graders. "This isn't a fun-filled romp we're planning. This is serious business." Cordelia gave me an evil look. "You'd do better to stay at work where you belong."

She heard the collective gasp of her colleagues and softened her tone immediately. "I meant to say, we are going to collect signatures on our 'save the anaconda' petitions. We'll be busy."

Ophie decided to move into passive-aggressive mode. "Sassy, honey chile, did you get me that Regina Mersky's cell number? I do so want to invite her to join us."

I began rummaging through my pockets, came up with the scrap I'd torn from my order pad and written the number on. When I handed it to Ophie, her smile encompassed everyone at the table. "Y'all are going to love my new friend when you meet her. Regina is the sweetest thing and I'm sure she could use a day in the fresh air." That was a jab at Cordelia for sure.

Ophie scraped her chair along the floor and stood. "Well, it has been a lively afternoon. I'd better get on over to the Treasure Trove and check if I have any messages. My clientele is quite demanding." She tossed a careless wave around the table and when she reached the door, she turned to me. "I bet Regina's sister-in-law would like to join us, too." And she sashayed out the door knowing she'd stuck another pin in her Cordelia doll.

The rest of the ladies began organizing themselves while Cordelia reasserted her authority, reminding them what time and where to meet in the morning and assuring them that she would have plenty of pens and clipboards for their petition drive. Miss Augusta Maddox walked over to me and in an uncharacteristically warm gesture took my hand. "Miguel is worried about Bow? Delia's Bow."

I nodded.

She squeezed my hand. "Well then I get his point. I truly do. Just don't like upsetting the natural order of things is all. Don't want the snake killed."

And she turned and followed the other ladies out the door.

I locked the door and began to clean off the tables where Ophie and her friends had planned their next venture. I pushed Robert Frost back into its proper place, scrubbed the tables and chairs and swept the floor. The whole time I was thinking about Augusta's comment. I'd always heard that a green anaconda was the biggest snake in the world, bigger even than pythons. So how did a snake like that fit in the natural order of things in southwest Florida?

I finished the cleanup, tossed my apron in the laundry, turned out the lights and locked up. I was in the Heap-a-Jeep when I realized that I could have my snake questions answered in a jiffy. I headed south on Estero Boulevard to visit Dr. Mays.

The parking lot was nearly as crowded as it had been the last time I was here. I was happy to see Miguel's SUV. If he was still here, I would get to visit with Bow. I was deeply disappointed that Bow couldn't come to live with Bridgy and me. But she is an indoor-outdoor cat and would never have adjusted to life in a fifth-floor apartment. Still, if I couldn't have her for a roomie, I was glad Bow had a happy home with Miguel. Of course the fact that he lived on the edge of the bay was a real problem now that the big snake was swimming around.

Cynthia Mays was one of the most organized women I'd ever met, and her assistant, Inga, was unflappable. The waiting room was crowded but peaceful. Bridgy came through the back door, carrying an adorable puppy. He reminded me of Sweetie, the Jack Russell terrier we had when I was in grammar school. If the brown circle around his right eye had been a little larger, they could have been twins.

"Sassy, meet Denny. Isn't he adorable? He's only five months old."

Our Sweetie loved to be petted on the top of her head right between her ears, so I gave Denny a gentle rub, and he rolled his head from side to side to keep contact with my hand. I could swear he gave me a smile.

I half hoped he was looking for a home, but Bridgy said that his owner was on her way to pick him up.

"How is the sheltering working out?"

Bridgy shrugged. "Inga would know. She keeps strict

track because the animals who are here to be sheltered while their owners are at work can't be housed with the animals who are here because they're sick."

Made sense.

All of a sudden, Denny tried to wiggle out of Bridgy's arms. A middle-aged woman dressed in pink hospital scrubs opened the front door and before she was completely inside, Denny was panting and wagging his tail joyfully.

Bridgy started to laugh. "Hold on, sweetheart. Is that your mama?"

The woman waved to Inga and then took Denny in her arms. She nuzzled him and gave him a tiny treat. She looked at Bridgy and said, "Thanks so much for volunteering. I felt so much better knowing if the snake came ashore near my house, I wouldn't have to worry."

Bridgy's cheeks pinked just a little. "I had fun. We even had a chance to play with his tug rope. He's a strong little fella."

The woman smiled her thanks and then went to the desk so she could sign the pup out on Inga's forms. As she left she waved a cheery good-bye and called out, "See you again."

"Where's Miguel?"

"Oh, he's helping with the cats. I think Bow gets a wee bit jealous when she sees Miguel get too close to another cat."

I asked, "How many animals come in for shelter?"

Bridgy thought for a minute. "Inga told me that today we have four dogs and seven cats. The number varies, depending on need. Remember Mr. Gerrity, Miguel's neighbor? According to Miguel, he only came in the one time because that day he had plans and didn't want to leave Tess alone. I'm sure there are one or two other pets that are here for a few hours once or twice. The rest are here because their humans have to be at work." She lowered her voice. "I hope this is very temporary because Dr. Mays and her staff are already stretched thin and it's not like the space in the back is unlimited."

On cue, Cynthia Mays came through the door at the back of the clinic. The tailored tan outfit under her long white medical coat was brightened by orange buttons on her blouse. "Sassy, I'm so glad you're here. We just got an emergency call. The patient will be arriving shortly. I was going to ask Bridgy if she could stay until all the sheltered pets are picked up. It would be wonderful if you could help. At least until I see what's going on with Duke."

"Duke?"

"Mrs. Whatling's golden. He's getting up in years. Mrs. Whatling is afraid Duke has seriously hurt his hip. Golden retrievers have a propensity for hip problems, you know."

I didn't but I nodded anyway.

"Doctor, I wanted to talk to you about the green anaconda. Do you have a minute?"

"I have until Duke and Mrs. Whatling arrive." And she ushered me into her office.

I wasn't sure how to begin.

Chapter Twenty-nine |||||||||||

Dr. Mays indicated the visitor's chair and asked if we needed to close the door. I hesitated and then said yes.

She sat, folded her hands and waited patiently for me to speak.

"I'm concerned about the growing rift in the community between those who want to protect the green anaconda and those who think it should be killed for the safety of their pets. This battle could ruin lifelong friendships and cause troubles that may never heal in the community."

She unclasped her hands and leaned back in her chair. "Sassy, you are right on track. In fact, there is a meeting at Pastor John's church in about"—she glanced at her wristwatch—"two hours to discuss how to head off a Hatfield and McCoy collision here in our tiny community. It's open to the public. Why don't you join us?"

I accepted enthusiastically.

I shook hands with Dr. Mays and went to find Miguel. He was sitting on the windowsill next to a big old gray tabby, stroking her back gently. She seemed content to lie in the sunshine and be adored. Bow, her trademark neck ribbon a saucy bright blue, was standing on Miguel's lap and swiping at a toy Miguel was bouncing above her head. The feather on a long string dangled from a stick that Miguel waved back and forth from one side to the other. Bow bobbed and weaved as if she was training for the Golden Gloves boxing championship.

Two cats were tumbling around a tunnel toy that looked like it was a scratcher as well. The rest of the cats were sleeping in circles of sunshine on the floor or just roaming the room.

"*Hola, chica.* Did that annoying woman continue to cause trouble after I left the café?"

Clearly Miguel wasn't going to forgive Cordelia Ramer anytime soon.

"Every time Cordy tried to stir the pot, Ophie took the spoon away. Say, are you going to the meeting in the church later?"

"I wouldn't miss it. As long as pets are allowed, I am happy to participate. Now here"—he threw a small purple ball at me—"have some fun with the cats."

And so I did, tossing and rolling the ball as the cats took turns chasing it. One pretty gray tabby with big yellow eyes had mastered the art of slapping the ball from top to bottom and sending it spinning across the floor. Two other cats dashed after it and as soon as they had it cornered, she of the yellow eyes would muscle the other cats out of the way and slap the ball, sending it off again. I had to laugh when Bow suddenly jumped from Miguel's lap and landed squarely on the purple ball. She rolled back so that the ball was securely under her front paws and hissed just long enough to scare the chaser cats away. Yellow Eyes wasn't intimidated. She stood a few inches out of claw range and stared at Bow as if daring her to start something.

I looked to Miguel for help, but he held up his hand. "Wait and watch. Perhaps they will settle this amicably."

I thought he was crazy but I followed his direction. Within a few seconds, Yellow Eyes arched her back but made no threatening move. Apparently bored with the game and the lack of a stronger reaction, Bow released the ball and leapt back onto Miguel's knees. Yellow Eyes promptly turned her back on the purple ball and pranced off to a scratching post in the corner.

Pet owners showed up sporadically to retrieve their animals and soon it was only Bow and Yellow Eyes left in the cat room. Bow had curled up for a nap in a bright warm patch of sunlight and Yellow Eyes was once again slapping the purple ball, albeit with less enthusiasm than she had when there were cats interested in chasing the ball around the room.

Inga, cat carrier in her hand, stepped into the room just as Yellow Eyes slapped the ball. It went careening across the floor and landed at Inga's feet. She picked it up and bounced it a few feet away, sending the cat scrambling after it. Bow heard the commotion and opened one eye, decided the activity was not worth opening the other and went back to sleep.

Yellow Eyes was about to slap the ball again when Inga swooped her up and said, "Come on, baby girl. Time for home and dinner."

I pulled out my cell phone, checked the time and said to Miguel, "That was fun, and it is almost time for the meeting about the green anaconda. Are you going?"

"Of course. I have Bow's carrier outside. I want to bring her as exhibit A—the prime example as to why the snake must be killed. Our pets are not safe . . . Ah, but you understand about the pets. I am preaching to the choir."

I nodded uneasily. As much as I understood the danger the snake presented to the small pets, I was inclined to a remedy that involved capture rather than kill. I hoped there would be a good turnout at the meeting and we'd find a solution that everyone could support.

Bridgy was talking to Cynthia Mays in the lobby and invited me to walk over to Pastor John's church with them. I thought the walk, short as it was, would do me good.

Inga was staying at the veterinary center with the night attendant and a community volunteer, so Dr. Mays was free. As we strolled across the parking lot, the yellow and orange ribbons of another dazzling southwest Florida sunset were peeking above the row of beach cottages that sat between us and the Gulf of Mexico.

"I never get tired of watching the sun go down in southwest Florida. I'm from Chicago originally. Sunset is not a big deal there," Cynthia said with a gentle laugh.

Bridgy told her that when we first moved to Fort Myers Beach we watched the sun go down every night for at least the first six months.

I nodded. "It never gets old and I never take it for granted."

As we walked to Pastor John's church, now and again a robust gust of wind coming inland from the Gulf carried a whiff of salt water and its inhabitants. I inhaled deeply. "That smell never gets old, either."

When we reached the church, I was surprised to see so many cars in the parking lot and said so.

"Well, if you think about it, there are residents who have strong feelings about both sides of this issue, and neither group wants to be underrepresented."

Cynthia had a point. Bridgy was quick to ask if there was any obvious solution, and Cynthia was quick to respond. "That's what we are here to determine."

Bridgy pointed to a spot at the far end of the church parking lot, where Cordelia Ramer was corralling a contingent of women wearing the long white tee shirts showing off their love for the snake. "Oh, darn. The Guy Bradley girls are front and center. I don't see Aunt Ophie, thank the Lord. Still, the night is young." Bridgy sighed, fearing the moment still might come when she would have to rescue her aunt from the middle of a brawl between the environmentalists who wanted to protect the green anaconda and the pet owners who wanted the snake caught and killed.

The hall inside was noisier than I expected, but it wasn't the sound of bickering. People were moving around, saying hello to friends and neighbors and scraping the floor with the folding chairs that had been placed in untidy rows as they settled in for the meeting. Pastor John was sitting at a long table facing the audience.

Cynthia Mays patted my shoulder. "We can't leave Pastor John all alone to deal with this crowd. I'll see you later." And she strode to the front of the room, exuding the confidence of a movie star who'd just won an Oscar, smiling and waving to anyone who greeted her. She took a seat at the table next to the pastor.

Miguel waved to us. He was sitting toward the front on the left side of the aisle, with Mr. Gerrity on one side and another man who I recognized from my volunteer time at

Dr. Mays's clinic. I was guessing that was the "kill the ana-conda" section. I was wondering where the "we're just here to listen and vote for peace" section was when Cordelia Ramer marched in her troops complete with their "save the anaconda" signs held high. I noticed that Miss Augusta and Blondie Quinlin held to the rear and weren't carrying signs. I wished the entire group was as sensible. The signs caused quite a stir on Miguel's side of the room. Pastor John marched purposefully down the center aisle, picking up a couple of younger men along the way.

He stopped directly in front of the Guy Bradleys. "Corde-lia, I already told you that you and your organization mem-bers are welcome but those signs are not. If you insist on bringing them to our meeting, then I must insist you leave."

I'd never heard him speak so forcefully. I found myself daydreaming about what would happen if he spoke that firmly to Jocelyn. I shook it off as a fantasy for another time.

The room filled with silent expectation. Then Cordelia meekly turned over her sign to one of the young men who flanked Pastor John, and signaled her cronies to do the same. After abandoning their signs, they walked down the center aisle, heads held high, and settled in on the right side of the room.

The men put the signs in a side room and came back. By the time they took their seats, Pastor John was back behind the table and calling the meeting to order. Bridgy and I took two aisle seats in the back row and waited for the fireworks to begin. I was surprised to see Mark Clamenta come in a side door and sit at the head table.

Pastor John gave him a nod of welcome and explained to all of us that we had come together to find a solution to the problem of the green anaconda snake that had been spotted numerous times in Estero Bay.

Someone from the front left yelled, "Kill him and be done with it." That caused a great deal of rumbling.

Pastor John pounded his hand on the table. "I will have order. Now, we have two guests here tonight who may help us find a solution that will satisfy everyone."

This time we heard murmurs from both sides of the room but no shout-outs.

"You all know Dr. Cynthia Mays. Listen carefully to what she has to say."

Pastor sat down and Cynthia Mays got up. She walked around the table and stood closer to the audience, which was restless at first, waiting for her to speak. She held up a hand to indicate patience or silence, I wasn't sure which, but it was enough to get everyone's undivided attention.

"We, as a community, have come together to solve a problem. We have a fundamental disagreement about the solution, but we do not disagree that having the green ana-conda swim in our waters and coming ashore on our island is a problem that could result in tragedy."

She stopped speaking, and swung her gaze slowly from one side of the room to the other and back to the center.

"I know that pet owners are concerned that if the ana-conda is caught and set free in the Everglades, it might once again find its way north. I agree that is a possibility."

I expected that sentence to lead to mumbling in the audi-ence, but it didn't.

Dr. Mays continued. "Throughout the United States there are dozens of serpentariums, or snake zoos. In fact, there are three right here in Florida."

She waited a minute to let what she had said sink in everyone's brain. "So I propose that we find a serpentarium willing to take this anaconda away from our community."

I was pleased to see heads nodding in agreement all over the room. Mr. Gerrity raised his hand. "I'd be happier if we could send the snake out of state. That way if he escapes, he won't find his way to Fort Myers Beach again."

Cynthia Mays concurred. "Excellent suggestion. We will focus on trying to find a location out of state."

A man two rows in front of us raised his hand. "I don't see Fish and Wildlife here. Who's gonna catch the sucker?"

The doctor smiled. "I'll let my colleague, Mark Clamenta, answer that."

Bridgy leaned in and whispered, "What does Mark know about snakes?"

Chapter Thirty

Mark Clamenta joined Cynthia right at the edge of the audience. "Hi, all. My name is Mark Clamenta and I've lived on this island for decades. I used to run a fishing boat off San Carlos Island. Now I'm retired and enjoying life, but nearly fifty years ago I spent some time in the jungles of Vietnam. Anyone else?"

A voice from somewhere up near Miguel called out, "Da Nang, 1970."

Mark gave the man a full salute. "Then you know, brother. Nam vets are at home with snakes."

The vet gave a high thumbs-up. "Damn straight."

Mark smiled. "We have veterans with service time spanning from World War II through the Iraq and Afghanistan wars. They belong to associations that meet in this church. I've spoken to the leadership of each group and everyone is interested in helping. Even as we are here talking, there are vets hunting down the equipment we'll need to find and capture the snake."

"Then what?" A voice came from the Guy Bradley seats.

"Along with Dr. Mays, we will secure the snake until arrangements can be made to transport it off island and out of our lives."

Cordelia Ramer stood, hands on hips and shouted, "And if none of your fancy snake zoos will take the anaconda, then what?"

Mark took a step toward her and I was actually looking forward to the confrontation, but Dr. Mays touched Mark's arm and crossed in front of him to get closer to the Guy Bradley ladies. "There are dozens of snake zoos all over the world. We will find the anaconda a home." She took a deep breath and swiveled her head to the other side of the room. "Any more questions?"

Several hands shot up.

In short order, Dr. Mays and Mark Clamenta established a committee to set up a round robin for telephone information to be sent out as quickly as possible. Bridgy volunteered to join that working group.

Not to be outdone, I volunteered to work on compiling a list of snake zoos. According to Dr. Mays we'd go for those most likely to be interested in the anaconda first and work from there.

After settling that the temporary shelter in Dr. Mays's office would continue to be supported by volunteers, Blondie Quinlin and another Guy Bradley member raised their hands and signed on. I wondered if Miss Augusta was annoyed that her animal allergies kept her from helping.

Pastor John stood and gave one sharp clap. "Well, that

settles it, folks. It looks like we've made great progress, and life on the island will get back to normal in a very short time. Thank you all for coming."

Before he got the last syllable out of his mouth, people were shuffling their chairs, standing and heading for the door.

I turned toward a familiar voice. "Wait. I have an announcement."

Everyone stopped, wondering what we hadn't covered.

Miguel gave his name and address and pointed to Mr. Gerrity. "This is my neighbor, Liam Gerrity. We both own pets who like the outdoors and we live in the two houses at the end of Orange Gate Drive beside the bay. We are so grateful that everyone has come together to protect all the pets, we have decided to celebrate with a cornhole party as soon as the anaconda is caught and shipped. Every volunteer will be invited. We will make sure to give every committee chair the details to pass along."

A big cheer went up in the room, followed by a round of clapping. Bridgy and I looked at each other. Cornhole? Miguel was surrounded by people, so we decided to head out, pick up my Heap-a-Jeep from Dr. Mays's parking lot and call it a day.

When we arrived at the Read 'Em and Eat the next morning, Bridgy marched right into the kitchen to ask Miguel about cornhole. I followed along.

"You're a chef. It's a food, right?"

He laughed as if he was sure she was teasing. "You never heard of cornhole?"

We both shook our heads.

"You come to the party and you will learn." And he bent his head to the veggies he was chopping and ignored us until we took the hint, put on our aprons and got to work.

Later that morning, George called to thank me for arranging a day out for Regina and O'Mally. "It was so friendly of Bridgy's aunt to take them along on her outing to that park, Ding Darling."

I bit my tongue. This was probably not the best time to teach George the difference between a park and a refuge, so I segued. "What are your plans for the day?"

"Well, Owen Reston and another lawyer from his veterans' legal defense group are going to go with me to meet with Goddard Swerling. I think they are in the best position to read him the riot act. I don't have the strength."

My heart broke to hear him so dejected. "How is Alan?"

"He's getting good care and seems more lucid each day, so I think that his arrest will come shortly. Too bad. I was hoping to take him to the condo for a few days. Give him a little normalcy."

I wished him luck, put my phone on vibrate and got to work.

The café was at its busiest. We had no tangible lull between breakfast and lunch. Not one table stayed vacant for more than a minute or two. Lunch was at full throttle when my phone vibrated in my pocket. I ignored it but when it vibrated for the third time in five minutes, I pulled it out and took a look. Ophie.

I waved the phone at Bridgy and then slipped out the front door. "What is it? How are Regina and O'Mally managing?"

"Everything is hunky-dory, but I wouldn't be surprised if that O'Mally doesn't skin Cordelia Ramer alive. Why,

Cordelia actually nagged at us to stop lollygagging and tend to our petitions. Who put her in charge?"

I, for one, was sure the Guy Bradley ladies did, but I didn't reply. I looked to heaven. Would Ophie ever get to the point?

Finally she did, sort of. "It is hot as blazes out here. Not a breeze to be had. So of course, every time I was able to drag Regina and O'Mally away from Cruella de Vil and her petition drive, I'd take them for a walk on a shady path and show off our flora and fauna. Did you know there are more than two hundred thirty species of birds in the refuge?"

"Ophie, we're busy here."

"Sorry, honey chile. Guess who I saw trying to be all smoochy smoochy–like with a man who wasn't having it?"

I wasn't up for an episode of *Entertainment Tonight*. If Ophie thought interrupting my day to report some vacationing celebrities seeking privacy was a priority . . . well I had no answer.

"Okay, don't guess. It was that part-time waitress you hired. The college girl. But he was no college boy, I can tell you that."

Why would I care about Elaine Tibor's love life? "Ophie, listen . . ."

"No. Y'all listen. At first, I thought they were cozy looking but Augusta said the girl was a might too possessive, clingy, you know. I think Blondie got it right when she said the fellow looked a tad uncomfortable. Like he'd rather be anywhere else but here."

I could hear the pride in her voice, like she'd dropped the bombshell of the century right in my lap.

"Ophie. I have to get back to work. Elaine is a single young woman. She can do as she likes."

"Don't y'all want to know who she was doing 'as she likes' with?"

I heaved a long and wistful sigh. Anything to end this call. "Okay. Who was she with?"

"Well, I didn't recognize him at first. But O'Mally knew right on. She grabbed Regina's arm and said, 'That's the man whose wife was murdered. What is he doing with that girl?' And then I took a closer look and I recognized him from the evening news. It was Tanya Lipscome's husband. Definitely. Y'all better tell Ryan and that handsome lieutenant."

"Ophie, we're really busy. Can't you tell them? You're the witness, after all."

"Much as I like the title, we're here on a mission. Y'all get a break sooner or later. Call Ryan then. Gotta go." And she clicked off.

Give her an assignment. The one sure way to get Ophie off the phone. I rushed back inside the café and pitched in to help Bridgy, who was practically roller skating around the room, serving and bussing at warp speed to pick up my slack.

A couple of hours flew by before I noticed an empty table. Then two. The rush was subsiding gradually at first, and then all at once we were down to two tables with folks who were lingering more than eating. Bridgy came out of the kitchen and signaled me to meet her at the counter. She set down a fresh pitcher of lemonade and then pulled some papers out of her pocket. "I know you don't want to talk about the ice machine, but Royal has a really good one on sale right now. And ours is at the end of its rainbow." She slid a piece of paper across the glossy countertop. "I did a lot of checking. Miguel even introduced me to the manager of the country club."

"You're kidding, right? I would think the club was a place you'd avoid."

She tossed me a dismissive wave. "We went a while ago. Long before our little adventure with Barry Baby."

My head snapped up, Bridgy's ice machine purchase forgotten. "OMG."

Bridgy waggled her fingers, signaling me to lower my voice, which I did. I lowered to an absolute whisper. "Ophie called."

"Oh Lord. They didn't get arrested, did they? I thought last night's meeting had cooled things down. I swear I will slap that Cordelia Ramer . . ."

"No arrests, at least none that I know of. Ophie, Augusta and Blondie took the Mersky girls on a side tour of Ding Darling, you know, looking at birds, turtles, frogs and butterflies. And who do you think they saw off in the trees all alone and snuggly?"

Bridgy was quick, I give her that. "Don't tell me. Barry Baby?" She glanced behind me. "Hold that thought." She hustled a check over to the couple sitting at Hemingway. Then she stood at the register, getting more impatient by the moment until they finally strolled over and paid.

Bridgy smiled and gave them a cheerful, "Enjoy the rest of your day," and then made a beeline back to me. "So, who is she? Do we know? Did Ophie recognize her? Spill."

"Oh, we definitely know her. Your Barry Baby was playing footsie on a side path at Ding Darling National Refuge with . . ." I tapped out a rather dramatic drumroll on the countertop. "Elaine Tibor."

Bridgy gave such a startled yelp that we both looked over at the three people sitting at Agatha Christie, but they were deep in conversation and didn't pay us any mind.

"I thought she was fooling around with Ellison." Bridgy's whisper had an edge of steel.

"Tutoring. She said tutoring."

Bridgy tut-tutted. "I *know* what she said but I thought it was code, like booty call."

"How do you get booty call out of tutoring? Honestly, Bridgy. Let's focus here. Could having an affair with Elaine Tibor be a motive for Barry Baby to kill his wife?"

Bridgy shook her head. "I'm not sure. I think he's a dog. Remember how he flirted with me the other day? I peg him as one of those 'any port in a storm' types. His son's tutor is a young girl and she's around a lot, so he thought he'd give it a whirl. Nothing serious."

My turn to tut-tut. "Work with me here. I'm trying to find a reason for anyone other than Alan to be the murderer."

Bridgy looked at the big round clock over the door and waved her arm to erase our conversation. "You have the Teen Book Club meeting today. Time to get ready. We can hunt for motives after the kids leave."

I glanced at the clock and saw she was right. I pushed Tanya Trouble's murder to the back of my mind. Well, not too far back.

Chapter Thirty-one

Holly Latimer and two of her high school classmates arrived early for the Teen Book Club. They sat down at Emily Dickenson, dropping book bags all around them.

I took out my order pad. "Hungry, ladies?"

"Grumbly-stomach hungry. Today is early lunch day because we have double-session Advanced Placement Math. We haven't eaten in hours. I swear I could absolutely faint." The girl with sun-bleached brown hair pulled back in a ponytail that reached her waist wrapped her arms across her stomach and doubled over.

I recalled that her name was Angela and she had a flair for the dramatic, so I humored her. "Sounds serious. Do you need menus?"

The girls telepathically tossed the question to one another and eye vibed the answer. "No, we're in synch. Your menu items have such fabu names, we never forget the ones we like."

The curly-haired blonde whose name I didn't know beamed a smile, and I noticed that the bands on her braces were a very patriotic red and blue, pulling back snowy white teeth. "I want a *Swiss Family Robinson* Cheeseburger. You know I love those cheeseburgers so much that I finally read the book. Obvi, it was mad awesome or I would have given up the burgers."

After some delightful teenaged giggling, Angela gave me a nod. "I'll have the same. Medium rare. Extra onions."

"Eww. Onions. Who'll want to kiss you with onion breath?"

Angela reached back and pulled her ponytail over her right shoulder. "You'd be surprised."

The giggles moved up several levels to gales of laughter. As it subsided, I looked at Holly, who asked if it was too late in the day for eggs.

"Never too late. How would you like them cooked?"

"*Green Eggs and Ham.* Hashtag *salsa verde* yum."

I took their drink order and came back with two waters and a sweet tea. When I thought of all the sugary drinks that I drank growing up, I was always surprised by the number of kids who came into the café and ordered water. Then again, so did their parents.

As I set the glasses down, the girls did that "talk to one another without saying a word" thing again. Then Holly muttered, "Angie" under her breath. Angela reached over and tapped Holly's arm saying, "No. You." The blonde stared out the window like she was sitting alone and waiting for someone.

Holly gave a decisive nod and took a deep breath. "Sassy, we were wondering if you needed any help, like, with finding Mrs. Lipscome's killer."

"I'm not looking for any killer." I crossed my fingers behind my back.

"Sure you are. And look what happened the last time we had a killer on the island. Nearly killed you, too."

I so wished people would stop reminding me about that. I found myself quoting Aunt Ophie. "Well-mannered ladies do not inject themselves into dangerous situations." I shook my finger in their faces and used the sternest voice I possessed. "You stay out of this. I am leaving the investigating to the deputies. You are to do the same."

Only the little blonde looked the least bit bothered by my harangue. Holly and Angela were bouncing happily in their seats. They looked at each other, did the metal-telepathy thing and then Holly yelped. "Too late. We already helped."

My knees actually buckled. I sat in the one vacant chair at their table. "You did what?"

"We helped."

All three girls were nodding at me like bobblehead dolls at hurricane speed.

I looked directly into Holly's eyes. "And what did your mother say?"

Ah, the power of "mom." The very thought got the girls squirming in their seats.

Holly looked at the salt and pepper shakers for a while. "We didn't tell our moms. Not because we're afraid to get into trouble or anything. We wanted to tell you first."

Again, the bobbleheads.

I was horrified at the thought of these girls doing . . . I don't know what. So I asked. "Please tell me exactly what you did so I can gauge the danger. And I will have to speak to each of your mothers. You understand that, right?"

The bobbleheads slowed to a more somber up-down, up-down. Full stop.

"Everyone knows that our neighbor Mr. Ertz, the wrestler guy, threatened Mrs. Lipscome. I even heard him once. Mega-loud and double cranky."

Bridgy came out of the kitchen and brought the girls' food order to the table. I pointed to Holly. "*Green Eggs and Ham.*" Then I swung my finger to Angela. "Extra onions." The final plate went to the curly blonde.

The girls started to open napkins and pick up cutlery. They realized I'd gone silent and looked at me, confusion in three sets of eyes. I nodded. They began eating with massive enthusiasm. I guessed they were right about lunch being far too early.

I was short on patience and I knew the other kids would be showing up very soon for the Teen Book Club. I needed answers. I gave them a few minutes and then said, "Okay, let's talk while you eat. Holly?"

"So, you know I live right across form Mr. Ertz. We"— she circled her hand around the table to indicate her coconspirators—"were on my patio and FaceTiming from my iPod Touch—it's fifth generation—to Angie's mad-awesome iPad."

Angela pulled a hot pink case out of her backpack and set it on the table. "Totes fabu, right?"

Fabulous though her new iPad may be, I was more concerned about whatever trouble the girls might have wandered into on their devices, so I asked the evident question. "Who did you FaceTime?"

All three girls rolled their eyes in perfect synchronization. Then Holly tried again. "I *told* you. Me and Angie. We Face-Timed each other."

Clearly I was losing my ability to understand. "I thought

we were talking about some, well, some investigating you'd done. Now you tell me you were on FaceTime while sitting next to each other on the patio. Sorry, not following."

Holly slowed down as if she was explaining to a two-year-old. "Okay, so, we set up the FaceTime and then we went to play soccer in the street. Daphne"—she indicated the blonde—"kicked the ball into Mr. Ertz's side yard, and then I ran in to get it and propped my iPod Touch up against the patio screen. Mr. Ertz and the man in the slick suit went right on talking."

Light was beginning to dawn. "And you three listened in on the iPad."

"Now you're catching on. They were talking about Mrs. Lipscome. The man we didn't know said that the world would be a better place without her. I mean, really, who says things like that?

"Mr. Ertz called her a female dog, you know, the 'B word.' Said he was glad the 'B word' was dead. Then the other man told Mr. Ertz not to talk like that otherwise the sheriff would consider him a suspect."

The door opened and the other three members of the Teen Book Club came in. I waved them to the book corner and Holly dropped her voice to a whisper. "Mr. Ertz said, 'Don't worry, they can't prove a thing.' Then he laughed like . . . like a jackal howling at the moon. It was scary."

I stood, ready to let the girls eat in peace and get the other young clubbies settled, when Angie said, "Wait. We took a screenshot." And she let her fingers walk around her iPad screen until she pulled up a picture. At first I thought it was grainy but then I realized I was looking at two pairs of legs through the mesh of the patio wall.

Holly said, "The hairy legs belong to Mr. Ertz. We don't know the man in the pants."

I looked closely. Gray sharkskin dress slacks. Goddard Swerling. He might have been there about the swimming pool lawsuit, but I knew for sure civil law wasn't his only area of expertise. Was his criminal law practice the real reason for their meeting?

I stood and motioned to the girls' plates. "Finish up and I'll stall the meeting with a plate of cookies."

Sounding like the little girl she was when I first met her, Holly asked, "You're not mad at us, are you, Sassy?"

I couldn't help but smile. "No. Not mad. Just worried for your safety. Let it go for now. Eat up."

The two boys sitting in the book nook nearly jumped on the plate of chocolate chip cookies I passed around. Jenna, who was the youngest of the teen group, took one and said, "No more, thank you."

They were still munching when the three teen detectives joined us. After some shifting of chairs and rummaging through backpacks, we were ready to talk about *Treasure Island*. Angela held up her hand, then remembering we were far less formal than school, asked, "Who picked this book? I wasn't here last month and I would have x-ed it right off the list."

Larry, a muscular boy who played tackle football and was an expert long-board surfer answered. "Me. I suggested the book. What's your problem?"

Angela grimaced. "Surfer dude. I should have known."

"Known what?" he snapped back.

"You'd pick a boy book all about pirates and sailing and such. We promised no girl books, no boy books."

I hadn't foreseen this dustup, but before I could interfere,

Holly offered an opinion. "It's not a boy book. *Treasure Island* is an adventure book. I don't know about you, but I love adventure."

Daphne agreed. "Sure. Girls love adventure. Like with the iPad, iPod thingy." She went no further, because Holly's glare stopped her in her tracks.

Jenna piped in, "Oh, new app? Tell me later."

Angela and Larry sent air daggers with their eyes and then pretended the other didn't exist for the next hour until Angela said, "Jim Hawkins was younger than we are and he had the courage to go on the *Hispaniola* with that violent and dirty crew. And then the mutiny! Even though he's just a kid, he is majorly loyal to Captain Smollett and Squire Trelawney. Hard-core, really hard-core."

Larry tilted until his shoulder touched Julio, who was sitting between him and me. Then he stage-whispered, "I thought she said it was a boy book. I thought she didn't like it."

Julio said, "I know, man." But I was probably the only one to hear him since Angela roared back, "I never said I didn't like *Treasure Island*. I only wanted to know who chose it."

I held up my hand. "Stop. Right now. You two can argue later if you wish, but we are not going to waste our time listening to you." I plastered a bright, cheery smile on my face. "Now whose turn is it to pick the next book?"

You'd think I asked them to walk on jellyfish. Not a word. Finally I picked up the cookie platter and passed it around. "Okay, finish these off. I'll pick the next book and email the name to you later on today. Anyone change their email addy lately? No? Good."

Bridgy met me at the counter. "What was that all about?"

I shrugged. "Who knows? Might be young love. Remember

how you and Mary Baronne's brother fought all through our junior year of high school and then he asked you to the Bishop Ford High School prom?"

"I forgot all about that. I do remember that I had a good time, but I think that was because Mary went with somebody so we hung out. How did we not rope you into coming along?"

"I was 'going steady' with what's-his-name, remember? He didn't go to Bishop Ford."

The kids finished their cookies and gathered their pile of books and bags and backpacks.

When Holly came over to say good-bye, I said, "Tell your mother I'm going to call later, or she can call me when it's convenient for her. You might want to talk to her first."

Holly, completely resigned to the inevitability that her mother would have to be told about the escapade involving Mr. Ertz, was back to her usual bubbly self. "No probs. I'll talk to her and ask her to call you."

She turned to give me a final wave as she and her friends bounded out the door.

My first thought was, if Lieutenant Frank Anthony was irritated when he thought Pastor John and a few veterans might wind up acting like what he called the "Estero Boulevard Irregulars," I could only imagine that he would go ballistic at the thought of three teenaged girls spying on suspects, real or imagined. I'd have to talk to the moms. I decided to call George while I waited to hear from Maggie.

Chapter Thirty-two

Before I got a chance to take my phone out of my pocket, Miguel came out of the kitchen, looking for the teens.

"I should have known they were gone. It is so quiet. I'm sorry I missed them. Holly and her two friends volunteer at the temporary animal shelter and I was hoping to recruit some of the others. Dr. Mays could use the help."

I thought Jenna wouldn't be a problem, but I suggested that if he wanted to invite the boys, he might get a better response if the girls weren't around when he asked.

Miguel laughed as he headed for the front door. "Ah, having been a teenaged boy, I well remember the fear instilled by teenaged girls. *Mañana, chica*." And he was gone.

I called and got George's voice mail. I left what I hoped was a cheerful message and then began wiping down the tables and chairs. A few minutes later my phone rang. When

I punched "Talk," it was Maggie. Holly hadn't wasted any time in confessing her escapade.

"Thanks so much for ending the girls' detective careers before they got into serious trouble. I can't image what they were thinking. Otto Ertz has a very short fuse. Why don't you and Bridgy come over later? I can show you the lay of the land and you can see for yourself how close the girls came to getting into real trouble."

I told her I was waiting to hear from George but Bridgy and I could probably stop by. No point in mentioning that I'd already scoped out Moon Shell Drive not once, but twice, with very little in the way of results. If the residents had secrets, the street wasn't giving them up.

While we were doing the final spit-and-polish cleaning for the day, once again, Bridgy brought up the dreaded ice machine. I pulled the paper from my pocket and looked at the numbers with the hope that the cost was less than I remembered. It wasn't. "This will absolutely break the bank, but if you and Miguel are sure we need to replace ours, this is a great buy compared to the prices we saw the other day. Order it, but make sure delivery is late afternoon so we don't have the mess of installing when we have customers."

Bridgy gave me her "How stupid do you think I am?" look, but at least there were no hands-on-hips poses involved.

We were putting the cleaning supplies in the cabinet when I mentioned that Maggie had invited us to take another look at Moon Shell Drive. I was surprised the usually sociable Bridgy was reluctant.

She was vague about her plans. "I have chores and I need you to go with me."

"Okay, but can't we stop by Maggie's first?"

Bridgy went outside to make a phone call. When she came back she said we could stretch half an hour but no more. As I turned out the lights she said, "I mean it, Sassy. I'm on a schedule."

When we turned onto Moon Shell Drive, I said it was beginning to be as familiar as our own street. Bridgy didn't find me to be amusing. I hoped once we got her "chores" done, she'd be in a better mood. Bridgy parked her fire engine red Escort ZX2 right in front of Maggie's house. I panicked for a moment, fearing that Barry Lipscome would see it and our cover would be blown, but then I realized that, a) the last time we were here I was driving the Heap-a-Jeep, and b) who cares?

Holly came running out to greet us. "My mom and Aunt Karen are on the patio. Come on in."

I looked at Bridgy, who tapped her imaginary wristwatch but followed along behind Holly.

The patio ran along the side of the house that faced Estero Bay. I took in the wide expanse of scrub pines and sea grape bushes. I pointed to a couple of small trees that were dwarfed by palms. "Those are unusual trees."

"Not so unusual along the edge of the bay. Called devilwood—they're from the olive family. They bloom tiny white flowers for about a minute near the end of spring." Maggie gestured us to seats around a table covered with a cheerful cloth decorated with waves and seagulls. "I thought you might want a drink before we explore."

I didn't even have to look at Bridgy. "We're short on time. Chores, you know." I thought Karen was looking well and said so.

"Oh, I feel great. Running at a hundred percent. I'm sort of stalling, hanging out with my sis for a while longer before

253

I have to go back to the real world. You know—the home, work, home, work cycle."

We all laughed. We knew the feeling.

Maggie stood. "Well, let's take a look around."

When Holly started to rise from her chair, Maggie ordered, "Sit."

Maggie opened the patio door facing the bay, and we stepped out into a small clearing with flowerpots scattered around. Most were filled with greens. I pointed to one that was overflowing with gray-green leaves and golden yellow flowers. "Those are pretty."

Maggie smiled. "I keep them for color. Clustered rockrose blooms year-round in south Florida. No matter what stage the other flowering plants are in—I always have sunshiny blossoms." She motioned to the road. "The first house you pass coming into the street is Cordy Ramer's. Next to it is Otto's. You can't see the Lipscomes' walled-in property from either of their houses or yards. Can't see it from here, either. Only the wall. So no one on this block could have witnessed anything. Unless the killer parked a car outside the Lipscomes' driveway gate. That we would notice."

I nodded. A parked car on this block would definitely stand out. Maggie walked about two feet past the turn in the road and stopped abruptly. "This is my property line. The rest of the waterfront land belongs to the Lipscomes. This is where they want to build the pool and block everyone's view of the bay. Well, Cordy and Otto's view. I'd still have a straight view from the house and a full expanse to the north, but my view to the south would be nonexistent."

We walked a few more steps. I stared at the wall ahead

of us. "So anything could happen behind that wall and no one could see a thing."

"Well, unless you were in the house, or, say, in a helicopter hovering above." Bridgy thought she was funny but I was totally perplexed by the lack of any way to even see the scene of the crime. Somehow, I thought if I could see it, something would trigger a clue of some sort. Too many mystery books, I guess.

Maggie walked us back to the car. We asked her to say good-bye to Karen and Holly. Sotto voce I asked, "How much trouble is Holly in?"

"Just enough to keep her from pulling any stupid trick like that again."

I'd barely fastened my seat belt when Bridgy tore away from the curb. She kept looking at the clock on the dash. When she came very close to running a red light for the second time, I complained. "Whatever it is, we can be a little late."

She shook her head. "No can do. I made an appointment and then I rescheduled it for half an hour later. I don't want to miss it."

She was heading north. I thought we were going over the San Carlos Bridge but we zipped right past it. Bridgy didn't stop until we were in Bowditch Point Park, and she slid into a parking spot outside of Tony's marina.

She looked at the clock and banged her hand on the steering wheel. "Yes. We made it."

I looked at her and shook my head emphatically. "I am not going kayaking. Much as I love it, today is not the day."

"I promise there will be no kayaks used in this investigation." Bridgy's impish grin led me to suspect that kayaks might be the least of my worries.

"Investigation? Investigation of what?"

"Just get out of the car and follow my lead. For goodness' sake don't contradict anything I say. Oh, and if anyone wishes you a happy birthday, say thank you."

I pushed my sunglasses up on my forehead so I could stare her down, but she dismissed me by saying, "Put on your sunglasses. You're going to need them."

We got out of the car and she led the way to the dock. Tony, the proprietor, a large, jovial man with a more-gray-every-day Poirot-type mustache, clapped when he saw us. "Right on time. That's how I like my customers. And where . . . Oh there she is, the birthday girl. Happy birthday, missy. You are in for quite an adventure." He pushed his straw porkpie hat a little farther down his forehead. "You must be really super friends for Bridgy here to arrange such a whoo-hoo birthday present."

Bridgy gave him a beatific smile. "Friends since childhood. There's nothing I wouldn't do for Sassy."

My smile was not nearly as beatific. It was more like grinning through a clenched jaw. What on earth was going on? Then I saw it. A snazzy green and yellow powerboat was sitting dockside. It had a cage and rigging up top that I would have recognized even if the boat didn't have the word "PARASAIL" printed on the hull. It was followed by a phone number. An extremely tan boater about forty or so jumped off the deck. He was wearing surfer shorts and a tank top that matched the yellow and green of the boat exactly.

"Hey, Cousin Tony, these must be our girls, right?" He made it sound like we were blind dates for the Saturday night movie. "And which one a yous is the birthday beauty?"

Timidly, I raised my hand. But there was nothing timid about the birthday smooch he gave me.

Tony growled. "Darrin, these *ladies* are my friends."

That was enough to make Darrin drop his hands from my waist but it didn't stop his banter. "Okay, Cos, but they're gonna have to go up in tandem. There's no way either of these fine ladies weighs a buck and a quarter." He turned to us. "That's the minimum weight for a single rider." And suddenly he was all business. "Okay, birthday princess, I know this is a surprise present for you, so let me explain the drill. First off, we usually don't run in the bay because of the San Carlos Bridge. That's why my dock is on the Gulf side of the island. No bridge." He looked at us, apparently expecting some acknowledgment of the wisdom of his location.

I did the "smile through the clenched jaw" thing again and muttered. "Smart."

He beamed like a three-year-old who'd wangled an extra cookie out of Mom. "But Bridgy here insisted that you always talk about how you long to see Matanzas Pass Preserve from above and she thought . . ." Here he puffed out his chest. "She thought parasailing would be the most exciting, close-to-nature way to give you a spectacular view for your birthday."

My jaw was aching from all the smiling my role as "birthday princess" required. Still I managed to catch Bridgy's eye and shoot daggers at her. She responded with a wide-eyed "what's your problem" look; all the while we both pretended to listen to the annoying Darrin drone on.

My attention swiveled back to Darrin when I heard him say that his deck hand was on vacation. No way we were getting on that boat alone with him. Tony gave us a wide grin. "I'm going to be the fill-in. And that means I'll watch out for your safety and take your pictures when you are five hundred feet above the boat."

I gasped audibly. Five hundred feet? In the air?

Bridgy gave me a quick elbow to the ribs and I put my "birthday princess" smile back into play.

Tony handed us each a lifejacket and surprised me by putting one on himself. Darrin said, "Hey, no Mae West for me?"

Tony chided him by suggesting that Darrin had any number of vests on board and should wear one of his own. Then Tony held out a hand to help Bridgy and me climb onto the boat. It was gorgeous and extremely pristine. No matter how haphazardly Darrin treated people, he treated his boat with loving care.

As if to prove my thoughts, Darrin got a glow in his eye telling us that she was the love of his life, an Ocean Pro 31. "And she's a winchboat—I can launch and retrieve parasailers by a winch system," he pointed aft. "See, there it is. Safe as a cradle."

But all I kept thinking about was being five hundred feet in the air with Darrin at the controls. If we didn't die during this caper, I decided I would kill Bridgy as soon as we were back on dry land.

Chapter Thirty-three

With our lifejackets firmly secure, we sat on the deck as the boat glided into the bay. Darrin had named her *Flyin' High*. And soon Bridgy and I would be testing out the name. The water was smooth as glass. Darrin kept telling us how lucky we were there was no breeze at all. "One good gust is all it takes—give you a right tumble."

Awk! "You mean we could fall if there is a sudden burst of wind?"

Bridgy rolled her eyes at me. "Honestly, Sassy."

Darrin tried not to laugh but it was an effort. He did guffaw a time or two before answering. "You don't have to worry, birthday princess, the wind would only give you a jiggle or two. I know my ROPES."

That was comforting. I supposed he meant that he'd examined his towline before coming to pick us up. Still I asked,

"Exactly which ropes did you check? Are you sure nothing is frayed?"

That sent Darrin and Tony into gales of laughter. When Darrin was able to speak coherently, he explained. "Not to worry, honey, ROPES is the acronym for the Coast Guard safety alert for parasail operators. Remember, Observe, Prepare, Ensure and Safety. I check the boat, the chute, harness and rigging, even the weather under those guidelines before every trip."

My nerves were still edgy but being on the water always had a calming effect on me, and this ride was no different. The few clouds in the sky were white and puffy like cotton balls that had tumbled out of their plastic bag.

A flock of blue herons flew across the bay from San Carlos Island and disappeared behind the trees on Estero Island. Somewhere a red-shouldered hawk was screeching *kee yarr, kee yarr.* I couldn't identify the fish swimming a few yards out from the boat, but I'd bet Tony and Darrin could. I was about to ask when Darrin began explaining our adventure.

"I'm going to secure your harnesses now while Tony steers the boat. Then I'll steer until we pass under the San Carlos Bridge. Once we have gone a ways on the far side, Tony will take over the boat and I'll clip your harnesses to the chute. Like I said, you two can go up in tandem. Once you are secure, I'll operate the winch. You'll rise in the sky smooth as silk, swaying like you're rocking in my granny's old chair."

Bridgy tilted toward me. "Nothing to do now but enjoy the ride."

I mumbled in agreement. Since we were heading south in Estero Bay, I was getting a glimmer of Bridgy's reason for us to parasail along the shore. Knowing her, it wasn't for the sake of adventure. I decided to play along. "I can't imagine what we'll see when we're up so high."

Bridgy started ticking off on her fingers. "Well, there's Matanzas Pass Preserve. I know you do love it. And I'm sure we'll be able to see the library, Pastor John's church, Dr. Mays's clinic." Then she added with an extra touch of innocence in her voice. "Probably be able to see our yoga instructor Maggie's house. Isn't it right on the edge of the bay?"

Bingo. Bridgy had figured out a way for us to see inside the walls surrounding the Lipscome house with nobody being the wiser. I gave her a kiss on the cheek. "You're the best friend ever. What a fabulous birthday present."

Tony beamed. "Ah, finally getting into the spirit of things. Happy to see it. Okay, we've passed under the bridge. I'm going to take over so Darrin can get you safely launched."

Darrin checked our harnesses. As we sat side by side, Bridgy teased Darrin. "Double-check everything, please. I don't want this to be the last birthday present I give Sassy."

"You'll be fine, and I suggest you let me give you a quick dip, sort of drag your toes in the water. Calm enough day for it." By the looks on our faces, Darrin decided he might have gone a bit too far. "Tell you what, when you feel yourselves dropping slowly and safely, yell 'boat' and I'll bring you back onto the boat. If you don't yell, I'll give you a dip, raise you up again and then bring you back on the boat. Good enough?" I nodded with far less enthusiasm than I felt a few minutes before. Darrin wasn't finished. "Okay, kick off your shoes. Good. Now give me your phones."

Bridgy started to protest but Darrin persuaded her by saying that not a week went by when some parasailer or another lost a phone because it rang and "The darn fool tried to answer it, way up there." And he flung a hand skyward for good measure.

We surrendered our phones and soon felt ourselves begin to rise. In a few minutes we were high above the boat and could see everything for miles around.

I didn't know how far our voices would carry so I whispered to Bridgy, "You're brilliant. We'll see every inch of the Lipscome property. This is like a close-up on Google Earth."

She agreed. "All true but now 'ohh' and 'aah' and smile like a good birthday princess. Tony has the camera out and he is snapping away."

So we smiled and waved. Tony pointed to our right and shouted up to us. "The preserve. See the oak hammock ecosystem."

I gave him my broadest smile and yelled, "Awesome."

Finally we traveled past the preserve. I could see the parking lot of Pastor John's church filled with cars. A lot of people were milling about. I elbowed Bridgy. "Was there an event scheduled at the church today?"

But if she answered, I never heard her. From high in the air I could see the bay front of the church and the bay front of the Lipscome property seemingly only a few feet apart. More startling, I could see that the wall that enclosed the compound had two breaks on the bay side. A wide opening by the Lipscome dock and a narrow one by the hot tub. There weren't even gates. If I wasn't in a parachute harness, I would have jumped up and down in my seat. But as it was, I didn't actually have a seat.

I smiled and waved to Tony while talking to Bridgy through my teeth. "Look. There are openings in the back wall."

"I see. Do you see the path a few feet in from the waterline?

It goes north past John's church and south to . . . wherever. Anyone could walk into the property and murder Tanya without having to park a car on the street."

I was trying to memorize the entire layout when Tony told us to prepare for Darrin to turn the boat around. Prepare? I guess he meant hang on tight.

We made a slow, wide swing in the bay, which gave me time to memorize the entire shoreline for the span of a couple of football fields on either side of the Lipscome house. I couldn't help but notice the crowd in the church parking lot getting larger by the minute. I wondered if I could talk Bridgy into taking a ride to find out what was going on. Then maybe we could follow the path to the Lipscome house. Lost in thought, it took me some time to realize that we were going lower and lower. Darrin was using the winch to bring us back to the boat. Without warning our feet splashed into the water. I screamed more from the shock than anything else. I'd forgotten that Darrin promised us a dip. Bridgy was laughing and clapping. Her joy was so contagious, I joined in.

Then Darrin raised us up and landed us safely on the deck, unhooked us from the bar connected to the chute and asked how we liked it.

We both rushed to overdo our quotient of "most fabulous ride ever." But apparently no amount of praise was too over the top for Darrin. He was basking in the glow and could easily have listened to us go on for hours.

Before our voices gave out, Tony saved us by asking, "Did you happen to notice the big doings down at the church?"

"I did." I was sliding my feet into my sandals. "We were wondering if there was a party and we weren't invited."

"Maybe it's a surprise for your birthday," Darrin chimed in. I blushed. I'd forgotten my cover story.

Tony saw my pink cheeks and gave Darrin a sharp look. "Don't be teasing the girl on her birthday." He turned to me and Bridgy. "Those vets meet at the church all the time for this and that. Well, they did this whole town a right solid. They captured the green anaconda that's been swimming around here for weeks."

My eyes popped. "They caught the snake? Are you sure?"

"Sure I'm sure. Couple of fellas come by and borrowed some equipment from me yesterday. When I heard what they were fixing to do, I was happy to lend it. Mine ain't the only business in town suffering 'cause folks are afraid of the snake."

"Not to mention the pets," Bridgy contributed helpfully.

"Did they kill it or capture it?" Either way there could be some more confrontations around town.

"Heard just a bit ago that they brought the snake in. Couldn't find out more 'cause I was helping with your birthday surprise."

"Well I thank you for that, I really do." I shook hands with Tony and Darrin, then I turned to Bridgy, who already had her purse open. "I'll let you settle up and meet you by the car."

As soon as I was off the dock, I whipped out my iPhone. Hit speed dial for Miguel. He answered in half a ring. "*Hola chica*. Bow is safe. The snake is captured and leaving Florida forever."

I didn't realize how much stress I was feeling about the anaconda until I heard Miguel, and my entire body flooded with relief. "Wonderful. Are you at the church?"

"*Sí*, everyone is here. Come. Celebrate."

Bridgy found me by the car. She raised one eyebrow.

"All is well. Miguel is at the church and invited us to come over."

"Hop in."

A few minutes later we pulled up in the side street next to the church. Maybe two dozen cars were parked haphazardly around the church lot, but most of the space was taken up by people laughing, joking and clinking glasses. Cordelia Ramer and her Guy Bradley contingent were walking through the crowd, passing out snacks and napkins. It reminded me of a miniature version of the annual Shrimp Festival.

We were still getting out of the car when Ophie was on top of us. Gone was her oversized tee emblazoned with the anaconda. She was feminine as can be in a light blue eyelet A-line dress with a navy blue sash and strappy navy super-high heels. "Did y'all hear? That Mark Clamenta is quite a hero, leading the team to capture the anaconda. And Dr. Mays found him a home, out of state. She's a wonder."

I was tempted to ask if Cynthia had found a home for Mark or the snake, but didn't want to risk a well-mannered ladies lecture. I was more interested in finding Miguel. Ophie did that "spin on her heels" turn that constantly amazed me, and trotted into the crowd.

I looked at Bridgy. "How does she do that without breaking her leg?"

"I don't know, but if she falls, perhaps her big strong hero Mark Clamenta will pick her up and carry her in his arms all the way to the medical center on the mainland." And Bridgy began batting her eyelashes fast and furious.

We fell out laughing until a familiar voice behind us said, "You're a little late to the party, ladies, but at least you're having fun."

Lieutenant Frank Anthony stood with his hands resting on the wide heavy belt that held his equipment. Ryan Mantoni gave us a quick wave.

I decided to take control immediately. "How is Alan Mersky doing? George is hoping to bring him home."

Frank turned his eyes heavenward as if looking for guidance as to how much he could tell, then looked directly at me. "Healthwise he is getting his balance back. Legalwise, he's in a pile of trouble."

"He's not the only person who could have killed Tanya Lipscome, you know. Plenty of people have motive. And anyone could have gotten into her property by walking along the bay path and stepping in by the dock." I settled my hands firmly on my hips, arms akimbo a la Bridgy when she's mad.

He sighed and shook his head. "I don't even want to know how you know that." And he waded into the crowded parking lot with Ryan at his heels.

Bridgy marveled. "He didn't even give you a dressing-down."

"I know. He must be very sure that the killer is not at large but safely tucked away in the hospital psych ward." That was a depressing thought, so I moved to cheerful. "C'mon, let's find Miguel."

Chapter Thirty-four

The next morning, the atmosphere in the café was joyful. Twice I caught Miguel dancing between the work counter and the stove. Then Miss Augusta and Blondie Quinlin came in chortling about the success of the Guy Bradley Environmental Action League's efforts to save the anaconda's life.

So when George came in, I shouldn't have been surprised at his mood. Although he had no interest in the snake, change was certainly in the air. It was so much more than the bright blue, green and orange Hawaiian shirt that replaced his somber New York wear. He was ecstatic. He could barely speak. When he put his hands on my waist and gave me a kiss on the cheek, I knew things had turned for the better.

"George, why are you wearing your happy face today? Have they arrested the real killer?"

I was immediately sorry I'd asked, because his shoulders

slumped and that worried big-brother look I'd seen so often lately crept across his face.

"Not yet. But the prodding from the veterans got Swerling to take his responsibility seriously and he went to court and got a judge to order bail. I'm going to make the arrangements in a little while. When Alan is released from the hospital we can bring him to stay with us at the condo, until we get him, er, settled."

"Come with me." I brought him into the kitchen to share his good news with Bridgy and Miguel, who were as excited as I was. Bridgy gave him a big ole hug and began dancing around the room.

Miguel, always practical, asked about Alan's favorite foods and insisted that he would make Alan's homecoming meal. George started some version of "we couldn't possibly impose," but Miguel refused to take no for an answer.

"It is settled, *sí*? No arguments. And don't you look chipper in your flashy shirt? This is celebration time. I insist you sit down and let me fix you something. Anything you want."

Ever the New Yorker, George joked about pastrami on rye before saying, "Those sandwiches you made us once. The meat and cheese with the pickle slices."

"Ah, a *cubano*. A Cuban sandwich. You want it to stay or to go? And what about some food for the lovely ladies?"

"I'm actually here to meet the men O'Mally happily calls Alan's defense team—Pastor John and the veterans."

Miguel looked past George and posed a question to me with his eyes. I nodded an assent. What would a few sandwiches cost us?

Miguel gave George his widest smile. "It is not good to hold a meeting on an empty stomach. I will make a platter of sandwiches. The brain works better when the stomach is happy. Go sit down. Sassy will get you a drink."

I led George to Dashiell Hammett and was handing him a glass of lemonade and a copy of the *Fort Myers Beach News* when Cady Stanton came in semi-shouting. "I have great news." Then he saw me serving George and stopped abruptly.

I hurried over and led him into the kitchen. Miguel looked up from the sandwiches he was making. "My, my, we have a lot of company today. *Qué pasa*, my friend?"

"The town turned down the pool."

He may as well have said, "The cow jumped over the moon." We all gawked at him, waiting for an explanation. When he realized that not one of us knew what he was talking about, he said, "The Lipscome pool. The project is dead . . ."

And when he recognized that the end of that sentence could easily be "dead as Tanya Lipscome," Cady dropped his eyes to the floor.

Trying to spare him embarrassment, we three all spoke at once, praising the wisdom of the town fathers and thanking Cady for telling us. I wondered if anyone else thought Tanya might still be alive if the town had acted sooner. We'd never know until we found out if the real killer turned out to be Otto Ertz or Cordelia Ramer.

I heard more voices in the dining room and peeked out the pass-through. Pastor John, Owen Reston and Mark Clamenta were circling around George, giving him pats on the back and doing that arm-punch thing men do when a team effort is going well. I was surprised there was no butt slapping, but of course this team wasn't playing a sport. They were saving a man's life.

I followed them to Dashiell Hammett and took drink orders. A refill on the lemonade for George, sweet tea for the pastor and water for the veterans. Miguel brought out a platter of Cuban sandwiches and set it on the table with a flourish. "Here, my friends. Enjoy." He looked at Mark. "Thank you once again for saving the lives of so many island pets. You must not forget to come this Sunday." He smiled at Pastor John. "Along with my neighbor Liam Gerrity, I am hosting a cornhole party to celebrate that the snake is gone from Florida forever. Later in the day. Long after the last service has ended."

Pastor said he would be delighted to come and Miguel returned to the kitchen. I stayed nearby for a bit until I was sure the men didn't require anything else. They chatted about fishing, and Mark Clamenta tried to get a commitment from George to go out on a half-day trip before he headed back north.

A trucker came in for coffee and a burger to go. When I was done serving him, I stepped back to George's table to refill glasses and bus the dirty plates and utensils. I offered coffee but no one was interested. As soon as I brought the plates into the kitchen, Miguel pointed to a plate of Robert Frost Apple and Blueberry Tartlets.

When I came out of the kitchen with the tartlets, Pastor John was waiting for me at the counter. He signaled me to come closer, so I leaned in. "I heard you went parasailing over the Lipscome house yesterday."

Ah, the island drums were beating once again. If you caught a marlin on a fishing trip two miles west of Lovers Key, there would be a dozen congratulatory messages on your answering machine before you set a foot on dry land.

Pastor continued. "You're not planning any sleuthing, are you? Sassy, we all remember what happened the last time you scurried off on your own. I want you to be assured that you are a cherished member of this community. We don't want anything *sinister* to happen to you."

I knew I was being gently chastised for past bad behavior and warned against repeating it. He didn't seem to care that by what he thought of as my risky behavior, I'd caught a killer and saved a life. Two lives if you count my own. Still I smiled, thanked him for his concern and promised I had no intention of doing anything the least bit dangerous. I didn't even have to cross my fingers because I had no clear idea of any path that would lead me or the sheriff's department to the person who killed Tanya Trouble. I really wanted to help Alan Mersky, but I had no whiz-bang ideas.

I set the plate of tartlets on the table, refilled Owen's water glass and fussed around, pretending to clean the dining room while I waited for the men to get down to brass tacks, a phrase my father used whenever someone didn't get on topic as quickly as he'd like.

Two grandmotherly ladies came in, both carrying tennis rackets. Apparently exhausted, they dropped roughly into the chairs at Robert Louis Stevenson. The older of the two had a straight gray bob and a baby pink designer tennis outfit. She pulled off her visor and began blotting her face with a wad of tissues. I was barely at the table with my order pad in hand when her not much younger friend said, "Water, please."

Judging by how red-faced they were I brought two glasses and then I filled a pitcher with water and lemon slices and set it next to the sugar bowl. The ladies drained their glasses in a few gulps. When they set the empties on the table I refilled quickly.

The lady in pink said, "Thank you. We overestimated our abilities and underestimated our ages." She shook her head. "We walked from our hotel to the tennis courts, played two sets and started to walk back, only to realize we'd run out of steam." She shook her red plastic water bottle. "And water. I finished this sometime during the second set. Are you starting to feel human again, Estelle?"

Her friend smiled. "Sure am." She turned to me. "We were mighty glad to see your little café. Time to rest and replenish as my daughter always says. May we have menus?"

I assured them that they didn't have to order anything. They were welcome to relax and sip water for as long as they liked but Estelle claimed she was famished, and her friend agreed.

I took their order for one *Green Eggs and Ham* and one *Swiss Family Robinson* Cheeseburger, then I fussed around the café straightening a chair here, aligning salt and pepper shakers there. All the time I was listening to the four men sitting in the rear of the café and debating the best defense for Alan Mersky.

The door opened again. Elaine Tibor, dressed super casually in a lemon yellow tank and denim cutoffs, waved and stopped at the counter. I realized instantly that we owed her a day's pay. I walked over to meet her. "Looking for your pay?"

She laughed. "How did you know? Grad students skimp along. Every penny counts."

"In that case, let me get your pay stub and give you cash rather than a check. Can you wait here a minute?" I went back into the office, found the pay slip I'd tacked to the bulletin board the day Elaine worked, and got out my accounts book to record the transaction. I was opening the lockbox we laughingly called our "safe" when Bridgy stuck her head in.

"What?"

"Elaine came in for her pay. With everything else I forgot all about it. I'm going to give her cash."

Bridgy gave me a broad wink. "Did you ask her about Barry Baby?"

I stuck my tongue at her and then began double counting Elaine's pay. When I was certain I had the correct amount, I tucked the money into an envelope along with her pay slip. When I pushed through the door into the dining room, Elaine had slid all the way down the counter and was avidly listening to George and his friends talking about Alan's defense.

Owen was saying, "There is no tangible physical evidence connecting Alan to Mrs. Lipscome other than the broken branch. Since Alan never locks his car and all the fingerprints on the branch were washed away in the hot tub, there is a strong chance this will never go to trial."

I had to call Elaine's name twice to get her attention but I understood why. Owen's comments would be fascinating even to someone unfamiliar with the case. Elaine clearly knew the family and would be doubly interested.

I pushed the envelope and a receipt across the countertop. "Here you go, count your money, and if you wouldn't mind signing."

Her cell phone rang. She pulled it out of her purse, took a quick look at the caller and punched the "Off" button, then glanced at the money in the envelope and signed the receipt, evidently in a great hurry. Her purse fell over and some of the contents spilled onto the counter. She scrambled to shove everything back and snapped the purse closed. But it was too late. I had seen a white gold and sparkly item.

Elaine stuffed the envelope in her pocket and nearly ran out the door, tossing "I'm late for an appointment," over her shoulder.

Not so fast, I thought. *Not so fast*. I ran into the kitchen, grabbed my keys, told Bridgy to watch the dining room and I ran out right behind Elaine. I was in the Heap-a-Jeep shifting into reverse gear when the passenger door opened and Owen Reston jumped in the seat.

"Pastor John sent me," was all he said.

I pulled out of the lot and could see Elaine's dark green Corolla a couple of blocks ahead.

Owen asked where we were going. He didn't seem surprised when I told him I had no idea. "You see that Corolla? The woman who rushed out of the café had Tanya Lipscome's fancy cigarette lighter in her purse. I'm sure of it."

"So why are we following her? She could have gotten the lighter anywhere. Maybe she borrowed it and forgot to return it. Now that the owner is dead . . ."

"According to Sally at the library, Tanya never let the lighter out of her hands. She loved to show it off. Claimed it cost tens of thousands of dollars. She would never lend it to the tutor."

"Tutor?"

"Elaine, the woman we're following, tutors one of Tanya's stepsons."

"And why, exactly, are we following her?" Owen turned in his seat to face me, to judge my response carefully.

"I don't know precisely. Oh wait, she's turning. I got a glimpse of the lighter and before I could ask about it she hustled out of the café. And she has some kind of relationship with Tanya's husband. Something isn't right."

I made a left and followed Elaine from one winding street to another.

Owen gave me an atta-girl cuff on the shoulder. "Okay, then. If we're following your hunch, I'm in. I love chasing down a hunch."

Chapter Thirty-five

We trailed Elaine up one street and down another. Suddenly we were back on Estero Boulevard. I fretted. "Do you think she spotted us on her tail?"

Owen seemed to think that was the funniest thing he ever heard. "Who are we supposed to be? Jim Rockford and Angel? Nah, she's just lost. This part of the island has few houses and a ton of small streets that dead-end abruptly in the tangle of mangroves and scrub pines bordering the bay. She probably picked the wrong one. See, I was right. She's turning again."

I signaled for a left. It was like following Alice down the rabbit hole. The barely there road was overgrown with vegetation and rutted with tire tracks probably ground into the spotty asphalt over the last dozen rainy seasons.

"Hold up, Sassy, and turn off your engine. She has to stop when she turns around that bend up ahead."

I did as I was told. "You know where we are?"

"The veterans' camp is on the other side of that thicket." He pointed straight ahead, then swung his arm to the right. "And Alan's hut is maybe twenty yards to the south."

"That's where she's going. Alan's hut."

Elaine turned the bend and cut her engine, just as Owen predicted.

"Why? Why would she go anywhere near Alan's hut? For all she knows there are a dozen deputies in there right now ripping it apart for the umpteenth time." Owen was having trouble seeing what was so obvious to me.

"Because she heard everything you said at the café about there being a lack of physical evidence to connect Alan to the murder. She is going to plant evidence. Frame Alan once and for all."

"Sassy." Owen was losing patience. "You realize that by now the deputies have searched the hut and the surrounding grounds more than once. It's too late to drop something that might be evidence and expect it to be credible."

"You sound like a lawyer."

"I *am* a lawyer."

"Let's see where she goes, what she docs." I jumped out of the jeep. Except for the *clee clee* of a few water birds lazily circling above, the thicket was deathly quiet.

Owen was right next to me. "Sassy, if you are sure that she is involved in this murder, it's time for us to take a step back and call the sheriff."

I knew he was right, but there was no time. Without witnesses Elaine could stash false evidence. One of us had to follow immediately behind and keep an eye on her. "I'll sneak in behind Elaine. You call Ryan Mantoni or Frank Anthony." I handed Owen my phone. "They're in my speed dial."

He seized my wrist. "Why don't I follow her and you call?"

"Because you know where we are and I don't. If I give them directions, they'll wind up driving all over the island looking for us." I yanked my wrist away. "Besides, some of the other vets are bound to be milling around the camp. I'll be perfectly safe." And I ran around the bend and past Elaine's Corolla.

I stepped lightly along the edge of the wood until I pushed in on the small path Elaine had taken. It seemed to meander among the trees and bushes. I recognized some species like the Jamaican caper, a tree I first learned about when Bridgy and I toured Mound Key with the Books Before Breakfast Club. I was pretty sure that the wide and pretty bushes with a faint turpentine odor were Brazilian pepper, like the ones Ophie planted in her side yard. She said that as long as you didn't crush the leaves, the handsome bushes wouldn't give off an odor. It was her great joy to rip off some leaves and crush them to give anyone nearby a whiff. The smell was so fresh that Elaine must have knocked off a small batch of leaves and stepped on them. The rest of the vegetation was a complete mystery to me.

I saw the veterans' camp immediately. Neat, quiet and almost certainly deserted. To keep my courage up, I hoped that someone was around. I could see Elaine off to my right, her yellow shirt moving slowly through the brush. I knew she was heading toward the area where Owen indicated Alan had set up his hut. She moved cautiously, not wanting to be noticed by anyone just as I didn't want her to catch sight of me walking behind her.

She crept stealthily for eight or ten yards, then quickened her pace. I looked past her. There was a clearing around a thatched hut with a rickety old lawn chair set out front. Four or five piles of branches and tree limbs were scattered about. This had to be Alan's hut. I sped up. I wanted to catch up with Elaine and confront her before she could do anything to harm Alan. She nearly caught me off guard when she swiveled a full one eighty to make sure she was alone. I ducked behind a gnarled mangrove just in time. A few seconds slower and we would have locked eyes too soon. Just as she reached the edge of the clearing, Elaine took something out of her purse. A ray of sunshine streamed through the mangrove leaves and glinted off the edge of an object with lots of tiny points of light. Tanya's cigarette lighter. I ran toward her, not caring if she heard me coming. I had to stop her. She got to the edge of the hut and turned again, checking her perimeter. She saw me coming. I ran faster. I knew Owen was somewhere behind me and to give him a fix on my location, I called out her name. Loudly. Twice.

Like a kindergartener who stole a cookie from the cookie jar, Elaine turned to me and hid one hand behind her back. She demanded to know what I was doing following her.

I smiled as if we'd just met in the cosmetic aisle at Walgreens. "I'm visiting a friend's house to pick up a few things. I'm surprised to see you here."

All the while I kept moving toward her. At first she took baby steps backward and mumbled something about a nature walk. Then a look crossed her face. She'd made a decision. It seemed to me I'd be safest if I made the first move. I planted myself in front of her, grabbed her arm and pulled it out from behind her back. Her hand was clenched around Tanya Lipscome's gold and diamond-studded lighter. Close up with the sun hitting it directly, it was a dazzling sight, and I was distracted by the pizazz. Elaine grabbed a branch from the nearest pile of wood and swung at my head. I ducked and pushed her. She fell back and landed on the folding chair, which crashed to the ground. She grabbed onto the hut and when she recovered her balance, lunged at me. It took all my strength to push her again. This time she bounced off the wall of the hut and came at me screaming ferociously.

I never even noticed Owen Reston come out of the thicket. He ran into the clearing with the speed of the Flash and grabbed Elaine from behind, pinning her arms to her sides.

I reached for the lighter, which had fallen on the ground between us. Then I thought the better of it. I looked right into Elaine's defiant eyes. "I'll leave the lighter for the deputies to find. Wouldn't want to smudge your fingerprints."

That's when Elaine crumbled. She fell back against Owen and began to wail piteously, like a wounded animal begging to be put out of its misery.

Between sobs she said, "He wanted to marry me. I know he did. But that tyrannical witch wouldn't give him a divorce."

We heard Ryan calling my name. He and a half dozen other deputies came crashing through the woods. Two deputies moved to stand on either side of Owen, who was still holding Elaine. Ryan gestured at Elaine and said to the deputies, "We better read the young lady her rights." As a deputy, whose name tag read "Kliner," began in a very professional and dignified voice, I realized it was the first time I had actually heard the warning in the real world, not on an episode of *Law & Order* or in a movie.

Owen stepped out of the way. Ryan gave him one of those manly punches on the arm and then pointed a hitchhiker's thumb at me. "Thanks for saving our girl here."

I harrumphed. "I didn't need saving. Owen was along for . . . company."

Ryan laughed out loud. "Well, then I'm glad you had company. When Owen called, I thought, here she goes again. And I sure didn't want to be the one to tell Lieutenant Anthony. Remember the last time?"

Why were people forever saying that?

I pointed to the lighter. "That belongs to Tanya Lipscome."

Ryan dropped a marker next to it and signaled another deputy to pick it up in whatever special way they gather evidence. Frank Anthony came up behind us. "Ah, the cigarette lighter. Her husband said she was never without it. Yet when we found Mrs. Lipscome, she had cigarettes on the table beside the hot tub but the lighter was gone."

Elaine started sobbing as if her heart was broken. All of a sudden she stopped crying and started talking in a monotone voice as though she was the only one who could hear.

"I went to see her. She was in the yard drinking a glass of wine. I told her that Barry didn't love her, that he loved me. She laughed in my face. She held up that stupid cigarette lighter and told me that it meant more to him than I did. Then she lit a cigarette and kept waving her hand, shooing me away like I was nothing. Like it didn't matter that her husband loved me. Me. So I left. But I came back." Her knees buckled, and Deputy Kliner straightened the folding chair and told her to sit. She dropped into the chair at once.

Frank Anthony winked at Ryan. "Wouldn't it be a wonderful world if Sassy listened to us as obediently as Ms. Tibor?"

Owen Reston joined in the laughter at my expense. I stuck my nose up in the air and ignored them all.

In the first few days after I tangled with Elaine Tibor in

the woods, some folks stopped by the Read 'Em and Eat out of curiosity rather than a desire for a tasty lunch or an entertaining book. Now and again people I barely knew made comments like, "How are you feeling after . . . you know?" or, "Tougher than you look, aren't you?" And then there was the ridiculous "Poor dear, are you having nightmares?" from a woman I'd never seen before.

Ophie spent much of her spare time with us, so she and Bridgy fended off the most aggressive curiosity seekers. Still, Fort Myers Beach being the town it is, intrusive busybodies were few and far between.

In a day or two, life was back to normal.

Chapter Thirty-six

When Bridgy pulled her sporty little Escort into the café parking lot on Sunday morning, the lights were on and Miguel was at work chopping, slicing and baking, seemingly all at once. Being superefficient, Miguel had already hung several signs around the café and two on the front door for good measure reminding customers that we were locking up at one o'clock sharp. Today Bridgy and I would finally find out what turns a party into a cornhole party.

As soon as the breakfast crowd lightened, Bridgy and I practically pushed Miguel out the door. We knew he had things to prepare for the guests he and his neighbor Mr. Gerrity had invited to the cornhole party. Bridgy took over the kitchen. I walked around with the coffee carafes, orange-topped decaf and brown-topped regular, offering refills to the few remaining breakfasters. The Merskys came in just as we'd reached a real lull.

For the first time since they had arrived in Florida, George and Regina were as smiley and bubbly as O'Mally. I led them to Dashiell Hammett. George looked around the room, and asked, "Sassy, can you sit for a minute?"

"Sure." I went to the kitchen, asked Bridgy to watch the dining room and carried out a tray with three glasses of sweet tea and an appetizer of corn bread and honey butter. While I put the tea and corn bread on the table, I asked how Alan was reacting to the news that he'd be free to do as he pleases once he's released from the hospital.

O'Mally and George exchanged a look. He hesitated. "I'm not sure Alan ever knew that he was going to be arrested as soon as the doctors gave the okay for a bedside arraignment. I guess it's safe to say that he understands that he'll be released from the hospital shortly. He has agreed to stay in the condo with us."

Of course I saw the fatal flaw in the plan. The Merskys couldn't stay in Fort Myers Beach forever. George continued. "We really came with questions. We've asked the deputies but their answers are vague. I thought you might be able to tell us how this woman knew Alan and why she framed him for murder."

Owen Reston and I spent enough time in the sheriff's office answering questions, making statements and answering still more questions, that there was very little we hadn't heard or at least discerned. The first part of George's question was easy to answer.

"Elaine was a graduate student who researched in the library. Now that we know of her relationship with Barry Lipscome, I'm sure she kept a close eye on Tanya Lipscome, who was a library volunteer. Since Alan had several run-ins with Tanya, Elaine probably witnessed at least one."

George pulled on his chin thoughtfully. "And Alan's car was so recognizable. Still, how did she know where to find his car so she could break off the branch and . . . hit the woman?"

"An accident of fate. Elaine tutored Tanya's stepson. She was familiar with the layout of the house, the street and the path along the bay. She was determined to demand Tanya give Barry a divorce. Elaine knew Barry was at a business event and she was sure his sons wouldn't be hanging out with the stepmother they detested. She parked her car in the parking lot of Pastor John's church and took the bay path so she could get past the Lipscomes' fence and confront Tanya."

O'Mally furrowed her eyebrows. "So she planned to talk to her, not clobber her."

"Originally." I heaved a deep sigh and tried to think of the most painless way to tell the rest. "Elaine found Tanya sitting on the patio next to the hot tub. Vicious words were tossed back and forth. When Tanya laughed and dismissed Elaine, she sealed both their fates."

Regina was shredding her napkin and looking totally frazzled. To give us all a break, I offered more sweet tea. When everyone's glass was full, I continued. "Elaine walked back to the church parking lot and by then a veterans' meeting had begun. Everyone remembers that Alan was present. Elaine noticed Alan's car, saw she was alone in the parking lot, opened the car door, tore a hefty branch from the tree limb that straddled the seats and went back along the bay path to physically threaten Tanya.

"When she got there Tanya was lounging with her eyes

closed in the bubbling water of the hot tub. Seeing Tanya relaxing like that enraged Elaine. She brought the branch down on Tanya's head more than once. Then she dropped the branch in the hot tub and walked back to the parking lot, got in her car, and, get this, drove down island to have dinner and drinks all by herself in an elegant waterfront restaurant to celebrate her impending 'engagement' to Barry Lipscome."

"She never." O'Mally was horrified.

"Oh yes. I heard her say so, quite nonchalantly, to one of the emergency medical technicians who examined us both after . . . er, when we were at Alan's hut."

Regina was dabbing at her eyes with the shredded napkin. "I'm sorry. I thought I was done crying. To think she could kill a woman and then let Alan take the blame . . ."

"George, what's next for Alan?" I thought we should look to the future.

"Well for now we hope he will stay in the condo. Regina has another month's leave from work. O'Mally and I will go home as soon as Alan is settled, and then we'll come back before Regina goes home. By then we'll know if we've gotten Alan the right medical help he needs. Now that we have Pastor John and the veterans groups to communicate with . . ."

O'Mally grabbed his hand and squeezed. "The future looks bright."

My iPhone vibrated. Miguel. "*Hola, chica. ¿Qué pasa?* It's after one thirty. The cornhole party is moving along without you."

"The Merskys stopped by . . ."

"Invite them. They have much to celebrate, *sí*." And he hung up.

George put his hands on the table and half stood. "Are we keeping you?"

"Not at all."

He slid back into his seat.

"But"—I gave the entire family a broad grin—"that was Miguel. He was calling to remind me to bring you to the cornhole party."

George laughed—a loud, deep belly laugh that was wonderful to hear. "I was wondering what this cornhole party is all about. Is it like a barbecue with grilled corn?"

"I have no idea. Come with us and we will find out together."

O'Mally jumped up and clapped her hands. "I'm in. I don't care a fig about the cornhole. I heard the word 'party.'" She began waving her arms and dancing around the room. "Conga line, anyone?"

Bridgy and I closed up the Read 'Em and Eat and the Merskys followed us down Estero Boulevard. We parked a block away and when we walked down Orange Gate Drive, it looked like all of Fort Myers Beach had turned out.

People were milling around on lawns and in the street. Tables and chairs were scattered everywhere, and maybe George's guess about grilled corn was right, because there was at least a half dozen barbecues going full blast. We were only a few steps into the street when Cynthia Mays rushed over to give me a big kiss on the cheek. "Isn't this awesome? Look." She pointed to a group of Guy Bradley members laughing with pet owners I recognized from the temporary shelter. "Your fears about enmity in the neighborhood were justified, but it all turned out well in the end. Everyone is friends again."

"And where did the anaconda go?"

Dr. Mays beamed. "We found her a lovely home in a zoo west of the Rockies."

"Her?"

"Definitely her. I examined the snake thoroughly. Ah, here comes Deputy Mantoni."

She reached out to shake Ryan's hand and asked him to extend her thanks to Lieutenant Anthony for all his help during the snake crisis. "Not as though he didn't have other things to deal with. Murder. On our island." She shook her head at the thought.

Ryan grabbed my arm. "Miguel is looking all over for you." He waved for Bridgy and the Merskys to follow.

I tried to stop to talk to Ophie and Mark Clamenta, who were sitting on folding chairs under someone's royal palm, but Ryan kept moving forward.

Bridgy waved to her aunt. "We'll be back in a few minutes."

And when Ophie replied, "Don't hurry, y'all," Bridgy asked if I thought something was brewing between the two.

I told her it was too early to tell. And she reminded me I was often wrong about that sort of thing.

O'Mally put in her two cents. "Never too early if the spark is right." And she hip bumped George, which started the rest of us laughing.

Miguel was as excited as I have ever seen him. "Finally, you are here. Welcome. The cornhole can begin."

Mr. Gerrity was supervising three or four men who were moving a slanted box with a hole in the top of the high end into the center of the street. Then they dragged a similar box farther toward the bay. Mr. Gerrity was yelling. "Twenty-seven feet. They have to be exactly twenty-seven feet apart."

Two men, one wearing flip-flops and the other wearing motorcycle boots, were trying to do a pace off and arguing about the effect their footwear had on the accuracy of the measurements, when a wizened, white-haired gentleman pulled one of those measuring wheels that surveyors use out of his shed. Problem solved.

Miguel looked at George. "You will play, *si*?"

George laughed. "Why not?"

"Okay, we will be on one team. Sassy and Bridgy on the other." He looked at us. "Agreed?"

"Sure, but you have to tell us the rules," I insisted.

Miguel shrugged. "*Ay*, rules. You are so fussy. Just like my Bow. Partners stand opposite each other alongside a board." He tossed me a blue bag, maybe five or six inches square. It felt like it weighed about a pound. "We take turns throwing bags at the hole of the faraway board. If the bag lands in the hole or on the board, you get some points. On the ground, no points."

I nodded. "Sounds easy. How do we choose who goes first?"

"We generally play 'ugly goes first' but since you ladies could not possibly qualify . . . I will go first."

Everyone laughed and Miguel showed us exactly where to stand and warned us not to step over the imaginary foul line. He said Mr. Gerrity would keep score and explain how we won or lost points.

Forget points, I was losing patience. "Okay, okay I get all that, but why is a game played with beanbags called cornhole?"

Miguel gave me a slightly superior smile. "Because the bags aren't filled with beans. They are filled with . . ."

I rolled my eyes and finished his sentence. "Corn."

Miss Marple's Orange Iced Scones

IIIIIIIIIIIIIIIIIIII

by Karen Owen

SCONES
2 1/2 cups all-purpose flour
1/2 cup white sugar
1/2 cup softened butter
3 teaspoons baking powder
1 egg
1/2 cup milk

Preheat oven to 375 degrees.

Place first 4 ingredients in a large mixing bowl. Use a stand mixer or hand to blend the butter into the flour, sugar and baking powder until it resembles coarse breadcrumbs.

Mix in egg and milk. Cover a baking sheet with parchment paper. With a spoon or ice cream scoop drop 12 equal amounts of scone batter onto the baking sheet. Leave 2 inches between the scone batter balls to allow for spreading. Bake at 375 until the edges and tops of scones turn a golden brown.

ORANGE ICING
1/2 cup powdered sugar
1 teaspoon grated orange rind
1/2 of a large orange, juiced

Place powdered sugar in a small bowl. Add grated orange rind to sugar. Squeeze the juice from the orange half over sugar and rind mixture. Use a spoon to mix the icing together. Icing should be fairly runny. Spoon drizzle over warm scones.

Best served with a pot of Earl Grey tea and a Read 'Em and Eat Mystery!